THE APPLE BLOSSOM CAFÉ

A Fairfield Orchard Novel

Emma Cane

Copyright

THE APPLE BLOSSOM CAFÉ: Copyright © 2019 Gayle Kloecker Callen. ALL RIGHTS RESERVED. This book is licensed for your personal enjoyment only. No part of this work may be used or reproduced in any manner whatsoever without written permission of the author, except in the case of brief quotations embodied in critical articles and reviews.

This is a work of fiction. Names, characters, places, and incidents are products of the author's imagination or are used fictitiously. Any resemblance to actual locales, organizations, or persons, living or dead, is entirely coincidental.

ISBN: 978-0-9980438-4-5

Cover art by Wicked Smart Designs: www.WickedSmartDesigns.com

Editing by Jena O'Connor: www.PracticalProofing.com

Praise for Emma's Books

AT FAIRFIELD ORCHARD
"If you enjoy small town romance with big families then you'll love this series."
Romancing the Readers

A SPICED APPLE WINTER
"Tender, spicy, and witty, this heartwarming story sweeps readers from the fall glory of October to the merriment of the holidays with a tried-and-true friends-to-lovers romance."
Library Journal

A TOWN CALLED VALENTINE
"Will leaving you smiling long after you've closed the last page."
Lori Wilde, *NY Times* Bestselling Author

Dedication

To my sisters-in-law, Linda Swenton, Melissa Swenton, and Erika Swenton, who've become sisters of my heart.

Chapter 1

Noah Fairfield stood alone inside the Apple Blossom Café, the first restaurant he'd been able to plan from the architectural drawings to the menu. In another week or two, as spring unfurled itself at Fairfield Orchard, so would his café, with a grand opening all his family members were helping to plan. Though it had been his dream, he wasn't going to stick around to watch it grow.

He moved between the tables to the wall of glass windows, beyond which he could see acres of apple trees, their pink and white blossoms a fragrant reminder of the earth's renewal. It was still early on this April morning, before his family's orchard opened for the day. He'd agreed to come back, because it was his turn to help rejuvenate the orchard. Their new customers needed something more than bar food in the tasting room, and Noah's café was going to give it to them. He had everything ready—except the new chef who would replace him when he headed back to Pittsburgh.

Not that he'd told the family *all* of his plans. Hell, he hadn't even told them his sabbatical from his Pittsburgh restaurant, La Folie, had actually been a dismissal. Last thing he wanted was for his family to feel sorry for him, or assume he'd lick his wounds by staying. He'd escaped the orchard and his conflicted feelings about his dad a long time ago, and he was never coming back permanently to Spencer Hollow.

He stood looking out at the orchard, arms crossed over his chest, frowning. It was a beautiful view, no doubt about it, but he'd take the view of the three rivers from Mount Washington in Pittsburgh any day.

Yet there was something about the smell of apple blossoms that truly made him know it was spring, no matter where he went. It brought to mind tractor rides between rows of trees, the buzz of bees enjoying their crucial work, blossoms falling around him like snow as he waded through long grass in anticipation—or dread—of the first mowing. It was also a tense time of year for a farmer, anticipating the fall harvest by monitoring the buds, searching for insects, and praying that frost wouldn't wind its way through the trees at night like a bank of deadly fog.

None of that was Noah's concern right now; he was focused on the Apple Blossom Café. He was about to step out onto the terrace for a deep inhalation of spring, when he spotted a woman and froze.

Gabrielle Eklund.

Or should he just think of her as Gabrielle, like all her fans did? He meant to back into the shadows before she could see him, but it was too late—she waved so cheerfully he felt his frown deepen until a headache threatened.

What was she doing here? And why was she looking at him with a friendly eagerness that seemed foreign on her? They hadn't exactly gotten along when they'd met a few months ago. They'd been in the same room together only a handful of times. She was an international movie star, an ex-girlfriend of his brother Tyler. She and Tyler had starred in a soap opera together a few years before and had steamed up the screen so much that Gabrielle had won an Emmy. Instead of being grateful to Tyler, she'd used him to restore her reputation last fall, then left town to film a movie. Noah thought they'd never see her again, now that she'd gotten what she'd wanted, injuring Tyler's reputation in the process. He could never trust a woman who'd hurt his brother.

The Apple Blossom Café

She was coming across the terrace, that beguiling smile still in place, moving with a languid grace that was sexiness incarnate. And God help him, like every other man in the universe, he felt something hot and urgent rise up inside of him. She was known as the most beautiful woman in the world, small and delicate, with curves that made a man wonder if his brain cells were leaking away. Her tanned, toned legs were shown off by a short, white casual skirt and strappy high-heeled sandals. She had long blond hair, the kind that seemed made of every color of gold, all mixing together in an exotic fall around her shoulders. With one hand, she pushed it back from her face, but it only fell sinuously in waves again—was that deliberate?

He looked into that gorgeous oval face, with wide lavender eyes surrounded by dark lashes. That's when he realized that she was just on the other side of the glass door, staring up at him as her brow wrinkled and her head cocked with bemusement.

"You're not locking me out, are you?" came her muffled voice.

He wanted to turn the bolt and keep her out, so he didn't have to resist the need to touch her. She'd be silken to caress. And that voice—even through the glass, the seductive, deep tones were alluring. He was just as weak as every other man where Gabrielle was concerned. He was determined not to show it.

He pulled on the door and slid it open silently. She crossed the threshold, and he told himself to step back. But he didn't.

"Hi, Noah."

"Hello, Gabrielle."

For what seemed like a long moment, Gabrielle looked up at him. That friendly smile started to fade as their gazes met and held. The pull of awareness, of temptation, moved through him almost like a shudder.

Gabrielle suddenly looked past him. Her lips parted, her eyes widened. "Oh, Noah, just look at this place! Tyler told me you've done a great job, but words didn't do it justice."

Hearing his brother's name was like taking a cold shower. He was grateful for the renewed ability to keep his distance.

He closed the door and turned around, trying to look at his café, rather than the way her hips moved as she seemed to glide with all the grace of…an actress on the red carpet. That's how practiced she was, he reminded himself.

He tried to see the café through her eyes, and because it was so new, still smelling of fresh paint, that wasn't difficult. The wall next to the terrace was almost completely made of windows, letting in the sun. Wooden columns rose from stone bases; the exposed dropped ceiling beams were draped with lights of all sizes, some twinkling about the beams, others hanging above tables. The tables themselves ranged in size from two-tops for intimacy to community tables.

She arched her neck to look up at the lights on the ceiling, then glanced at him. "Did you always know?"

"What?"

"Did you always know that being a chef was what you were meant to do?" She wasn't smiling now. She watched him with serious eyes, suddenly deep and unknowable. Tyler had told him once that there were depths to Gabrielle that Noah had never seen.

"Since I was a teenager, I knew I wanted to cook." He pressed his lips together, inwardly grimacing at how husky his voice sounded.

"Why?" she asked.

"Why?" he echoed, confused.

"Why cooking?"

"Why do you care?"

The Apple Blossom Café

She blinked at him. "I'm trying to be friendly. I didn't mean to pry. We're both in creative fields, and I was just...curious."

He regarded her warily. Was he supposed to spill his guts about something so personal, tell her what it was like to grow up with an alcoholic dad and how that had led to the discovery of his passion for food? He didn't do that with anyone, let alone a woman who was almost a stranger—especially not a woman whose every move made lurid headlines around the world.

So he shrugged. "I'm not very deep. I like cooking, and I discovered I was good at it."

He thought he glimpsed disappointment in her eyes. He was momentarily curious, but he let it go.

"Yet you're not going to stay here and cook."

"Nope. Going back to Pittsburgh after the grand opening."

"And who'll be the chef then?"

"I'm in the process of figuring that out."

Gabrielle walked past the tables where the chairs were stacked upside down on top. She put her hands on the bar and eyed the shelves behind, made of apple crates.

"Shelves for all the hard cider?" she asked over her shoulder.

"Yes." He didn't want to be curious about her, but he was. "So why are you here, in Spencer Hollow, I mean? I thought you'd gone back to your career."

When she glanced up at him, desire stirred again. It made him uneasy to be attracted to a woman who'd been in his own brother's bed.

"This little corner of Virginia is a beautiful place," she said. "I'm thinking about buying the house I've been renting. It's on the creek that winds down from the Blue Ridge Mountains. And there's your adorable little college town of Charlottesville not too far away, if I want a little more to do."

"Why don't you live *there*?"

She went pale. "Are you worried about me being around, that I might throw myself at Tyler?"

He shook his head. "It wouldn't matter. My brother only has eyes for Bri. He moved into her place."

She swallowed and nodded, her stiff shoulders relaxing. "If you think I might try to come between them, other people might, too. I don't want that." She studied his face with concern. "You really believe I would be bad news if I stayed? I would only be here a few months of the year, between movies. Six months at the most. It's so peaceful, and people are getting used to me and almost treat me like a normal person. But I would never willingly cause Tyler grief..." Her voice trailed off.

He'd never seen this vulnerable side of Gabrielle, and it made him uncomfortable. "He'd be the first to say you should do whatever makes you happy. I just don't know why you'd want to stay here. It's not all that great."

He'd read that she hadn't had an ideal childhood, but Tyler said she was pretty private. After all, everything about a celebrity had to be managed just right, to put a false front before the world.

"You're crazy," she said good-naturedly. "Spencer Hollow is a gorgeous place, and so peaceful. Though living in New York and L.A. can be fun, sometimes I just need to get away."

He nodded, eyeing her though he tried not to. She had a presence, a bigger-than-life vibe that was probably one of the reasons she was so successful. That, and her ability to use men to her advantage, he reminded himself. There were a lot more men in her wake than just Tyler. A failed affair was one of the reasons she'd ended up hiding out at Fairfield Orchard last fall.

The silence grew dense and uncomfortable again. Gabrielle didn't look at him, as she meandered behind the bar, her movements slow and deliberate. She never seemed to do anything impulsively.

The Apple Blossom Café

"I used to be a waitress in my struggling days," she said.

"Don't tell me you're asking for a part-time job during your downtime."

She laughed, and the sound lingered, deep and husky.

"No, I need that downtime, where I have nothing to do but read or cook or relax."

He arched a brow at her. "Someone told me you like to cook."

"Nothing that would impress you," she insisted.

"You once asked for fat-free cheese at a party," he said dryly.

He thought she stiffened just a bit—that had been her reaction then, too. Had he wanted that reaction, a way to keep the distance between them?

"No food judgment from the chef," she said, her voice a forced lightness.

Where was the usual snide comeback? She seemed to be trying too hard, and he didn't know why. Was she trying to get along to appease Tyler and Amy?

"Okay, no judgment," he said. "To each his own."

"Are we both on vacation, then?" she asked. "I heard you've been home for a few days, getting the café ready to open."

"Yep." He didn't say anything else—he was hardly going to tell Gabrielle he'd been fired when he hadn't told the rest of his family.

"I'm looking forward to working my way through your menu."

"I hope your entourage sticks by your side to fight off the crowds."

She turned and leaned back against the bar, elbows resting on the top behind her. The position thrust her breasts out a little too much, and he wished her scoop-neck top was a bit looser. Or that she were one of those celebrities who disguised themselves from the public with baggy clothes. Nope, not Gabrielle.

"My entourage?" she echoed.

"Your bodyguard—or maybe you have a fleet of them."

"Like they're cars?" she asked dryly. "Not a fleet, no, but sometimes a strong man is necessary."

Those words lingered in the silence, as if they had a double meaning.

She tilted her head and eyed him. "So, are you saying your café will be crowded, or that my fans will be getting in the way?"

Their gazes met and held in a challenge that seemed to be closer to their usual interaction.

"Maybe I'm saying both," he shot back.

She cocked her head, that polite smile lingering. "You can't say you'd turn away my fans as customers."

"Of course not." He cleared his throat. "Speaking of your entourage, where's the bodyguard I remember?"

"You mean Smalls?"

"Yeah, the big guy in the suit. Intimidating, but a little out of place around here in the clothes department."

"He has a very professional air about him. I gave him the weekend off. I might give him a few weeks off, he and Marcella, his backup. I get really tired of being followed around."

He leaned back against the bar next to her, crossing his arms over his chest. "Isn't that kind of dangerous? I remember the threats you got last fall."

She glanced sideways at him, a corner of her mouth curled up. "You were watching my Twitter feed, were you?"

"My brother was pretty worried, so I heard about it."

"Yeah, well, that's died down, thanks to Tyler. I won't forget how he put himself on the line for me, and how close I came to ruining his relationship with Bri."

The Apple Blossom Café

"He said fake-dating wasn't your idea." Noah hadn't believed that was true. He studied Gabrielle, even as she looked away, not meeting his eyes.

"That doesn't matter," she murmured. "I went along with it after my managers asked him to pretend to date me. It wasn't fair to Tyler."

"But it worked," he said dryly.

She sighed. "It worked. The crazies stopped calling me—well, I won't even repeat what they called me after Brock died, and I dared to go on with my life. I thought my career was over."

"'Going on with your life' and getting photographed kissing a European playboy only a few weeks after your boyfriend's death aren't quite the same thing."

"Look at you, the possessor of some isolated facts, but not the truth."

She was prickly now, and it made those eyes flash at him. "No? Then what's the truth?"

"Now it's my turn to ask why you want to know."

Chapter 2

Gabby was almost glad she and Noah had started to bicker again. There was something about Noah Fairfield that put her on edge, made her feel both conflicted and wary. He was wearing skinny jeans and army boots, with a blue buttoned-down shirt that brought out his gray eyes. His dark brown hair was a little long on top and combed back. He wore sideburns, and a few days' stubble. He looked rumpled and moody, and far too sexy.

And it was frankly weird to have a guy be so…normal around her. They were always either awed and incapable of making conversation or trying to be all macho, as if she'd only be attracted to an alpha male. She'd had enough of that, thanks. She should be happy Noah wasn't starstruck; she wasn't quite sure why she felt conflicted.

"I don't need to know all your secrets," Noah said. "I was making conversation."

She should end this topic, but then words spilled out of her mouth. "It's not an easy conversation when it's about a tough time in my life. And for your information, Brock wasn't my boyfriend when he died."

Noah frowned. "The press didn't seem to know that."

"They did not. Our managers were waiting for the right time to tell the public I'd broken it off with the big jerk—sorry for speaking ill about the dead."

"You don't sound all that sorry," he mused.

"It was what it was. Though America thought of him as the boy next door and lined up in droves to see his movies, he

The Apple Blossom Café

treated me like crap. The movie-going public wasn't to know that, of course. We had to keep up appearances. And then he died speeding in that car—thank God he didn't take anyone else with him."

"Including you?"

"I knew never to get in a car with him," she said bitterly.

Gabby couldn't believe she was going on about the past to Noah. He was practically a stranger. What was it about the Fairfields that made her think they could be trusted? It had been a long time since she'd trusted a man other than Tyler.

"I'd pretended to be a grieving, love-sick girlfriend for two months," she continued. "I couldn't take it anymore. I thought Europe was far enough away."

Noah rubbed his chin whiskers. "So that's how you got photographed with the playboy."

She nodded, and the silence stretched between them. It actually felt good to have some of the truth out in the open, especially since he'd seemed hostile toward her after his brother got caught up in her mess. She didn't want to make things uncomfortable for anyone; she wanted to continue feeling welcome at Fairfield Orchard. She liked hanging out in the new tasting room.

Noah broke the silence first. "I hear you're back from filming a movie. Did it go well?"

"I think so—I hope so. It would have been more fun if Tyler had accepted a part."

"He says he's done with acting and seems to mean it."

She shrugged. "We'll see. Sometimes the acting bug bites your ass and doesn't want to let go."

He snorted and she thought he'd been suppressing a laugh. It seemed to be a hard thing, to make Noah laugh. She wondered why he was so intense, so…grumpy, for lack of a better word.

Not that she'd spent much time around him. Maybe only *she* brought out the grumpiness in him.

She sighed. "I hope it turns out well. They delayed production because of the scandal last year, and the producers were still leery about me. Although that's nothing compared to the producers of the movie coming out in two months. I had to get away from all of them for a while."

"And an island in the South Pacific didn't strike you as a better choice?"

"Are you wishing I wasn't here, Noah?" She held her breath, knowing how important his answer was to her plans.

"I didn't say that." He glanced out the window nonchalantly.

It was hard to read him, but she found her breath easing.

"I don't need a reclusive vacation," she said. "I want to be somewhere where I feel comfortable, normal."

"And Spencer Hollow is it."

"I think so. Like I said, I'm going to put an offer in on my rental house. It's in the woods near the creek, so it has a little privacy. And there are horse trails—maybe I'll buy a horse. Not that I've ridden much, but it seems like a relaxing thing to do. And don't say anything else about my entourage. I don't need an assistant here—that's what email and texting are for." She pushed away from the bar. "Please tell Tyler and Bri I'll give them a call to meet up."

"They're going to be at the tasting room after hours tonight. Family and friends, that sort of thing."

"I don't want to intrude…" She let her voice trail off.

"You're not intruding. They probably want to hear what you've been up to."

And just like that, Noah had issued an invitation. She'd take it as a good sign. "Thanks, I'll stop by." Now wasn't the time to press her luck, so she stepped past him with a smile. "See you later."

The Apple Blossom Café

And then she escaped. Immediately she felt lighter, more at ease. There was something about Noah that left her unsettled. Regardless, step one of her plan had gone relatively smoothly. Maybe she should even have asked him her favor right away, but she sensed he needed more time before he'd let her into his kitchen. Another man might be flattered that she wanted to shadow him for her next role—as a chef—but Noah was too private. She sensed that his kitchen was his retreat, his domain. Having her follow him around for days on end? That would take some persuading on her part.

She took a deep breath, trying to concentrate on the gorgeous spring day at the orchard. Branches in the nearby apple trees swelled with green leaves and pink blossoms. Bees buzzed, the air smelled heavenly, like apple-blossom perfume. She raised her face and let the sun touch it, even as she knew the peace wouldn't last long. She heard the employees walking across the grounds, heading for the little country store, and the ancient barn that had been converted into useful space again. It rose above the café, the top floor a tasting room with a wrap-around deck, and the lower still closed, as if anticipating the next Fairfield venture. A patio connected the barn with the café, a pergola overhead to shade the customers. Beyond the café was the large gazebo, enclosed on one side, the open front facing the patio and the sloping grounds far beyond.

Gabby and Tyler had christened the gazebo with a scene from their play last autumn. She'd performed with the local Skyline Theater Guild, and though she'd done it as a volunteer, it had been her first time on the stage since high school. Tyler was the brother she'd always wished for—and then she winced, because she already had a brother, whom she hadn't talked to in a few months. Kevin wasn't like Tyler, a big brother combined with a dear friend, who'd helped launch her career a few years back on the soap *Doctors and Nurses*.

She crossed the grounds, and instead of ignoring the whispers and the pointing, she waved as if she was just another resident of Spencer Hollow. She wanted her neighbors to treat her like everyone else. Two young employees of the country store gave a little scream and rushed toward her. She briefly stiffened, remembering a time or two when a fan had gotten too close, and Smalls, her bodyguard, had had to intervene. But Smalls wasn't here.

Few people knew she'd come home; no one could be lying in wait. Gabby relaxed and signed one woman's bank statement, and the other woman's envelope. She asked them questions about their jobs at the orchard, wanting them to see her as a person instead of a celebrity. She wasn't certain she'd succeeded, because after the conversation, they backed away with wide, giddy eyes. It would take time, Gabby told herself.

Then she realized she'd called Spencer Hollow home, even if only in her mind. When had that feeling happened? True, she'd decided to buy a house, though she'd only spent a few months here. They'd been good months, though, where she'd put the ghost of her ugly relationship with Brock and the fallout behind her; where she'd renewed her friendship with Tyler and found new friendships with his sister and his girlfriend. Mrs. Fairfield had welcomed her like a long-lost niece.

Mrs. Fairfield, mother if the Fairfield clan, was a well-loved woman. Gabby had seen that herself last Christmas, when Gabby had performed the holiday play with Tyler. Mrs. Fairfield had had a breast cancer scare a few years ago, and was now enjoying retired life with her husband, traveling the country in their RV. She was a wonderful mom—unlike Gabby's. She reminded herself that her mom had often worked two jobs trying to support them, since Gabby's dad had left them when she was still a little kid. It didn't make up for her mother's ready anger, her favoritism where Gabby's brother was concerned, the way

The Apple Blossom Café

Gabby had to abandon all of her after-school fun once she was old enough to babysit.

She shook off the depressing memories, rolled down the car windows and just breathed in the smell of apple blossoms. It was with a sense of peace and contentment that she drove down the twisting mountain road and into Spencer Hollow. The heart of the little village in the foothills of the Blue Ridge Mountains was only a four-corner stop sign—they didn't even have a traffic light. There was Brianna's family store, MacDougall's, with different wings built over the decades, kitty-corner from Jefferson's Retreat, the tavern that kept up the colonial ambiance in their décor, since President Jefferson had once owned land nearby—Fairfield land.

Gabby took a right at the stop sign and headed west toward Bucks Elbow Creek and her new house, with the sun shining in dappled patterns through the trees.

~oOo~

The house was empty, except for the memories. Noah came downstairs early that evening, free to make as much noise as he wanted in his family home, where he'd once had to whisper and tiptoe because his father was often suffering from a hangover. He reminded himself that his father had been sober for eleven years, that he'd spent those years trying to make up for his mistakes. Their mother had forgiven the man, and Noah told himself he had, too. No one was perfect.

But the memories of shame, worry, and disappointment weren't so easy to banish, as if ghosts lingered in the empty house.

Noah had showered after a day spent preparing the café, scheduling staff interviews, unloading boxes, setting up his kitchen.

Not *his* kitchen, he reminded himself. Another chef would make it his or her domain. But right now, it seemed like his; over the last few months, he'd conceived and designed it, chosen the industrial stove and cooking stations, even the best knives. He was proud of what he'd achieved and excited to show it to the world.

Just for a few weeks, of course.

Though he would have continued to work through the evening, Tyler and Amy wanted him to relax in the tasting room with them, and he couldn't say no to that. They didn't know he was running out of time here, that he needed to see everything settled and thriving so that he could go back to Pittsburgh and find his life again. His brother and sister had discovered a new peace at the orchard, reset their lives, found people to share it with. He was happy for them, but it left him feeling on the outside more than ever.

He left the house and walked up the lane to the public grounds of the orchard. There were still cars in the lots, since the tasting room didn't close for another hour. There were even people gathered on the deck, though the evening air was chilly. Many were tourists from Charlottesville and beyond, but one local raised a hand in greeting. The man had gone to school with one of Noah's younger brothers. Noah nodded back. People remembered him, though he'd been gone for over ten years. Memories were long in small towns, and that was good and bad.

Inside the tasting room, he paused as he always did, caught by the view at the far end of the room, where an entire wall of the old barn had been torn out and replaced by a giant window. The original beams still crisscrossed it, and as twilight approached, LED candle pillars had been lit on those beams. There were deep leather sofas and chairs, and two long bars through the center of the room, where glasses hung overhead, and patrons could taste flights of cider and discuss. He saw Tyler behind one of the bars, holding court, as always, his sandy brown hair bedroom-rumpled in a style that was no accident. Tyler was no

The Apple Blossom Café

longer on national TV, but he was a celebrity people still came far and wide to see.

In one corner was a display counter of make-your-own-basket picnic foods, from fruits to specialty chocolate, to the goat cheese made by Carmen Rodriguez, daughter of their cider maker and manager Carlos. A set of lit shelves displayed the history of the orchard, and eighteenth-century artifacts from the archeological dig last summer—broken pottery, buttons, and pieces of a flintlock musket.

A baby grand piano took up space in another corner, where Theresa MacDougall, Brianna's sister, played a jazz selection. They'd hired her part-time last Christmas, and the background music soothed and relaxed even someone as tense and distracted as Noah.

Although he wasn't sure how relaxed people could be, after he saw Brianna holding Theresa's eighteen-month-old David. David bounced on his aunt's knees, watching his mother and clapping—to the beat, Noah noticed, shaking his head with amusement.

The little boy leaned over and reached for something. "Doggie!"

Amy's Alaskan husky Uma perked up her pointy ears and suffered David's attention.

Tyler saw Noah and waved him over. Noah sat down at the bar, and Tyler put a glass of Shenandoah Blue in front of him.

"My favorite," Noah said, and sipped the hard cider, savoring the flavor before swallowing. "It never disappoints."

"I'll tell Carlos. But I have an idea for a new flavor."

"Spill," Noah said.

Twenty minutes later, a change came over the room, rippling out behind Noah. Tyler looked past Noah's shoulder, then smiled. Others in the room whispered and pointed eagerly, and

Noah swung around on his bar stool, already knowing what he'd see.

Gabrielle stood in the doorway, nothing disguising her face or the sweep of her long blond hair, chin raised almost defiantly. She wore knee-high boots, tight dark jeans, and a sweater that draped around her body almost like a coat. If only it hid her curves, but he wasn't that lucky. The sweater hugged her body, following all the feminine slopes.

There was something about Gabrielle's beauty that had the power to hypnotize, and he saw more than one man almost blank-faced with awe. Noah was about to turn around, the better to keep traitorous thoughts of her at bay, when he saw her face light up at the sight of Brianna, Amy, and Amy's fiancé Jonathan Gebhart, a history professor at the nearby University of Virginia. Carmen Rodriguez, daughter of their manager, had arrived, too, and she jumped up to greet Gabrielle with an eagerness that betrayed her as a fan. Noah had always thought of Carmen as cool, unflappable, and businesslike—but, apparently, she also worshipped Gabrielle.

After rolling his eyes, Noah leaned back against the bar and watched Gabrielle greet everyone with hugs. He had to give her credit—she seemed to appreciate her new friends and be genuinely happy to be back in Spencer Hollow.

When Gabrielle leaned over to hug Brianna, she awkwardly reached around little David, who leaned back against his aunt and stared wide-eyed at the stranger. Instead of smiling at the little boy, Gabrielle almost seemed uneasy.

"And who's this?" she asked.

Brianna nodded toward the piano player. "My sister Theresa's little boy, David. You might have seen him during the play."

"He's grown."

Brianna kissed his head. "David, can you say hi?"

"Hi," he said faintly, waving a little plastic truck.

The Apple Blossom Café

Brianna sighed. "Makes me want to be a mom, and I haven't even gotten married yet."

Noah glanced knowingly at his brother, who was watching Brianna as if he'd just seen a vision of his future and wanted it so desperately. Too much bliss for Noah's taste, and he turned back to their friends, only to see Gabrielle frown, as if the thought of motherhood interfering with her career was unthinkable. He knew you sometimes had to be selfish to get ahead, had practiced it too much himself. He didn't want to think Gabrielle shared such a flaw, especially not about kids.

"Gabrielle, I hear you might buy a house right here in the Hollow," Carmen said brightly.

"Please, call me Gabby," she said. "Gabrielle feels like a public persona, not me."

"Is it your real name?" Noah heard himself asking.

She turned to smile at him with that same bright eagerness from that morning. "Hello, Noah, I didn't see you there. Yes, it's my real name. And Tyler!" She stepped closer, hugging Tyler, and then there was an awkward pause, as if she wondered if she was supposed to hug Noah, too.

He thought they'd just nod and go their separate ways. To his surprise, she put her arms around his neck and gave him his own brief hug. He froze, arms at his sides a moment too long. Her hair brushing against his smelled exotic, her sweater was warm from her body. He put his hands on her hips because it would be rude otherwise—yeah, right, that was the reason. She was soft and curvy, all woman—and he suddenly knew something else was going on. She might be a great actress, but he knew an act when he saw one.

For some reason she couldn't seem to hide her emotions from him. Perhaps it was because they annoyed each other—or could it be that she was feeling this same pull of desire?

No, that was ridiculous, he told himself as she stepped away, smiling up at him but not quite meeting his eyes. Gabrielle could have any man on the planet—in the universe.

As Gabrielle sat down beside their friends, Tyler turned to deal with a sudden rush of customers who wanted to be near both Tyler and Gabrielle.

Tyler pushed a tray of cider bottles toward Noah. "Take this over to our table, will you? I'm swamped."

"Make sure to pose for selfies," Noah teased.

Tyler shrugged. "I'm popular—what can I say? I'll try to keep the crowd from Gabby. I promised her a fun night."

Tyler was always taking care of people these days, as if now that he was happily in love, he wanted everyone to be just as happy.

Noah took the tray to the tables his family and friends had pulled together. He presented the drinks with a flourish, and Amy laughed as she chose a glass of cider Tyler had put there just for her. Amy didn't drink the hard stuff—another way their father's choices had affected her.

Gabrielle chose a bottle of Monticello Legacy, gave him a grateful smile, then turned to Amy. "Did Tyler tell you I want to buy the house I'm renting?"

"He did," Amy responded. "You'll be happy here, I promise."

"The Hollow has certainly been good for all of you." Gabrielle took a sip of her cider.

Noah retreated back to the bar, where he could still listen.

"Would you be my Realtor?" Gabrielle asked Amy.

His sister beamed. "I kept telling myself to let my license lapse, but I didn't. I'd love to help."

The two women chatted about the logistics of buying the house, Jonathan chimed in with details about the house he and Amy had owned since the holidays, and Noah was free to watch. He wasn't the only one watching. Everyone in the room stared at

The Apple Blossom Café

Gabrielle, some surreptitiously, and others with open fascination. He tried to imagine what it must be like to be looked at, whispered about, judged, twenty-four hours a day.

Then again, it was the career she'd chosen, and celebrity was a side-effect. Hell, maybe she enjoyed being the center of attention.

But then she wouldn't be contemplating buying a house in Spencer Hollow, Virginia.

After a last call provoked good-natured grumbling, the customers eventually departed, leaving just close friends of the Fairfields. They pulled more leather chairs and sofas around the stone fireplace that was the centerpiece of the glass wall. To Noah's surprise, Gabrielle took a seat right beside him on the sofa, gave him a smile, then turned her face toward the view. For a peaceful moment, Noah simply enjoyed the sky, etched with clouds, deep purple and pink. Out of the corner of his eye, he found himself just as captivated by Gabrielle's pure and beautiful profile, until he forced himself to look away.

And then everyone started talking at once and he winced.

"For a guy who grew up with a big family," Gabrielle said quietly, "you don't seem to appreciate the noise."

He glanced over to find her regarding him with an amusement he didn't appreciate. "I've lived alone for a long time now. I got used to the quiet."

The couch squeaked as she turned to face him, drawing her legs up beneath her to get comfortable. "I've been in restaurant kitchens. They aren't known for peacefulness."

"True. Which is all the more reason to appreciate my own apartment each night."

"Apartment, not a house, huh?"

"It's Pittsburgh. I like living in the city."

"A far cry from the Blue Ridge Mountains."

"Exactly."

"So you're not a nature lover?"

"What's with all the questions?" he asked.

She blinked those big lavender eyes at him. "Just making conversation with my new neighbor."

"Unless you're moving to Pittsburgh, we're not neighbors."

"We are for right now. Tyler even said I could crash at the family home if I needed to."

Frowning, Noah took a deep breath, imagining running into her in a shadowy hallway late at night. What did she wear to bed?

She gave a low, sexy laugh. "Calm down, Chef. I have a place to live, remember? You're so easy to tease. Has anyone ever told you that lightening up will make you less prone to heart attacks?"

"Enough with the medical diagnoses. All you did was play a doctor on TV."

She put a hand to her chest. "Is that humor? I never would have believed it."

He continued to frown; she continued to look at him with laughter brimming in her wide eyes. For a moment, she stirred something lighter inside him, almost made his mouth quirk up in an answering smile. She affected him too easily.

"Gabby," Amy called, breaking the spell, "I hope you'll be around for our 200th anniversary this fall." She turned to Noah. "You'll be here, too, right?"

"We haven't even made any plans yet, last I knew," Noah said.

"And I won't know until you have a firm date," Gabrielle said. "Please let me know as soon as you do. I'd enjoy celebrating such a momentous occasion."

Momentous occasion? Noah thought, eyeing her.

To his surprise, Gabrielle patted his knee like an old friend. "Don't look like that. It's an incredible milestone—two hundred years since Thomas Jefferson sold the land to your ancestor."

The Apple Blossom Café

"I know that, but I don't know why you'd think it was so important."

Amy rolled her eyes and turned away, as if leaving her incorrigible brother to Gabrielle, whose expression softened in a way he couldn't read.

"Because you've all become my friends," she said quietly. "You don't understand how important that is to me."

"You must have hundreds of friends," he scoffed.

"Acquaintances. Colleagues. That's not the same thing and you know it. Do you have such a surplus of friends that you take it for granted?"

It was his turn to blink at her. "Well…no."

"You don't take it for granted or you don't have a lot of friends?"

His head was spinning. It was a good thing she didn't wait for a reply.

"Your family members are your friends," she said, nodding as if in confirmation. "I get the feeling you don't trust people easily."

Amy was looking between the two of them wide-eyed, before turning away and shaking her head.

Noah leaned across the couch toward Gabrielle, not anticipating how it would sink under his weight. It made feather-light Gabrielle practically fall into him. She braced herself against his leg, her touch hot through the denim. Or was he imagining that?

"Stop psychoanalyzing me," he said quietly, "especially in front of my family."

"Oh."

Her murmur was a soft puff of air across his face—his lips. And then he looked at hers. She was so close he glimpsed her tongue just behind.

Emma Cane

"You're too skeptical about everything, Noah Fairfield," she whispered.

And then she looked at his mouth. For a moment, he couldn't breathe. What the hell was he doing? What was *she* doing?

Noah abruptly stood up. "I've got food to bring up. I promised another new appetizer."

There were murmurs of appreciation, but Gabrielle looked at him knowingly, as if she suspected the true reason he was escaping. He didn't want her to know he was just another man who desired her. It gave her a power over him, made him feel frustrated and uneasy.

"Why don't you hold up a second?" Tyler said. "We're still discussing the anniversary."

Noah leaned against the mantel rather than sitting back down near the temptation that was Gabrielle.

"Shouldn't we table this discussion until Rachel is here?" Amy asked.

"It's better to have some ideas ready," Tyler said. "We can run them by Mom and Dad, too."

Of course their parents would come for such a big event. Tyler and Amy seemed so excited to include them. They'd forgiven Dad long ago. Noah told himself he had, too, but he couldn't forget. It made him feel…apart from them. It always had. He didn't want that but didn't know how to change things. They'd stuck around longer than he had, had more memories of their dad sober these last eleven years. The logical thing would be for him to do the same thing, to just relax.

He couldn't. Everything at Fairfield Orchard was tied up with his screwed-up childhood. Now he was building something new here, leaving a legacy. He wanted it to change his feelings, he wanted to enjoy it—was he even capable of that?

The Apple Blossom Café

He listened to them brainstorm ideas for fairs and festivals, cider-tastings and craft shows. They might dress in eighteenth century costumes and re-enact the day Thomas Jefferson sold the land to their ancestor—that was Tyler's idea, of course, and Noah wondered who would be playing Jefferson. He shook his head, his mouth quirked in a reluctant smile.

And Gabrielle smiled back at him.

As if she'd been looking at him the whole time.

Noah turned his back. Thinking about Gabrielle was complicated and confusing, and would get him nowhere. Let her flirt with someone else—maybe there *wasn't* anyone else, and that was the problem. He was the only available man in the room.

It was time to create another masterpiece in the kitchen, to go back to where he was most comfortable.

Chapter 3

Gabby knew Noah thought he was showing a mask to the world, and maybe he was, to his family. They seemed to see him as steady, calm, laconic Noah, an introvert in a family of extroverts, as far as she could tell.

She expressed emotions for a living, and she was beginning to see a hell of a lot of emotions locked behind those gray eyes. She saw the way he'd shuttered those eyes at the mention of their parents. Perhaps it was only because she, too, had a complicated relationship with her mom.

She watched him leave.

"I can see who you have your eye on," Brianna said, laughter in her voice

With a touch of guilt, Gabby turned to the other woman, who was smiling, her face dusted with cheerful freckles, her auburn hair swept to one side.

"Not in the way you think," Gabby said. "He's a friend."

Brianna smirked.

Gabby decided to change the subject. "So what's the Skyline Theater Guild up to?"

"Basking in our success," Brianna said smugly. Then she laughed. "All because of you, of course."

"Oh, please. All I did was act. You did the hard work of resurrecting the company." Gabby hadn't meant to steal the spotlight in the small community theater holiday play, but they hadn't been able to find the right heroine, and she'd offered to participate, wanting to help them raise money for Alzheimer's research.

The Apple Blossom Café

Gabby had also been intrigued to give the stage a try, a new challenge for her. When her co-star had broken his leg just before the show opened, Tyler had stepped in to take his place. Of course, that hadn't helped the scandal brewing around them…

"My father truly enjoyed helping to manage the production," Brianna said.

"And you didn't do a bad job yourself. I know you've stayed involved."

"I have. Our newest project has been to get the youth theater program up and running again."

"That sounds wonderful." Gabby remembered how theater had been one of her salvations when she was a teenager, a way to escape her critical mother, or the endless hours alone in the house while her mother worked. Watching her brother had been a chore Gabby hadn't relished, and all too soon, it became the only thing she was allowed to do. "I loved performing on the stage when I was younger," she said wistfully. "I'm so glad you've given the local kids a chance to experience the same joy. If you need a volunteer, I'd be happy to help."

Brianna shot her a glance. "Are you serious? A six-week session starts next week."

"Perfect, I'll be here a few weeks, and then gone for a week, if that's okay."

"Of course it would be okay! But is it too much? It's a couple hours a day after school, Monday through Friday."

"I'm in. Unless you think I'll be a distraction." Gabby felt like she kept saying that to people; her celebrity always made her self-conscious that she was annoying her friends who weren't in the business.

"They'll just have to get used to you," Brianna said, as if unconcerned.

Gabby could have hugged her for it.

"I'm not letting this opportunity get away," Brianna continued. "What would you like to do? Since you're new to it, you'd probably be someone's assistant: assistant lighting director, assistant costume coordinator, assistant director—"

"Assistant director?" Gabby interrupted. "At least I have some experience at that. Who's directing?"

"Aaron Ho."

"He directed us last fall," Gabby said. "At least *he* wouldn't mind me following him around." At first Aaron had seemed overwhelmed by her celebrity and her experience being directed by some of the world's best, but she'd gradually won him over. Soon he'd been ordering her around like a pro. "If you don't think Aaron would mind, I'd like to assist him. And if someone else already has the position, I could always follow Noah's grandma around—is she still the lighting director?"

"She is," Brianna said, smiling. "That's a good backup plan. Have you worked with kids before? We'll have all ages, second grade through high school. Welcome aboard!"

Brianna cheerfully reached over to shake her hand, and Gabby responded automatically, even as she was swamped by old guilt and sorrow.

As always, her mind raced to do the math—her daughter would be eight by now, the child she'd given up for adoption right after she was born.

She'd rarely been around kids since that terrible time in her life, often by design. Yet here she was, volunteering to work with children. And she hadn't even thought about how it might affect her, just volunteered. Could she do it?

Of course she could. But now she needed to think about something else. "The kitchen is easy to find, right?" She started to get up.

Brianna caught her arm. "You probably should let Noah go. It always takes him a while to shake things off."

The Apple Blossom Café

"Maybe he needs to be distracted." She gave the other woman a crooked smile. "Besides, he needs help carrying things from the kitchen, right?"

Brianna shook her head. "Good luck."

After giving Uma a good petting, Gabby opened a door to the new staircase at the back of the barn, leading down to the ground floor where a corridor connected the barn to the café's kitchen. In the kitchen's back hall, she peeked into a brand new walk-in cooler and freezer. Past the dish pit, chrome gleamed beneath bright lights, highlighting the mis-en-place work table, and the cooking line with its grill station, flat top range, and deep fryer. It seemed like only yesterday Gabby was standing in the cold line, helping to prep salads back when serving paid the bills.

Noah was slipping on a chef coat when he caught sight of her and frowned. "Why are you following me?"

"I thought you might need some help. Not with the cooking," she hastily added, when one of his dark eyebrows shot up, "with the tasting or the carrying."

He still waited.

"All right, I felt awkward, with all the harmonious family conversation. I can't exactly relate." Gabby was surprised she'd blurted out the truth—it wasn't as if she was used to confiding in people. And Noah wasn't exactly a people person who encouraged confidences.

He began to move again, fastening his coat. The crisp white emphasized the dark buttoned-down shirt he wore beneath. He had these big broad shoulders she really liked. When men looked at women, it was usually for their breasts or butt, sexual things. Her—she liked a man's shoulders.

"What are you making?" she asked brightly.

"Crepes. I'm experimenting with my ideas for the daily apple special." He moved past her, saying, "Give me a hand, will you?" before stepping into the cooler. As she reached the entrance, cold air wafted toward her as Noah began to hand out ingredients: milk, butter, apples, a tub of crème fraiche, eggs, and a lemon.

She decided silence might serve her better, so she simply watched him work. He ignored her at first, his face intent. But his body language wasn't tense; she'd made a study of people, and she knew tension when she saw it. Whatever was going on in the outside world, in his kitchen, Noah was in control, at ease, yet focused.

She'd always found light-hearted charmers attractive; maybe she'd never given brooding, serious men a try. Such intensity had always made her uneasy. She'd never looked for deep relationships—which was probably why she'd gravitated toward Brock, America's favorite son. Of course, he'd hidden some pretty ugly flaws behind his charm.

Gabby cocked her head and studied Noah. What did he hide behind those lowered brows?

He stirred together a flour-based batter, then set it aside. His eyes were intent, and he moved with skilled ease as he chopped apples so quickly she almost couldn't see his hands move. She needed to learn to work with food with that same surety. What if she just asked him to help her?

But no, he was still uneasy around her, distant. He preferred to be alone—she sensed he only tolerated her now because he didn't want to make a scene with his brother's friend. She had to work harder to make him relax, to get him to like her. That had never been difficult before now.

"You're so intent and focused," she murmured.

He didn't look up. When a lock of his hair fell over his forehead, she wanted to push it back and linger.

Hmm, that was strange.

Feeling a worktable at her back, she boosted herself up to sit and watch him work.

The Apple Blossom Café

"Of course I'm focused," he said almost impatiently. "This is important."

"I wasn't suggesting otherwise," she said mildly.

He gave her a brief glance from beneath those dark brows. She sent him a smile that only made his frown deeper.

"It's hard to be driven," she continued. "Doesn't it make you exhausted?"

"No more than anyone else who wants to do their best work. Are you exhausted after a day on the set?"

"Completely drained. Even then, I still have a difficult time falling asleep—the overwhelming day keeps running through my mind. Does that happen to you?"

"Sometimes."

He added lemon juice, cinnamon, and ginger to the apples, and gave the bowl a toss. In a pan, he caramelized sugar, then added the apple mix, which sizzled until a wonderful aroma filled the air.

She inhaled deeply. "Smells good."

Again, he didn't answer, only started heating another skillet.

"I think restaurants serve an important function," she said. *That* sounded awkward.

But it did get him to look at her again, and those blue eyes were intense.

"Besides an entertaining and rewarding meal?" he asked.

"That's important, of course. There's something about good food and a welcoming restaurant that makes you feel like you belong."

"Hmm."

At least he wasn't ignoring her.

"Maybe because many of us don't have big welcoming families anymore," she continued, then added, "present company excepted, of course."

Emma Cane

He occasionally stirred the pan of apple ingredients, while ladling out a small amount of batter in the other skillet, rotating it until it coated the bottom.

"Did you have much family?" he asked.

It wasn't her favorite subject, but she had to keep him talking. "I have a younger brother whom I'm not very close to, and a mother I see…occasionally. My dad ran out on us when I was six."

He looked up at her sharply. "I'm sorry."

With a shrug, she said, "It was a long time ago. I guess an alcoholic father is almost the same thing as one that leaves."

He stiffened. "How did you know about my dad?"

"I'm sorry—Tyler told me." Had her big mouth ruined their tentative friendship?

Noah expertly flipped the crepe in the air so that the other side could cook. "It was hard for my father to get over what happened to him in Vietnam, but he never left us. I can say that for him."

There was a wealth of unsaid things beneath his words, and Gabby knew better than to try to wrest more out of him. Noah barely knew her—why would he confide in her and make getting to know him easier?

Breast cancer scare, alcoholism, Gabby thought. Noah and his siblings hadn't had it easy. And here she'd thought a Fairfield childhood had surely been worthy of envy, after what she'd endured. But then everyone had things in their past that molded them into the adults they'd become. She thought about Noah's grumpiness, about his refusal to work at the orchard. What happened in childhood stayed with a person forever. She certainly knew about that.

As he made a few more crepes, she found herself saying things she normally kept to herself. After all, knowledge about a person meant they had power over you. She'd lived by that

The Apple Blossom Café

motto. "I can understand some of what you've gone through. My brother is an addict."

He shot her another look. "I'm sorry."

"You apologize for things that aren't your fault," she pointed out, smiling.

"It's the polite thing to do."

She chuckled. He didn't smile. "Oh, you're serious."

"I wouldn't joke about a subject like addiction."

"I didn't mean—hell, I guess when things are awkward, I make a joke. And it doesn't have to be awkward. My brother has gone to rehab." *Again,* she thought, but didn't say that aloud.

"That's a step in the right direction. Do you see him much?"

As Noah started a third bowl, whipping the crème fraiche with powdered sugar and vanilla, Gabby thought about Kevin, who was half the reason she'd left home. "Sadly, not much. There's definitely tension between us. I've paid for the rehab, several times, and he's always relapsed. I want this time to be different… Did your father go cold turkey, or did he slide back into drink?"

"Though he made promises for years, he ended up stopping completely because of a close call."

"What happened, if you don't mind telling me?"

"I wouldn't have brought it up if I minded."

"Of course," she murmured, biting her lip to keep from smiling.

"He was hung over and working at the orchard, driving a tractor and pulling a wagon of kids. He was miserable and not paying attention and almost flipped it." He poured brandy into the apple mixture, then lit it.

She inhaled swiftly, his story overshadowing the flaming appetizer. "That must have been terrifying."

"He quit drinking. Hurting his own children didn't make him quit, but hurting others? That was enough."

What could she say to that? It was probably true. "I don't think an addict thinks about it that way."

"I don't think they think at all," he said dryly. He covered the pan to put out the last of the dying flames, then tossed the mix, coating the apples.

"It is an addiction," she said, "an illness."

He shrugged and placed another crepe on the covered stack he'd been keeping warm in the oven.

"I know it in my mind," she murmured, "but in my heart..."

Their gazes locked, as if they'd had the same thoughts, saw the world the same way. It was a long moment, and she didn't know what to make of it, the way his eyes regarded her solemnly, making her feel as if he saw to the bottom of her soul—saw all her secrets.

And that was too much. She wasn't sharing her shame, her regrets. She just wanted him to relax around her, wanted him to teach her. She gave him a well-practiced smile. "You're sure I can't help. I love to cook."

"So you've told me. But this is my kitchen, and you'd be in my way."

Damn. "I'm very good at carrying plates. Remember, I was a waitress until I was cast on *Doctors and Nurses*. You can trust me."

After arranging crepes on a platter, he started spooning caramelized apples onto each, adding a scoop of the crème fraiche mixture before folding.

He'd turned off the stove/range and was plating the appetizers, dribbling a caramel sauce over them that had been simmering while he'd cooked the rest.

"Can I have a taste?"

"No fingers."

"I'm not a barbarian." She jumped down from the table lightly, found a spoon and leaned over the pan. After scooping some up, she blew on it, and saw that Noah was watching her

The Apple Blossom Café

intently. When he realized she was looking back, he bent over the plates again, wiping the edges with a towel.

She put the spoon in her mouth and closed her eyes. The gooey warmth coated her tongue, and she moaned. "This is delicious."

When she opened her eyes, he was standing right in front of her. She should have been startled; instead she felt a thrill of excitement deep down in her stomach at those broad shoulders which looked so strong. She could feel the warmth of his body, felt lost in the hot, dark gray depths of his eyes.

He leaned down and kissed her. They both tasted of caramel, and she thought it might seem an erotic taste for the rest of her life. His mouth was hot and urgent moving over hers, and he gripped her upper arms and pulled her against him. It brought forth another moan, one he shared.

She'd kissed her share of men—maybe too many. She should be jaded; instead she was wildly excited, her heart hammering, her skin tingling. When she put her hand on his chest, felt his own heart's rapid response, anticipated the feel of those shoulders, he surprised her by suddenly setting her away and letting go.

She blinked up at him, shocked. Had a man ever rejected her kiss?

"I shouldn't have done that," Noah said between gritted teeth, even as he stared at her mouth.

"It's not like I said no," she answered dryly.

He stared at her for another long minute, then sighed and looked away. "So you were going to help me carry these plates."

"You don't want to talk more about what just happened?"

"No. I'm sure men kiss you all the time."

She almost snorted. "What kind of woman do you think I am?"

"I didn't mean that the way it sounded."

She put her hands on her hips. "Then what did you mean?"

"You're beautiful. From what I've read, you don't lack for dates."

"Dates? What have you read?"

"You know what journalists write about you."

"I tend to avoid what's written about me in tabloids and online. Why don't you tell me?" she asked sweetly. This wasn't going as she'd planned. The unexpected kiss had startled her, unnerved her about her plan to sweet-talk Noah into letting her job-shadow him. She didn't want him to think the kiss had been an attempt to seduce him into complying.

Noah sighed. "I don't stalk you online. You always make the headlines."

"You know the last guy I dated died in an accident last year. I made *all* the tabloids."

"How am I supposed to know who you're *technically* dating," he asked with a trace of sarcasm. "*Technically,* you dated my brother just a couple months ago."

"You know we weren't dating. Hasn't your brother explained that you can't believe everything you read about actors?"

"I know that."

"If that's true, how can you possibly believe the number of men I've supposedly dated, the number I've kissed?"

"I just know you're the most beautiful woman I've ever seen, and I can only imagine men lose their heads over you."

She stared up at him in surprise. She was partly flattered at the praise, especially coming from a man like Noah, whom she suspected did not flatter for empty reasons. And she was partly dismayed, because so few people ever looked beyond her face and saw the woman beneath. Tyler had been one of those people; she was disappointed Noah wasn't the same.

She'd begun a friendship with Tyler before she was "glamorous." He'd known her as a fellow actor, without the

The Apple Blossom Café

makeup or the expensive clothing. Noah only knew the woman Gabby let the tabloids see. She had to change that perception, let him see she was approachable, that she was just like anyone else.

"Men don't lose their heads over me; they avoid me," she said quietly.

"I can't believe that," he scoffed, lifting up his platters and gesturing to the two she could carry.

She did so and followed him across the kitchen. "I'm telling you the truth. I seem to intimidate men. The truly good ones don't want to be splashed all over gossip websites with me. They want to lead their own private lives, not have every decision they make subject to public scrutiny."

Noah put his back to a door to open it wide. He was staring at her, really listening to her—she thought. She hoped.

"In answer to your question," she continued, "no, I'm not kissed often, unless it's on a movie set. And that kiss…it was really good, Noah. And it meant something to me that you wanted to kiss me. I hope…I hope it was for a better reason than that I'm pretty."

She moved past him and down the hall, then to the stairs that led up to the tasting room. It was her turn to push open the door with her backside, and she gestured Noah to go in first. He gave her a searching glance from beneath lowered brows, as if he was really looking at her, seeing past the good looks she'd gotten from the genetics lottery.

In the tasting room, Brianna gave them a curious look, but no one else seemed to notice anything amiss. Noah was as taciturn as always, and Gabby was really good at acting like nothing had happened.

She was surprised by how much she continued to think about Noah's impulsive kiss, even when she arrived home later that evening. It was difficult to forget the feel of his body against hers—it had been a long time, almost a year, since she'd let herself be intimate with a man. It was so hard to trust anyone to want her for the right reasons. And to just give in to a man's kiss? She was still surprised by her impulsiveness.

As she turned on lights in her great room, she forced herself to put the tempting thoughts away. She had business with Noah, and she wasn't going to complicate it with flirtation. Instead, she remembered the comforting feeling of being surrounded by a family, even if it wasn't hers.

And that made her think of her brother, Kevin. He'd called again—she'd seen the message pop up on her phone. Kevin probably needed more money, or maybe their mom was bothering him or—something. He was always complaining. Or relapsing. With a sigh, she listened to his message. To her surprise, he sounded almost cheerful. He said he was doing well and wanted to tell her about his new job. Before she could think too much about it, she called him back.

"Gabby, hi! Thanks for calling me."

Kevin sounded far too enthusiastic, which made her uneasy.

"Hi, Kevin. You sound good."

"I feel great—thanks to you, of course." He sounded sincere.

"You're welcome. I'm always glad to help."

"I'm determined that this time you won't regret your generosity. And that it will be the last time."

She'd heard that before, and he knew it. "Are you still in New York?"

"Nope, I took a job in DC. I'm doing community outreach for the rehab facility. I figure I know what I'm talking about, so I can be convincing."

"That sounds like a good way to help people."

"That's my hope. The things I've done with my life…" His voice trailed off, and he sighed.

Gabby tensed, knowing this was the point in their usual conversations where he got down on himself, or their childhood,

The Apple Blossom Café

and she usually heard echoes of his feelings of betrayal because she'd left home to start her own life.

"Enough of that," he said with that cheerfulness that seemed so startling. "What are you up to?"

She wanted to stare at the phone. Kevin was asking about *her*? Without the usual jealousy? She wished she could just trust that he'd really recovered this time, that they could have the sibling relationship the Fairfields seemed to have.

"Well, I finished filming, and I've taken some time off."

"Let me guess—back to that little town in Virginia."

She frowned. "How did you know?"

"I was going through a rough patch last fall—"

An understatement.

"—but I caught pictures of you during that little play you helped put on."

"You're making it sound like we did it in the backyard and charged a dollar to the neighbors."

"We did that once," he said quietly.

"I remember. You played Skeletor, and I was working with He-Man to defeat you."

"You never wanted to be the weak heroine, waiting to be rescued."

"Of course not."

"But...I don't want to play the villain anymore," he said quietly.

"You're not a villain, Kevin. Stop thinking that way."

"That's nice of you to say."

They were speaking in almost hushed tones, as if so shocked by their words, they couldn't say them out loud. She sank down on the couch and pulled her knees to her chest.

"Why don't you come visit me?" she asked impulsively. "I'm just hanging out. You could tell me about the job."

"Gabby, I—"

He stopped and had to clear the huskiness from his voice. A wall of reserve inside her seemed to melt a bit, and she blinked at a surprising sting of tears.

"I—I don't know if I can get away that easily," he continued, "being the new guy on the job and all… I'm really grateful for the invitation. It's lonely in a new city."

"I totally get that. I'm only a couple hours away, in Spencer Hollow, just west of Charlottesville. Oh, but you know that from all the media coverage during the play."

"I do." There was a long pause. "Well, it's getting late. I'll let you get some rest. Good night, Gabby."

"'Night, Kevin."

The phone clicked into silence, and now she really did stare at it, even as the screen darkened to black. Almost from the moment he'd been born, Kevin had been the proverbial weight around her neck. She'd been forced to babysit him on and off, and when it had become full time, she'd resented him terribly for "ruining" her high school life, her school plays and musicals, the only "good" kids who'd let her in. Their mom had held her responsible for everything that had happened to Kevin—and then he'd gotten into drugs, and her mom had insisted that that was Gabby's fault, as if she'd picked his friends. Leaving had been all she could focus on, and when she did, she tried not to look back on the dysfunction she'd left behind.

But she'd found that "dysfunction" wasn't just her family, it was her. Her mom and brother weren't the only ones to make terrible mistakes. An innocent baby had paid the price, born into a world unwanted by its mother.

Stop that, Gabby ordered herself. Why was she thinking about the little girl she'd only named in her heart, unable to speak the name aloud because that would have made her too real?

Because she'd seen Theresa McDougall's little boy at Fairfield Orchard. She'd been surprised by her strong reaction to the

The Apple Blossom Café

toddler. It wasn't as if she never saw kids. She'd always known she was too busy to give a child the love and attention it needed—that would be unfair. She'd given up her little girl because of the total poverty she'd been living in at the time, sleeping on men's couches, making too many mistakes.

How could she fault her brother, when she herself was so guilty?

Chapter 4

Noah almost squinted at the sun as he drove down the mountain side and into Spencer Hollow. The big yellow ball was right in his eyes, and he was still surprised that it was just after dawn, and he was awake. That didn't often happen in his restaurant world.

He was surprised about a lot of things lately—which led him to think about the kiss he'd boldly planted on Gabrielle, famous movie star, Tyler's ex-girlfriend.

What had he been thinking? he asked himself for the hundredth time. So she'd liked his caramel sauce; so she'd made the most incredibly sexy moan when she tasted it; so she'd closed her eyes and looked as if he'd sent her to the most sensual heaven. But with only his food.

Then he'd kissed her. He was still surprised she hadn't slapped him—no, punched him. That would be Gabrielle's style. He would have deserved it. He'd pulled her against him like a caveman, and she'd gone right along with it.

She was messing with his head, no doubt about it. He'd come home to Fairfield Orchard, ready to continue being angry with her on his brother's behalf, but instead...he wanted her. And he couldn't control the desire that simmered just beneath the surface every time he was with her, threatening to erupt. He'd kissed his brother's ex, fulfilling the fantasy of every other man on the planet.

But...why had she returned the kiss?

Maybe he didn't want to know.

Noah pulled into the parking lot of Feel the Burn, the gym in an old Victorian storefront next door to the firehouse. It wasn't

The Apple Blossom Café

like the gyms in Pittsburgh, with their chrome and glass and high-tech equipment. The Hollow's only gym was just some cardio machines and free weights that the fire fighters used when they were off duty. Noah had bought a month's pass.

Inside, a few of the men greeted him. He'd been coming every other day or so, reconnecting with a couple people he went to high school with, including Madison, a few years younger than he and a fire fighter with the muscles to carry a man to safety. He'd seen her prove it recently, too, challenged by one of the guys in the department to demonstrate how long she could carry him.

Madison was working out, wearing a tank top and doing impressive bicep curls. She smiled at him, her face damp with perspiration as she continued with her reps. Noah started running on the treadmill, listening to an audiobook, his headphones connected to his phone. He got lost in the world of the mystery novel but couldn't miss that Madison was watching him.

Then Noah was distracted by the next woman who walked through the door. It was Gabrielle, dressed in expensive leggings and a matching jacket. Her hair was pulled back in a ponytail, a casual style he'd never imagined her wearing. She wore a ball cap and sunglasses as if trying to disguise herself on the street. Inside, she took off the glasses as she looked around. Though she wore little makeup, she was stunning. He'd kissed her just last night and was still feeling a little stunned himself.

He wasn't the only one who noticed her, and the whispers began to circle the room.

Gabrielle bestowed her megawatt smile on everyone. "Hello!" she called to no one in particular. "This looks like a fun place to work out. Can I talk to someone about joining? Any yoga classes?"

Though most of the men gaped for several minutes too long, Madison took pity on her and gave her the lowdown on how to join, the hours, etc.

"No yoga classes," Madison added reluctantly. "I bet someone would work out with you, if you wanted."

Gabrielle looked right at Noah, and he glanced away, pretending to be engrossed in his running and in his book. Surreptitiously he paused the book, having totally lost track of what was going on between the detective and the suspect. He was not about to get caught up in the very public drama that always surrounded Gabrielle.

"Do you like yoga?" Gabrielle asked Madison.

"Sorry, no."

Madison gave Noah an embarrassed look which he couldn't read. But that made Gabrielle face him. She turned up her smile, it reached her eyes, and even Noah got a little breathless.

"Noah!" Gabrielle called.

He cocked his head, pulling out his ear buds. "Hey, Gabrielle. I'm just working out."

God, that sounded lame. Why else would he be here? And why did he keep looking at her mouth? He wasn't about to taste it again.

To her credit, she didn't chuckle. "It's a great little place. I don't suppose you like yoga?"

He shook his head emphatically—he was not going to get down on the floor with her in impossibly sexual positions.

"That's a shame." Gabrielle looked at the treadmill next to him with speculation.

He held his breath as she unzipped her little jacket, and he caught a glimpse of her breasts.

"I'd like to learn yoga," said a firefighter with bulging muscles that looked far too inflexible.

"Me, too," called another man.

The Apple Blossom Café

With a wave, Gabrielle left him. They cleared a place in the corner for her, and soon she was teaching a class of eager men as if she'd been born to instruct.

Noah should be happy. But this was worse, so much worse. There were mirrors in that corner, and he couldn't get away from reflections of the great Gabrielle bent in every kind of position, her leggings hugging the muscles of her calves and thighs, not to mention what they did to her ass...

He wasn't the only one watching. He was joined by every other man in the gym—five of them—as well as several guys outside the building, looking through the front window with cameras dangling around their necks. The paparazzi had found her, and he felt a stirring of sympathy. Famous actresses got paid well and had to accept the lack of privacy that went along with it. Then he reminded himself how easily bystanders could get pulled in.

"Hey Noah!"

Gratefully, he looked at Madison. "Yeah?"

"How's it feel to be home?"

"It's not permanent," he quickly said.

"I know that," she said with patience.

Out of the corner of his eye, he saw Gabrielle coming toward them. "Madison," Noah said impulsively, "why don't we have dinner tonight and catch up? It's been awhile since I've eaten at Jefferson's Retreat."

Her face brightened as she nodded. Gabrielle's stride didn't even break as she found her water bottle on a bench near her jacket, took a drink, then moved past him once again, giving him a distracted smile.

After agreeing on a time to meet up with Madison, Noah expected to feel relieved. But he didn't. He was forced to watch Gabrielle and the firefighters. She was so charming as she walked among them—some of whom had obviously never stretched a day in their lives and needed her personal attention. Noah's gut clenched every time she adjusted someone's arm or laughed at a comment. He'd always appreciated beauty, and hers was almost painful, as if she'd cast a spell on him. He thought of her revelations about her previous relationship. After years of hearing Tyler's experiences with fame, Noah knew not to believe everything he read. The fact that he wanted to believe the worst about her only showed him how desperate he was to keep his distance. Disappointed in himself, he put his ear buds back in and turned on the book.

~oOo~

Gabby finished her impromptu class with the firefighters and stood with them for several minutes. They were big, friendly men, eager to talk to her—unlike a certain chef.

She glanced at Noah, as she'd done too many times while she'd supposedly been paying attention to her yoga students. He was running on the treadmill, his stride long and confident. Occasionally he mopped his sweaty face with a towel or glanced at the treadmill screen to monitor his pace. He was wearing a t-shirt, damn him, so she couldn't check out his bare shoulders as she wanted to. He seemed focused on whatever music he was listening to. Country, rock, classical, or maybe rap. She told herself her curiosity was simply because she was looking for a way to strike up a friendship.

Because that was all they were going to have, if his blatant dinner invitation to Madison was any evidence.

Gabby made her excuses to the disappointed men and put her towel and water bottle back in her bag. She should be glad Noah was ignoring their impulsive kiss. He'd never agree to help her if he thought she was seducing him into compliance. People often assumed she used her looks to get what she wanted, and it irritated her no end, as if she didn't have brains and talent. She didn't want Noah to believe something so shallow about her. He

The Apple Blossom Café

and the rest of the Fairfields were her friends, and she wanted to deepen that friendship, since she planned to spend a lot of her free time in Spencer Hollow.

She glanced up at the big plate-glass window, only to see that the crowd of photographers had grown. She was no longer surprised and puzzled that they thought her workouts were worthy of photos. She always told herself they were just doing their job; that didn't mean she wanted to wade through them and their shouted questions just to get to her car.

"They're persistent."

She jumped, but it was Noah, speaking right over her shoulder, silent in his approach. His hair was darkened with sweat, and his t-shirt clung to him. She quickly looked away, knowing exactly how it felt to have her chest ogled.

"That's your car," he continued, "the little red one, right?"

"The one they're leaning on?" she asked with faint sarcasm. "Yep, that's the one."

Some photographers were now waving to get her attention, and a few started snapping photos through the window. Noah quickly turned his back, and she did the same.

"You sure you want to be photographed with me?" Gabby asked. "You know what happens, the rumors that start."

"To be honest, it's the last thing I need." She frowned, and he added, "When I visited Tyler in New York, women would stop him for his autograph, occasionally follow him around, but it was nothing like this."

"New York's different. People mind their own business, most of the time."

"Even the paparazzi?"

"Well, no," she admitted.

He glanced over his shoulder at the window again. "Want a ride home? I can drive around to the back and pick you up there, so you can avoid the herd."

She didn't run away from the paparazzi, or she'd be running all the time. Noah didn't need to know that. Besides, spending time with Noah could help her cause. "That would be nice, thanks. Meet you in five?"

"I'll be there."

Gabby made a show of waving good-bye to him, then going to the back of the gym as he left. She imagined he got a lot of questions as he unlocked his car. After saying good-bye to the firefighters, she waited inside the back door until she saw Noah's SUV.

Once outside, she jumped in and slammed the door. "Step on it. I always wanted to say that."

The corner of his mouth gave a faint quirk, as if he almost smiled as he sped away. Not that he had far to go, just a couple miles, but she'd enjoy the ride while she could.

She bit her lip before she could say, *Madison's cute*. That would sound bitchy and jealous, and she was neither. She glanced at Noah. "How much longer will you be in town?"

"Until after the grand opening of the café next week."

He kept his eyes on the road as they drove through the four-way stop by the MacDougall's store.

"Are you excited?"

He glanced at her from beneath an arched brow. "It's business, not a movie opening."

"That's business, too. I can still be excited and hopeful that everyone likes it."

"True. I do want it to be a success."

"Perhaps you're nervous more than excited," she teased.

"You have no idea," he said dryly.

"Now that's cryptic."

"Not really. A family restaurant is different than a movie."

"In some ways." She gestured down the drive toward her rented house. "Take a right."

The Apple Blossom Café

They were almost there. How could she keep him talking? "Have you found a chef yet?"

"Not since we discussed this last night." He pulled the car to a stop in the driveway.

She was making a mess of things. "Did you want to come in for a drink? The view from the terrace is beautiful."

"I can't, sorry."

She unbuckled her seatbelt and turned to face him. "Oh, I wanted to tell you—you know how we were discussing my brother last night?"

He nodded but didn't turn off the car.

"He happened to leave me a message, so I gave him a call. He's doing well, clean and sober, and has a new job in DC with the rehab facility. He sounds good."

"I'm glad," he said quietly. "Much as I don't get home regularly, family is still important to me."

There was a long moment of silence. There was still the tension of the kiss they hadn't spoken about, and she was desperate to find a safe topic of discussion.

"I don't want you to be late for whatever you're doing today," he finally said.

He was kicking her out. She sighed.

He cocked his head. "Nothing exciting to do in the Hollow? I'm shocked."

"I didn't say that. I'm going to do some volunteer work with the Skyline Theater Guild."

"You have time for another play?"

"Not this time. I'll be back and forth to L.A. But I'm going to work with the youth theater. Bri talked to Aaron Ho, who'll let me be his assistant director for the next few weeks. I start today."

"Herding kids—fun."

"You don't sound enthusiastic. You'll change your mind when you're an uncle."

"I didn't think kids were your thing."

"What?" she asked sharply. "Why would you think that?"

He put up two hands. "Ease up there. I only meant that you didn't seem to warm up to Theresa's little boy last night."

She put aside her dismay that she hadn't done a better job hiding her emotions and tried to make her voice sound light. "How closely were you watching me?"

He narrowed his eyes. "Too closely."

She caught her breath. They looked at each other for a long time. She forgot what they'd been discussing, lost in a moment fraught with dark possibilities. Oh, this wasn't a good idea.

He seemed to think the same. "Have fun, Gabrielle."

"Gabby. My friends call me Gabby. Gabrielle is my actress persona."

For a moment, she thought he'd say "Gabrielle" and confirm her place in his life as an acquaintance, nothing more.

"Gabby." His voice was soft and deep.

She fumbled for the car door, knowing she'd better not push her luck. "Do you have a fun day planned?"

"Interviews."

"Good luck."

She shut the door, and he put the car in gear and backed down the driveway, turning at the end to swing around and drive toward the road.

She stood there for a long time, arms crossed over her chest. There weren't many men who'd resisted her, especially one she'd already kissed. She wasn't *trying* to sway him physically. Yeah, she knew she cleaned up well, but it was often the whole package, the fact that she was a "movie star."

Noah didn't seem at all starstruck by her, and for the first time, she considered if perhaps that…bothered her. Had she

The Apple Blossom Café

thought she'd get her way with him? Did she actually want his attention more than she wanted his help?

That kiss had been the last thing on her mind when she'd fallen asleep, and the first thing she thought about in the morning. Noah had showed her how he felt about it by asking another woman to dinner right in front of her. It was the smart move to make.

And yet it irritated her.

Chapter 5

Much as Gabby told herself she was going to try to live like a normal person in Spencer Hollow, the close call with the paparazzi made her leery. She didn't want to admit to herself that sometimes Smalls and her other bodyguards came in handy. But no, she was going to be a regular person again. And she didn't want to arrive for her first day with the kids trailing paparazzi, like a movie star there to do some charity work.

She knew there'd be cars waiting at the end of the driveway to follow her into the village. She remembered there were a couple bikes in the garage, so after putting her hair up in a ponytail beneath a ball cap, she went to examine her options. The antique bike with the wide flat seat and basket on the handle bars made her chuckle. She gamely pedaled it down neat dirt paths between pine trees, the horse trails that interlaced the countryside. In the village, she swung around the north side to avoid the main crossroads, and approached the Spencer Hollow Community Church's back door. She brought the bike into the hallway and left it there, along with her cap and sunglasses. She knew her way around the building after performing there last fall.

She entered the church hall, where all the chairs were stacked along the walls, with the stage at the far end. She saw Brianna and several other adults gathered around a long paper-strewn table near the stage.

Brianna glanced up. "Hey, Gabby!"

Since Gabby had worked with most of these people before, she exchanged a lot of hugs, and then shook hands with several new volunteers.

Aaron Ho wore his trademark scarf around his neck, and he gave Gabby a hug that almost spun her around. "I can't believe

The Apple Blossom Café

you want to work with me!" he cried with exuberance. "You have so much more experience."

"Not directing," Gabby countered, smiling at him. "You did a great job with our play last fall. And I'm sure I can count on you to show me the best way to work with the kids."

He reddened and waved off the compliment. "You'll be doing me a favor, too. I've taken a job as an adjunct professor in the theater department at UVA, and I'm feeling busy and overwhelmed. But I would never disappoint these kids."

"How exciting for you! I'll help any way I can."

As Brianna called for the volunteers to begin assembling, Gabby went to say hello to Mac MacDougall, Brianna's father. He'd been the production manager before a recent diagnosis of Alzheimer's disease had begun to slow him down. Brianna had re-opened the theater guild as a way to share lasting memories with her dad, even though he might not remember them. Mac still worked occasionally at the store, although he'd given up the day-to-day management to Brianna.

It was obvious from Mac's blank expression that he remembered Gabby, but not her name. She felt a pang of sadness, then shook his hand. "Hi, Mac, it's Gabby Eklund, a friend of Tyler's. Your daughter agreed to let me volunteer with the guild."

"Gabby," he said with relief. "You did such a great job starring in our last play."

He remembered. She was happy to know his condition hadn't worsened very much in the few months she'd been gone. "Thanks. Now I'll be working behind the scenes. I hope you'll give me some pointers."

He laughed but didn't have time to say more because children began to push through the doors at the back of the hall. There were several dozen of them, ages maybe eight to sixteen. Brianna settled them down for a discussion of the play that had been chosen, as well as the many parts they could audition for. Gabby helped collect paperwork their parents had signed. The younger kids briefly looked at her as if they might know her from somewhere. The teenagers were openly shocked, some of the girls giggling as they raised their phones for photos.

"No phones," Brianna called. "You know the rules. We're here to experience the theater, and there are only so many hours in the day. Miss Gabrielle would like some privacy while she's here. Let's not make that difficult for her."

"We'll find another time for pictures, I promise," Gabby added, smiling.

For the next hour, Gabby walked beside Aaron while the kids received their audition scripts and worked in small groups. Aaron went from group to group, making suggestions, several times deferring to Gabby for her input.

Between groups, she murmured to him, "You're the director—you don't need my opinion."

"Thanks for saying that, but the kids obviously want to hear from you. They're pretty excited."

"I don't want to make things difficult for you."

"You're not. They'll settle down when they get used to you. I did," he added, elbowing her playfully.

Gabby laughed, even as she noticed a group of kids onstage. "Are we practicing auditions?"

"No, that's the stage crew. Some of them are new to the job and are learning what's involved."

One girl stood out to Gabby. She was older, fifteen or sixteen. Though she was listening and not causing a disturbance, she seemed a little...bored. The girl noticed Gabby, reddened, and looked away.

She was just a few years older than Gabby's own daughter.

Stop it, Gabby told herself, nodding at whatever Aaron was saying. It had been years since she'd done this to herself,

The Apple Blossom Café

comparing random kids to the one she'd given up. Helping the youth theater was supposed to help her get over this—and it was obvious she needed help. Taking a deep breath, she turned to focus her attention on Aaron.

It didn't always work. There was something about the girl—her name was Sarah, Gabby finally learned—that called to her. Sarah wore her dark hair short and fashionably shaggy, with a blue streak down one side that made Gabby smile. Sarah was endearing as she played the professional elder, helping to divide the stage crew into groups for different tasks, speaking several times to one particular girl, who ended up being her younger sister. Gabby knew all about keeping track of a sibling, so she empathized with Sarah even more.

When it was almost time for the kids to be picked up by their parents, Gabby posed for pictures and answered questions for a few minutes. Sarah listened politely but didn't crowd in around her like some of the other kids. Eventually, Sarah took her sister's arm and pulled her toward the door. Gabby watched in bemusement.

"They're quite the twosome," Brianna said as she came up next to her. "Sarah has to watch over Zoe after school while their parents work."

Zoe? Gabby felt a stab of grief at hearing the private name she'd given her own daughter. It wasn't as if she didn't hear it regularly, but there was something about this particular girl, her big dark eyes looking up with such love at her sister. She gave herself an inner shake; it was a struggle to remember their discussion. "I can sympathize with Sarah. I have a little brother."

"And I have a little sister. We have way too much in common."

Gabby gave Brianna a frank look, thinking of Tyler, and both burst out laughing.

"Want to have dinner with me?" Gabby asked, after wiping her eyes.

"I'm meeting Amy and Carmen at Jefferson's Retreat. Come join us."

Jefferson's Retreat. Noah was having dinner there with Madison the firefighter. Gabby shouldn't bother them.

"I'd love to, thanks."

~oOo~

Gabby drove to the parking lot of MacDougall's General Store. She wished she'd accepted Brianna's offer of a ride, because several photographers followed her to MacDougall's parking lot. How could she have asked Brianna to drive, when the poor woman only lived a couple blocks from the restaurant?

Gabby wore her hat and sunglasses, but it didn't do much good. When Carmen and Amy pulled up in the same car, and Brianna came out of the store to greet them, several cameras caught their every move.

"I'm sorry," Gabby said, wishing she could give the paparazzi the finger.

"Don't be," Carmen said, waving at the photographers. "It's so exciting to live in your shoes for a little while."

"You'll get tired of it, I promise you."

"How long did it take you to feel that way?" Amy asked.

Gabby hesitated, then admitted, "A few years."

Chuckling, they all crossed the street. The emboldened paparazzi followed close behind, calling to Gabby to pose for them and answer questions, but after pausing to give them a smiling photo, she ignored them.

There were half a dozen people standing around or sitting on benches outside, obviously waiting for tables. Noah sat beside Madison, who was dressed in a short skirt that showed off her muscular legs.

The Apple Blossom Café

Although her three dinner companions went up to hug Noah and his date, Gabby hung back. She hadn't really thought this through. What had she intended to do, after all?

More photographers joined the others, and now they were taking photos repeatedly, their shutters clicking, as if hoping they could sell one of the photos for a chunk of money. Though Gabby ignored them, other dinner customers could not, as they were blocked or crowded out of the way. Customers began to glance at Gabby with annoyance, one even with downright hostility when a photographer stepped on his foot. Though Gabby wanted to build a home in Spencer Hollow, to become a normal part of the community, instead she might end up alienating all her new neighbors. It was a bleak, helpless thought. When one couple gave her a dirty look and departed for their car, her face heated with mortification.

Noah sent her a frown she could read too well. *What the hell are you doing here causing a problem during my date?*

She hadn't meant to annoy him. Was she so desperate for his attention—for his help, she insisted to herself—that she had to disrupt his life?

"The hostess says there's room inside at the bar," Carmen said. "Come on, Gabby."

Gabby followed the three women inside, relieved to leave Noah to Madison.

Inside Jefferson's Retreat, time turned back to the eighteenth century, with candlelit ambience of antique lanterns shining on framed paintings of men in breeches and tricorn hats bowing before bewigged ladies. The women jostled to stand near the bar, and soon Carmen was telling a funny story about the milking machine on her goat farm malfunctioning. Gabby found herself almost relaxing. It was difficult to totally feel at ease in public; she'd spent years learning to guard her expression. Suddenly that seemed overwhelmingly sad.

Emma Cane

Fifteen minutes later, a table opened up for them, and they were seated not far from Noah and Madison. Gabby deliberately chose the seat with her back to them. She was determined to enjoy the company of her new friends. A glass of wine helped loosen her up, but people kept staring; a woman asked for an autograph just as Gabby was chewing her meat; a drunk guy wanted her to settle a bet he had with his buddies at the bar.

Gabby answered him with a funny joke and he left.

Brianna gave her an amazed look. "This happens to you a lot?"

"Unless I have a bodyguard. And sometimes even then."

"How do you enjoy being outside at all?" Carmen asked.

All three women looked at her with wide, sympathetic eyes.

"It's okay," Gabby said lightly, though inside she was tense and uncomfortable. "It's part of the job. Fans are the reason my movies are a success."

Reassuring the women did nothing to brighten her own mood. She wanted Spencer Hollow to be "home," where she could be herself. So far, it had been a challenge.

She was used to being the focus of attention, but tonight it was like nails on a chalkboard. To make things worse, she could hear Noah's occasional laughter, something she'd seldom heard. He was obviously having a good time with Madison; Gabby couldn't make him laugh. Why would he want to let her hang out in his kitchen?

She excused herself for the ladies' room, and afterward, headed down the small corridor to the back of the building. It was good to be alone. She was beginning to see why so many celebrities built themselves walled fortresses to hide behind. She didn't want that kind of life.

She pushed through the door, and instead of another parking lot, she found a courtyard with tables stacked to one side. They must use this for outdoor seating during the warmer months.

The Apple Blossom Café

She smiled faintly at the old-fashioned well in one corner, and the lanterns on the wall, keeping up the colonial theme. Hugging her sweater closer, she sank down on a bench near the well and just took a deep breath, inhaling the scents of budding spring plants and listening to the night insects talk to each other.

"Need some company?"

Startled, she looked up to see a tall man silhouetted against the building's lights. She knew his voice.

"Hi, Noah." She cocked her head. "I'm fine. You can go back inside."

"I didn't ask if you were all right. I asked if you needed company," he said mildly. "Move over."

She moved over. The bench wasn't very big; she felt the brush of his hip against hers.

"I thought you did a good job trying to have fun," he said. "Not that you were successful."

"My back was to you, Noah."

"Not for the whole evening. I think I'm starting to be able to tell when you're acting by the look in your eyes."

"I'll work on that," she said dryly.

He let silence be his answer.

"Everyone acts some of the time," she finally said. "Otherwise humanity would be squabbling constantly. Why does it bother you that I do it?"

"I'm not really sure."

His voice was slow and deep, even thoughtful, as if he was trying to understand himself, too.

"I just know you want to be happy here," he continued, "and I warned you it's not some kind of utopia."

"Spencer Hollow isn't the problem; it's my foolish belief that I can find a place to be…myself."

Emma Cane

"You're expecting a lot out of a place when you haven't spent all that much time here. And, to be fair, you haven't really given it a chance."

She turned to look at him. "I can't believe Noah Fairfield is actually defending his hometown."

He shrugged those broad shoulders. The shadows recessed his eyes, outlining his cheekbones in bold relief. The firm lines of his mouth were highlighted, inviting.

She forced herself to look at the building again. "You should go back inside to Madison. She's probably wondering where you are."

"She left."

Her startled gaze returned to him. "Was she called in to work? I didn't hear a siren."

"No, it wasn't work. We parted amicably. She decided things weren't going to go anywhere with us because she said I couldn't stop looking at you."

Their eyes met, and she didn't look away. For a long moment, the simmering tension rose slowly up inside her. It was always beneath the surface; she couldn't escape this fascination with Noah, and the way even his somberness drew her. Though he seemed to isolate himself, he worked in a profession that was meant to be social, to please other people. The contradiction fascinated her.

"So what are we supposed to do about…us?" she whispered.

"I have no idea."

She gave a rueful smile. "You could say you want to kiss me until I'm breathless."

He was so still that she could tell he was holding himself back. Even his fists were clenched. She put her hand on his, where it rested on his thigh.

The Apple Blossom Café

"I want to kiss you until *both* of us are breathless." His voice was hoarse now, and it made something deep inside her shiver with excitement.

"Come home with me, Noah."

She couldn't believe she'd said the words. She wasn't the sort of person to trust a man with intimacy so soon—not since the terrible consequences of her rash decisions when she was too young.

"I want to. But you're here with—" he began.

"I'll say good-night. Bring your car around to the back to pick me up."

He arched a brow.

She squeezed his arm. "It's not that I don't want to be seen with you. I wouldn't subject you to the craziness, Noah. Do you want your face splashed all over the internet or the tabloids?" She almost said, *Remember what happened with Tyler,* but bringing up his brother, a man she'd once briefly dated, seemed like a bad idea.

He hesitated for what seemed like a long time. Would he think it through and decide the consequences weren't worth one night's passion? She wanted him with a desperation that felt overwhelming. It had been a long time since she'd been with a man, even longer since she'd been with one who fascinated her as much as Noah did.

"All right," he said, standing up, "I'll meet you beyond the courtyard."

He drew her to her feet. She thought he was only being polite until he pulled her into his arms and kissed her. It was open-mouthed and deliciously wet, hot and passionate, made even more so by the knowledge that this was leading to even more, and soon. She slid her hands up his back and held those broad shoulders for the first time, sagging weakly against him with pleasure.

Emma Cane

He lifted his head. "Can you get away quickly?"

She pressed her hips to his, feeling his erection through his clothes. "For that, yes."

He smiled, a broad, uncomplicated smile that made her feel such a shock of pleasure. To make such a somber man smile had to be one of the best things in life.

She kissed him once more, quickly, then went into the building. At the table, Brianna, Amy, and Carmen were mulling over the dessert menu as she approached.

"There you are," Brianna said. "Are you feeling all right?"

The perfect segue. And she'd only feel a little guilty. "I am, thanks, just a little headache." Something was aching, all right. "I'm going to head home. I really appreciate the lovely evening."

Amy was watching her, brow furrowed, and Gabby had to wonder if Noah's sister suspected they'd been together.

What did it matter? They were adults—as long as Noah didn't suffer from Gabby's harsh spotlight.

"Good-night," Gabby said. "I'm going to avoid the paparazzi by going out the back door. Thanks for putting up with my crazy fan club."

She did her best not to seem rushed, but it was difficult. She knew what awaited her.

And he was there, inside his dark SUV. She jumped into the front seat, hoping no one saw her. Sometimes the paparazzi did remember to cover several entrances, although maybe not in this small town, where it was no secret she planned to live part of the year, so she wouldn't be hiding.

"You didn't change your mind," she said with relief.

"I was thinking the same thing about you."

They grinned at each other.

Chapter 6

On the barely two-mile drive to the waterfront home, Noah didn't question his decision to take a risk. He glanced at Gabby as they passed beneath a streetlamp, and she looked cool and remote, so confident. Even her profile had an unbelievable beauty, perfectly shaped nose, generous lips, cheekbones that movie screens couldn't do justice to.

What was she doing with *him*?

He put the thought from his mind. It didn't matter. They were willing adults who wanted a little fun. They had made no promises to each other, had put their disagreements behind them—maybe they hadn't even been disagreements, just two people resisting the irresistible.

They turned down the driveway, and one by one, the motion-detector lights blinked on as they followed the curve. He came to a stop in the driveway and turned the car off. The silence was thick.

"Are you certain you want to do this?" he asked quietly. "You've had some time to reflect. You might have changed your—"

"Noah, stop with the polite, pretty words and get into my house before I jump you right here in the car."

He didn't need to be told twice. They were in the back hallway when they fell on each other, pulling off sweaters and shirts.

"Where's your bedroom?" he demanded, his mouth on her throat, his hand kneading a handful of her ass.

"Upstairs," she gasped, arching. "If you can't reach my bra, I can—"

"Stop telling me what to do," he said mildly. He bent and tossed her over his shoulder. She gave a giggling gasp.

There were low lights in the great room, and another at the top of the stairs. He barely noticed, because she was taking her turn exploring what she could reach of his body. He almost staggered at the sensations, but thank God her bedroom was to the left. A wall of windows overlooked what was probably the creek; in the dark it seemed ghostly.

The bed was large, the counterpane glowing white in the shadows. When he upended her onto it, she fell back on her elbows. Her hair spilled down from the knot that had been holding it atop her head, and she looked incredibly sexy and sultry. He started to pull off his pants, and she watched him as if it were her own private show. When he was naked, her smile died. She reached for him, but he wasn't certain he could take her touch at that moment. So he pushed her skirt up her thighs. She went still.

"Now you can take your bra off," he whispered.

She did, and he almost choked at the bounty before him. Her skirt was caught around her waist, and the smallest thong hid her from him. He dispatched with that, barely keeping himself from ripping it off in frustration. It was worth his patience, when he pulled the bit of lace straight up, then spread her legs. He was poised over her, so ready to be inside the heat of her.

"Now," she whispered.

"You're ordering me around again." He braced himself over her and took one of her soft, sweet nipples into his mouth.

She groaned. "I won't...do that...again."

He didn't respond, losing himself in her gasps and moans. He rubbed his cheek against her other nipple before licking it with slow strokes. Then he kissed a line down her trembling stomach,

The Apple Blossom Café

past the narrow line of curling hair. He hesitated, blowing gently on her dampness, until she cried out her frustration.

"Are you going to tell me what to do?" he teased.

"No! But—please." The last came out as a ragged whisper.

He couldn't play with her any more. He licked her while she shuddered and spread herself even wider for him. He sucked and stroked, reached to caress her breasts, until her arching tension took her over the edge into shudders of release.

And then he went searching for his pants and a condom.

Gabby lay all sprawled with delicious abandon as the last waves of pleasure worked their way out through her fingers and toes. Damn, Noah knew what he was doing. She wanted more. Where was he?

"Noah?"

"Right here, though I'm shaking like a kid putting on his first condom."

She was shocked and delighted that he'd admitted to such vulnerability. This was Noah?

He was over her and inside her before she could even take another breath. The plunge of his entry was shocking, thrilling, and those magnificent shoulders were all hers to touch—not to mention how they'd taken her weight as if she were a fragile flower. Now she gripped his hips with her thighs, as if afraid he'd leave her.

She didn't think Noah the sort of man to leave a job half done.

"Gabby," he murmured, bending to kiss her.

She liked hearing him call her Gabby instead of Gabrielle, as if he knew he was with *her*, not the movie star. Joined, unmoving, they kissed for a long time, as she explored his lips, then held his face and kissed his nose, his cheekbones. She would have kissed more, but then he began to move inside her, and she gave up any vestiges of rational thought.

She strained against him, their hips undulating. She caressed his chest, his nipples, fanned her hands down his arms where he braced himself. He paused deep inside her, his body trembling, as if he was trying to make the moment last. Then he picked up speed, thrusting deep until he came to his own shuddering climax, his head arched back, his expression intense.

When he collapsed on top of her, careful to support his weight, she did as she'd longed to, and gently pushed the lock of dark hair off his forehead. Coming up on his elbows, he leaned down and kissed her mouth softly.

"That was…unexpected," he murmured between gentle kisses.

"What was?" She was lazily sliding her fingers through his hair.

"Sex."

When he slid out of her and rolled off the bed, she watched him walk to the bathroom to remove the condom, admiring that masculine back, narrow hips, and the roundness of his butt. When he came back, she hoped he wouldn't start getting dressed. He didn't, instead stretching out beside her. With a sigh of relief, she cuddled against his side and used his shoulder as a pillow.

"I don't think it was all that unexpected," she mused, pressing her mouth to the sweet saltiness of his skin. "We'd been dancing around it every time we saw each other. Or maybe sex with *me* was unexpected. You did bring that condom for Madison." She gently bit him.

"Ouch. I did not. Men are always prepared."

Not always, she thought, but wouldn't let the past touch this drowsy feeling of pleasure.

"So you don't wish the date had ended with Madison instead of me," she teased.

The Apple Blossom Café

"Gabby—God no. I only asked her out because you were right there, and I was trying to convince myself to get over my obsession with you."

"You know how to make a woman feel good, Noah, in a lot of different ways."

"I'm glad."

The words were just a rumble. His eyes were closed. He was such a man, she thought, amused.

She poked his shoulder. "You were obsessed with me?"

He opened one eye and looked down at her.

"And don't say many men are obsessed with me. Those men don't know me. I might as well be a *Playboy* centerfold to them, rather than a real person."

"Are you looking for compliments?"

"Just the truth."

"I haven't been able to stop thinking about you since you came back. You irritated the hell out of me last fall, but when I saw you again…" He gave her breast a caress.

She shivered. "You mean you saw my boobs."

"No, you disappointingly had them very well covered."

"Huh." She wasn't displeased.

His touch eased, his eyes closed.

"What happens next?" she asked quietly.

The tension that rippled through his skin was faint, but detectable.

"You got to see me up close and personal."

"What do you want to happen next?"

Oh, he was wary all right. "What do *you* want to happen next?" she asked.

"Sex with you on top?" He rolled her onto her back and leaned over her, kissing the breast closest to him.

"Specific, a nice touch." She let out a blissful sigh. "I mean after that. Are we dating?"

"I don't know. I'm leaving soon."

"Would you be happier if I just stop talking and we see what happens?"

"If you want honesty, then yes." He sucked her nipple into his mouth.

She gasped and arched, then said shakily, "Okay, I can do that."

"You can?"

"Yes. No strings attached tonight. We've had a great time."

"We're not done."

"Okay." She reached into her nightstand for another condom. "Roll over, Chef. My turn to call the shots."

He did as she commanded, and his hair looked sexily messy, his expression casually charming. Another side of him she hadn't seen before—she was seeing a lot of Noah Fairfield tonight.

She straddled his thighs and took her time unrolling the condom down his hard length, until he was reaching for her with a lot more desperation.

He sat up and held her against him, kissing her deeply, his tongue expertly taking her mouth as she wanted him to take her body. He gripped her shoulders and arched her back until he could reach her breasts with his tongue. He played with her, making her shudder and moan, until he eased her toward him. She caught her breath and sat back up again, sinking on top of him and taking him deep inside. She pushed him back and rode him as she wanted to, pausing at crucial moments until he strained against her with need. Only then did she pick up her speed and bring them both to satisfaction.

It was her turn to collapse on him, and this time there was no more conversation. She almost fell asleep there, with him still inside her.

"I need to go," he murmured against her hair.

"Must you?"

The Apple Blossom Café

"I'm training my servers first thing in the morning."

"Damn." She rolled off him. "Do you want to shower?"

"Sure, but don't join me. I won't be able to go home."

"Another time then."

He looked at her, as if about to speak, then got out of bed and shut the bathroom door behind him.

Thoughts of his work at the café made her remember her desire to job-shadow him. She winced, drawing a sheet up over her nakedness. She wanted the help of a private man who'd probably prefer to be focused on his kitchen—and now she'd slept with him. Would he think she'd seduced him deliberately to get her way?

Damn. This was getting complicated. She would just have to explain everything.

But she didn't want to ruin what had been a great night or start a conversation that could go on too late. A few minutes later, he bent over to kiss her good-bye, smelling like soap and man. He didn't say he'd call her, though they both knew he would.

As she went into the bathroom to take out her contacts and get ready for bed, she thought about her chef, who'd just stirred things inside her like a master. And she smiled.

~oOo~

Noah looked up from his phone when he heard the knock on the café door. The servers had gone, but he knew who it was. Gabby had texted earlier, asking if she could drop by to see him. Though he'd eagerly said yes, he'd made sure they'd be alone.

After that text, memories of her in bed had made it difficult for him to concentrate on instructing the servers. He only had himself to blame. Gabby was a captivating lover, generous, unpredictable, light-hearted, and sexy in a way that was beyond what was captured on screen. And he had thought *that* woman was sexy.

He smiled when he saw her face through the glass door, then unlocked it, saying, "Good morning."

She laughed. "It's already afternoon. You've worked part of the day away."

She sailed past him into the dining room, the scent of her flowery perfume inspiring sudden erotic memories. When she took off her jacket, she was wearing a gauzy cape top that made him think of a beautiful butterfly. He felt like he stood there dumbfounded by the way she seemed to overpower the room.

She put her hands on his chest and leaned up to give him a quick kiss. "Whoops, I did that right in front of the windows. We didn't even talk about whether you wanted to keep us private."

He put his hands over hers on his chest to keep her there, then stared into her expressive lavender eyes. "You wanted to keep this private in the restaurant last night."

"I did *not* want to keep us private—I didn't want you exposed to the nastiness of online gossip. But your family and friends? I'm fine with that, if you're fine."

"That works."

"We don't need to create drama where there is none—though drama is what I do for a living."

She teased him with her lovely, impish smile, and he found himself relaxing.

"Speaking of drama," she began.

She sounded a little more hesitant, and she glanced at their joined hands instead of into his eyes. Noah tensed, though there wasn't any reason. A woman like Gabby was unpredictable, and he really didn't know her well at all. He said nothing, just waited.

"Look, I had a favor I was building up to ask you," she began, "but then this attraction between us overwhelmed me—"

The Apple Blossom Café

"So, I'm overwhelming," he said, doubt in his voice, even as he tried to imagine what kind of favor Gabby would need from someone like him.

She smiled. "Definitely." Her smile faded as she stared up into his face. "In my next movie, I'll be playing a chef. I was going to ask if you'd mind me hanging out in your kitchen, sort of job-shadowing you as if I was a high schooler who wanted to learn about her chosen career. Before I could ask, this amazing thing happened between us, and now I'm worried you might think I meant to seduce my way into your kitchen. I'm not that kind of woman, I promise you."

Without volition, he thought again about how her fake-dating his brother had almost ruined Tyler's reputation. She'd certainly used Tyler, though Tyler had insisted it had been her manager's idea, and that she'd tried to refuse.

"I'm not having any luck reading your expression," she said slowly. "What are you thinking? You can say that you're too busy, and I'll understand."

It was pretty obvious she didn't think he'd say no. He imagined she wasn't used to people turning her down about anything. And he felt a little more uneasy. *Had* this all been a plan to get what she wanted? He didn't think so, but he didn't know her well enough to be certain.

And what did her motives really matter? he told himself. They were going to keep having great sex, after all.

He squeezed her hands and then let them go. "I'm thinking that it will be difficult to keep my mind on cooking when I could be putting you up on the counter and showing you my other talents."

She smiled, though she was still searching his eyes as she took a step back. "Is that a yes?"

"Yes."

She let out her breath, as if she'd been worried. But did he believe that?

"Don't feel forced," she insisted. "I could try the head chef at Jefferson's Retreat. I did some research on him and he's had some solid training."

"Please. I ate there—it wasn't bad, but—"

"You really are an arrogant chef," she said with a laugh.

"I'm not saying that. He just doesn't have the experience I do."

"The big city experience, huh? Don't you mean the awards? Yeah, your family brags a lot about your culinary accomplishments."

He kept his expression neutral, although it took effort. He was surprised how jarred he was to remember that his latest accomplishments had ended in failure. Who was he to judge another chef? But Gabby had researched the man—would she research him? It would be easy to find out he'd been fired, that he was the subject of avid speculation in the Pittsburgh foodie circles.

He didn't really care if she found out, but he didn't want her pity or concern. It was not like she was his girlfriend.

The door suddenly opened, and Gabby took a big step away from him. That was good; he didn't need the scrutiny being seen with her would lead to.

It wasn't a tourist ignoring his "closed" sign, but his Grandpa Fairfield, white-haired, his glasses reflecting the dangling lights of the café. He was dressed in well-worn khakis and a black buttoned-down shirt with "Fairfield Orchard" stitched on the pocket. He'd worked at the orchard his entire life, having inherited it from his own father. He still showed up every single day. Though he smiled at Noah, he brightened on seeing Gabby.

"Miss Gabrielle," he said, his voice full of the smooth warmth of a Southern gentleman.

The Apple Blossom Café

"Mr. Fairfield," she said, taking his outstretched hand and holding it between her own. "How good to see you again."

"I hear you might be calling our neck of the woods home soon."

"In the very near future, I hope. Amy has already contacted the owners about my purchasing the place. They're interested."

That was fast, Noah thought, leaning back against the bar with his arms crossed over his white-coated chest.

"There's no place better to raise a family," Grandpa said.

To Noah's surprise, Grandpa Fairfield glanced at him after speaking those words. Was he still trying to persuade Noah to move home permanently, since it couldn't have anything to do with Gabby and him?

"So I hear," Gabby said. "I'm convinced. Not that I have any family plans," she added quickly.

She didn't look at Noah as she said those words. He smiled inwardly, wondering if she was trying to reassure him.

"Am I interrupting?" Grandpa asked, glancing from Gabby to Noah. "We were going to talk about the dessert menu, but I can come back."

"Not at all," Gabby said. "I don't want to intrude."

There was a lot of looking going on, as she gave Noah a pointed glance that he read easily. She'd leave if he wanted her to, but if it was café-related, she'd obviously like to stay.

"Neither of you is intruding," Noah said. "Grandpa, Gabby is going to hang out here to do some research for her next movie."

"That's wonderful," Grandpa said with enthusiasm. "Is it about an orchard?"

Gabby shook her head ruefully. "Sorry, no. I'll be playing a chef."

"No one better to learn from than our Noah here. Did you know he won the prestigious Drayton Award for upcoming chefs?"

"I did," she said, glancing at Noah with smiling eyes.

Noah took three chairs off the nearest table and gestured to them. "Sit down, Grandpa. I wasn't sure what you wanted to talk about, but I thought I'd give you the ideas I've been mulling. I'm still in talks with several chefs, one of whom, if I hire him, would like to make the desserts himself. Another woman wants to—"

Grandpa held up a hand. "You're getting ahead of the conversation. You don't need to bother your chefs about the desserts. I'd like to volunteer."

Noah frowned. "What do you mean? You want to bake for the café?"

"Who do you think created some of our best fudge and apple pie recipes?"

"Uh...I thought Grandma might have."

"You thought wrong." Grandpa shook his head toward Gabby, as if including her in his disappointment. "Unless Grandma claimed that. If so, I'd have to put her over my knee."

"Grandpa, stop!" Noah said, hoping he wasn't reddening. There were so many things wrong with that statement.

Grandpa and Gabby were chuckling.

"Anyway," Grandpa continued, "I've continued to work in the store kitchen. I'd be happy to help you. I even have some ideas—if I wouldn't be stepping on your toes."

"Of course not."

They spent the next hour sketching out ideas for a rotating selection of desserts every day, many with the requisite apple ingredient. Gabby was surprisingly good at knowing when to speak up and when to simply absorb. Noah could feel her watching him occasionally, and although he wanted it simply to be because they'd had mind-blowing sex—or so *he* believed anyway—he could also tell she was studying him, perhaps even dissecting his mannerisms, how he spoke about the food, everything. She'd asked to job-shadow him; he just hadn't

The Apple Blossom Café

believed it could feel so…intense. She even watched his hands, for God's sake, and they weren't even in the kitchen yet.

At last Gabby gathered her purse. "I have to go, gentlemen. I have a phone meeting with my team about the promotion schedule for the upcoming movie."

"What's it called?" Grandpa asked. "I really enjoyed *One If By Land.*"

"Ah, you're a historical fan," Gabby said. "Thank you. The next one will be released in June. I'm hoping it will be just as big."

"I watched you in *Doctors and Nurses*," Grandpa admitted, clearing his throat. "I never thought I'd watch a soap opera, but with my grandson in it, how could I not? You deserved that Emmy."

Gabby pretended to fan herself. "The compliments keep coming! Thank you. I'm pretty sure Noah here didn't watch." She patted his arm.

Noah wasn't going to respond, then Grandpa said, "Of course he did."

She turned those lovely eyes up to Noah, blinking rapidly as if to emphasize her surprise. "Did you, Noah?"

He shrugged. "Tyler *is* my brother."

At the time, he'd envied his brother mightily every time Tyler had been in bed with Gabby. TV show or not, their scenes had been pretty hot.

And now Noah had slept with her, too. He felt a twinge of uneasiness. It had been years ago that Tyler and Gabby had been an item. In the heat of Gabby's sexiness last night, Noah hadn't even given Tyler a thought. Would it bother Tyler that Noah was seeing her? Should it bother Noah?

It wasn't like he was marrying her, he reminded himself. And even the words "seeing each other" might be taking it too far.

Emma Cane

For all he knew, Gabby had given him one great night, and now had what she wanted.

Gabby stood up. "But did you *like* the show, Noah?"

He stood up, too. "You were good. Are you looking for more compliments?"

She laughed, giving him a flirtatious glance. "I don't need compliments, thanks. It's just nice to know you like the work your brother did. I thought he deserved an Emmy, too." As she slung her purse over her shoulder, she asked, "What time should I be here tomorrow?"

"I won't be doing much cooking yet, if that's what you want to watch. Still just organizing the kitchen and staff. I couldn't even give you an actual schedule."

"So I can stop by whenever I'd like?"

"Sure." He was reading a wealth of meanings into everything she said.

"I'll do that." She gave him a wink that only he could see before turning to his grandfather. "Have a good day, Mr. Fairfield."

It took a lot of willpower not to watch her hips sway as she walked out the door.

When she'd gone, Grandpa Fairfield studied the door and shook his head. "That is a young lady who can stir things up in this sleepy little town."

"Like she did last fall?" Noah asked wryly as he sat back down.

"Oh, no, she didn't plan all that. Sometimes an apple starts rolling down a hill and it's hard to stop it. Her presence isn't hurting the orchard, that's for sure." He eyed Noah closely. "Is she bothering you, wanting to follow you around?"

"No."

"I know how you are about your kitchen."

"It's not going to be my kitchen," he said patiently.

The Apple Blossom Café

"It could be."

"Grandpa—"

"Sorry. I don't want to pressure you. I did that to your father, and that was the biggest regret of my life." Grandpa's voice was very solemn.

Noah's father had wanted to leave the orchard but had felt guilted into staying in the family business after his Vietnam service was over. Unhappiness and PTSD had both contributed to his alcoholism.

"Grandpa, my dad made his own choices. You didn't force him to stay, and I don't feel like you're trying to force me."

The old man nodded a few times. "That's good. I've noticed that you've been a little...quiet since you've come home this last time."

Noah had to force himself not to squirm in his seat like a guilty little boy. "The café is always on my mind, I guess." He couldn't decide if Grandpa suspected that something was up with Gabby, or the true reason Noah was able to stay home for a couple weeks. "I'm fine. I'll be back to normal once the café is up and running and proves successful."

"I'm not worried about that, my boy. You're a success at everything you put your mind to."

And Noah's stomach churned a little more.

Chapter 7

After a tiring afternoon on a group Skype session with her team, working out her movie premiere schedule, Gabby was glad to go back to the ambience of the theater, even if it was only a small church stage. Her paparazzi stalkers still hadn't caught on to her biking method of escape.

The kids arrived after school before she did, and they seemed to all be watching the door when she arrived, their upturned faces as cheerful as a field of sunflowers. Gabby experienced a strange moment of both happiness and dismay, but she was used to trying to live up to people's expectations.

She spent the next two hours moving from group to group, working on their audition pieces. Some children had already memorized their parts and needed help with the emotions; others needed some encouragement and methods in the ways of memorization. Having worked on a soap, Gabby was a pro at memorizing quickly. She used to receive pages and pages of dialogue every evening for scenes to be shot the next day. It had been a relief to film movies, where the pace could be a bit slower. Although not always.

After working her way through the actors, she drifted backstage. She found Sarah standing at the light board, twirling her blue strand of hair around one finger as she concentrated.

"Hi, Sarah."

The girl jumped, her eyes widening as she saw who it was. "Hi, Miss Gabrielle."

"Is this what you'll be doing for the play?"

They spent a few minutes in a discussion about the light board, and how Mrs. Fairfield had promised to train her. Noah's

The Apple Blossom Café

grandmother had taken a theater course at UVA on stage lighting. Gabby hoped she could be as enthusiastic and active as the Fairfield grandparents were.

Not that she planned to have grandchildren to amaze with her talents, she reminded herself. *None that you personally will ever know,* that insistent voice whispered in her head.

"Was that your sister I saw you leaving with yesterday?" Gabby asked Sarah.

"Yes, ma'am. She can't be left alone after school. It's a good thing she likes the theater group."

"You're very lucky you share some interests. That'll help you stay close when you're older."

"I don't know about *that,*" Sarah said, sounding more like a typical teenager.

Gabby chuckled. Sarah seemed responsible and not at all bitter about her responsibility to her sibling—unlike Gabby in her younger days.

They were called back to the church hall for a snack, and Gabby answered questions about working as an actor. She continued to watch Sarah's brisk but obvious devotion to her sister and thought what a good job her parents were doing raising her.

Afterward, she walked her bike across the street to Feel the Burn. Surprisingly, no photographers had found her yet. She imagined what it might be like someday, when her life was so boring in Spencer Hollow that they left her alone here. It seemed a distant dream.

She parked her bike in a rack beside Noah's SUV, and felt a thrill of anticipation. Their encounter last night had been on her mind a lot, especially when she'd been at the café with him. Even when his adorable grandfather had arrived, it had been difficult not to rub her foot along Noah's calf, or reach for his hand.

Emma Cane

Much as Noah had said he didn't care if his family knew about them, she imagined he hadn't meant his grandfather.

But at Feel the Burn, she would get to see him all sweaty as he exercised. She almost rubbed her hands together in anticipation. With her backpack slung over one shoulder, she went inside and saw ten firefighters' faces turn toward her with anticipation. So many had crowded into the small gym that they must surely be running out of equipment. Noah was doing bicep curls with free weights in the back. They exchanged nods, but nothing else. Now she knew how Tyler and Brianna had felt last fall, when they'd been hiding their relationship because Gabby had supposedly been dating him. She felt a momentary wish to claim Noah for herself, especially when she saw Madison not too far away, taking a water break.

"Hi, Gabrielle!" several men called.

She waved, "Hi everyone."

There were a few women working out, who weren't quite as thrilled to see her. One lifted up her phone as if for a picture.

Madison touched the woman's arm. "Let her work out in peace."

"Thank you," Gabby said, sending a meaningful glance to Madison before saying to the other woman, "If you promise not to take a photo when I'm stained with sweat and beet-red, I'll be happy to pose with you now."

They took a selfie, and two of the men asked for photos of their own, and then everyone left her alone after she said she wasn't going to do any yoga that day.

"Have to switch up the exercise routines," she said brightly.

She really wanted to lift weights with Noah but thought that might be taking too much of a risk. She got on a treadmill, put on her ear buds for some music, and had the perfect sight line to watch Noah work out. Today he wore a tank top—hallelujah—and she got to see those magnificent shoulders put through their

The Apple Blossom Café

paces with some military presses, lat pulls, and chest flys. His hair flopped onto his forehead whenever he bent over. The more he perspired, the higher her engine revved, the faster she ran. He caught her eye once, smirked knowingly, and worked out even harder. At last she couldn't take it anymore and jumped off the treadmill. She took a quick shower, dressed in leggings and a jacket, said good-bye to her workout companions, and headed outside.

It was dark now, without the lights of the city distorting the crisp star-studded sky; she inhaled the scent of the Blue Ridge Mountains and thought, *Ahhhh*. Her immersion in village life had gone well in the gym—maybe the rest of the Spencer Hollow villagers would soon be able to treat her just as normally.

She eyed Noah's SUV, tried the door, and found it open. Apparently he hadn't picked up big-city paranoia. She put her bike in the back, sat down in the front seat, and waited.

When Noah emerged a few minutes later, he opened his door, leaned in—then saw her.

"Hi," she said. "I had to see you. Watching you work out—that was just unfair."

He slid inside and closed the door. "You didn't get enough last night?"

"No." Her smile faded as she remembered his skin pressed against hers. She wanted to jump his bones—when was the last time she'd had car sex?

"Want me to cook you dinner?" he asked unexpectedly.

"That sounds great."

They were relatively silent on the drive back to Fairfield Orchard. The atmosphere between them was pleasurably tense with the knowledge of what they both knew they'd be doing together later that night.

The house was dark as they drove up. She said, "When I lived here last fall, so did Tyler and Amy. Now it's just you alone in all these rooms."

"And Rachel, soon."

Rachel, the sister who'd stayed home to run the orchard with their parents, when all the other siblings had scattered for college or the military. After fifteen years learning everything about the business, a year ago she'd decided to see the world because she knew the orchard was in good hands with the twins. She'd gone off with a travel-writing friend, and except for occasional visits, had let Amy and Tyler do whatever they wanted for the struggling orchard.

"She's coming home for your grand opening?" Gabby asked.

"Coming home for good."

"She is?" Gabby said, startled. "I thought she'd eased her way out."

"I never thought that. Rachel loves this place. She just needed some time away."

"She'll have the big old family home to herself when you go back to Pittsburgh."

"Yep."

"Will your parents do the same thing, get sick of traveling and move home?"

"I don't think so, at least not permanently."

"What you're saying is, we have to take advantage of having the house to ourselves."

He glanced at her, and oncoming car lights lit his serious, intense expression. "Definitely."

The house was down a small lane past the public grounds of the orchard. Gabby had spent a few weeks living there when she'd been hiding from the public eye, so it still reminded her of feeling warm and safe. On the front porch, she stood beside Noah as he opened the door, then followed him through the

The Apple Blossom Café

comfortable living and dining rooms to the kitchen, beyond which was the heart of the home, a family room with a big fireplace.

Once in the kitchen, she leaned back against a counter and watched as he opened the fridge door and scrutinized what was within.

"Is this my first lesson?" she asked.

He glanced at her with a frown. She was starting to know him well enough to know it wasn't an angry or hostile expression, more one of curiosity.

"Lesson?" he echoed. "I thought you were just going to watch and learn."

She gave him a slow smile. "I love to watch."

He straightened and regarded her with intensity. "If you're not careful, you'll get nothing for dinner."

"Perhaps I don't want to eat right now," she whispered.

He closed the refrigerator door, approached her, then parted her knees. When he stepped between her thighs, she inhaled swiftly and wished she'd been wearing a skirt. As he cupped her face gently, she tilted her head for his kiss, He didn't lean forward, only looked at her for a long moment. She couldn't read his expression as he stroked her cheeks with his thumbs. Their eyes met and held for a long moment.

Hoarsely, he said, "Take your hair down."

Breathless now, she removed the ponytail holder and shook out her blond hair. It fell down her back, almost to the counter.

Noah threaded his fingers through, then pulled it forward. "Your hair is so beautiful."

It was her own color still, but she didn't spoil the moment with that little piece of vanity. She liked that it wasn't just her face he thought beautiful. And by their conversations, maybe he even found other things about her beautiful, not just what was on the outside.

His hands still in her hair; he tilted her head back, baring her throat to his kisses. She moaned at his gentleness. It didn't have the driving urgency of the previous night; they had time for exploration. He parted her jacket and cupped her breasts through her shirt.

He froze. "You're not wearing a bra."

"Watching you work out gave me ideas."

He tipped her back until she was on her elbows on the counter, then with both hands tightened her shirt over her breasts. Her nipples were hard points of eagerness. When he bent and took one in his mouth through her shirt, she moaned. But she could only take such exquisite torture for so long. She shrugged out of her jacket and reached for the hem of her shirt, pulling it over her head. Things got urgent then. Noah was tugging off her leggings and thong, lifting her hips.

As her backside hit the cold granite, she gasped and laughed at the same time. "Should we take this somewhere else?"

"No." He pulled a condom out of his pocket and loosened his pants.

"Then at least take off your shirt," she commanded, her hands already lifting it for him.

Impatiently, he yanked the shirt off, sheathed himself in the condom, then had her by the hips. As she gripped him with her thighs, he entered her in one smooth motion. She lost her breath at the pleasure of it, then found his mouth with her own. They rocked together, their slow gentleness forgotten. She urgently moved against him, pleasure rising up her body with heat. When he bent to take her breast into his mouth again, she lost herself in an explosion of pleasure that shuddered through her. Noah picked up his pace, every movement of his body inside hers drawing out her pleasure. When at last he groaned through his climax, she sank back on her elbows again and smiled up at him.

The Apple Blossom Café

"Wow," she murmured, watching with appreciation as his chest rose and fell with each heaving breath.

When he tried to step back, she crossed her legs behind his hips and held him there. He looked down at her, his expression intense, his breathing still fast. She didn't know why she wanted to keep him inside, to hold onto their moment of connection.

He ground into her slowly. "Did you want to come again?"

"I—no, I just…never mind." She lowered her legs and let him go.

"I'll be right back," he said, crossing to the bathroom off the kitchen.

What the hell was wrong with her? she wondered. She liked being with Noah—it wasn't as if she feared he was going to toss her out the door once they'd had sex. But she'd enjoyed being a part of him for such a brief moment, and prolonging it had suddenly seemed important.

That was ridiculous. She jumped off the counter, then found some spray under the sink.

Noah returned as she was scrubbing the counter and practically stumbled to a halt. "I never thought I'd find Gabrielle cleaning my kitchen naked."

"That's because it's Gabby cleaning your kitchen so you can cook me an incredible meal." She was mildly annoyed by the "Gabrielle" mention; it made her feel again as if she wasn't a person to him, but a celebrity. She handed him the bottle and sponge. "Here, you finish. I'll be right back."

She picked her clothes up off the floor.

"Must you?" he asked.

Because his voice was a little hoarse, she smiled at him. "I must. What if one of your nosy relatives drops by unannounced, wanting to cheer up lonely Noah?"

"Oh, right."

Emma Cane

When she emerged from the bathroom, he was chopping vegetables; eggplant, tomatoes, mushrooms, peppers, and onions were spread around him like a Thanksgiving cornucopia. The eggplant was already chopped and salted nearby. She came over to watch. They didn't speak as she studied his movements. He chopped so quickly, the peppers and mushrooms seemed to miraculously fly apart.

"Do you want to try?" he asked.

"It's not like I've never chopped vegetables before," she said dryly.

"You like to cook," he said, before she could say the same.

They shared a smile.

"What are we making?" she asked.

"Ratatouille, the perfect French countryside dish." As they chopped vegetables together, he said, "It never even occurred to me that someone could drop by while we were…"

"Doing our own cooking on the counter?"

He gave a brief chuckle. "Something like that. When I'm with you, I can't think about anything else but—kissing you."

"We've managed to have some good conversations," she pointed out.

"I spoke coherently, then? I'm glad to hear it," he added wryly. He tossed the garlic and onions into a sizzling pan, and a few minutes later added the peppers.

After squeezing the liquid out of the eggplant in a colander, he added it to the pan, along with tomatoes and zucchini. With his fingers, he sprinkled bay leaves and marjoram, salt and pepper, then left it all to simmer.

He leaned back against the counter and looked at her. "You settled your promotion tour?"

She nodded. "I'll be traveling to ten different major cities around the world—with some more added in as necessary. Appearances and press interviews every day. Even after the

The Apple Blossom Café

movie opens and I'm home, I might be doing radio interviews for weeks."

"It's probably grueling, answering the same questions every single day."

She shrugged. "I'm not complaining. It's part of the job. Any success I have is because of the fans. They have questions; I'll answer them."

"Over and over."

She smiled. "Yes, over and over. I feel like I should change things up, but really, there's only so much you can say without giving away the entire plot of the movie. And I can't do that."

"What's this one about?"

"I tried something very daring—which was the problem when I had a scandal last fall. In this one I'm playing the villain, and they were horrified that I might seem like a villain in real life."

"A villain?" He eyed her as he stirred the Ratatouille in the pan. "A cold-blooded killer or a thief? Frankly, I can't imagine you as a killer."

"I'm very convincing." She practically purred her answer, standing close to him.

He arched an eyebrow. "So, you're a killer."

"You'll just have to see the movie and find out."

He sighed.

"All right, all right, you're too persuasive."

His smile turned wry.

"I actually play a secretary whose husband is murdered, who ends up doing things she never imagined to get the justice she thinks she deserves."

"Doesn't sound very villainous."

He set out butter and a loaf of crusty French bread. She looked at it longingly. She knew she should stick with the vegetables; the press tour was coming up, but...she was going to have some of that bread tonight.

She tore her eyes away. "Wait until you see what she does. I'm not normally squeamish, but—ick."

"Maybe the murderer deserved it?"

"But does she have the right murderer?"

"Sounds complicated."

"And challenging. I loved it. And it horrified me to think that the hard work of the rest of the cast and crew could be ruined because I thought I couldn't play the part of the grieving girlfriend for one more minute and had to run off to Europe. It was foolish and short-sighted," she added bitterly.

"You weren't Brock's girlfriend when he died."

"No, I wasn't."

"Yet you'd been close to him once. I imagine his death and what happened afterward could have clouded your emotions for a while."

"Why Noah Fairfield, are you trying to make me feel better about ensnaring your brother in my scandal?"

"Well, I wouldn't go *that* far."

She laughed and went to set the table, feeling lighter about earning Noah's forgiveness.

They ate at the dining room table, candles making the atmosphere romantic. They looked into each other's eyes, played footsie under the table. She was just about to suggest they find another room to play in when the front door opened and closed.

Gabby turned shocked eyes on Noah and whispered, "Can you imagine this happening an hour ago?"

He frowned, not exactly amused, she guessed. He was still far too sober sometimes. She kept wondering if he'd always been this way or if something had happened to cause his mood. As he left the dining room for the living room and she followed behind, she thought about the times when he seemed to hesitate instead of getting lost in conversation, as if there was something he didn't want to say. It intrigued her rather than offended her.

The Apple Blossom Café

She could hardly fault anyone for keeping secrets from a person they were only casually seeing.

Ahead of her, she heard Noah say, "Rachel!"

Gabby entered the living room to find Noah's oldest sister dumping a large suitcase and a backpack onto the floor with a weary sigh. Rachel gave a tired smile and stepped into Noah's open arms.

Rachel had chin-length sandy blond hair that looked tousled from traveling. She had Amy's stubborn pointed chin and Noah's gray eyes that now looked weary, as if she'd spent a long day traveling. The strength in her shoulders spoke of years working on the farm.

When Rachel finished hugging her brother, Gabby stepped up to his side. Rachel's eyes widened a bit, and Gabby could imagine why. Though she'd met Rachel during the run of the play, they'd only exchanged the briefest of conversations.

"Gabrielle?" Rachel said, giving a confused glance at Noah, even as she smiled. "It's nice to see you again. Oh, that's right, I heard you're planning to buy a house in the Hollow."

"News travels fast," Gabby said.

"Amy has become an excellent texter since she moved home from Charlottesville." Rachel gave Noah a meaningful look. "I hope I'm not intruding,"

Gabby smiled. "Of course not. You live here, and Noah told me you'd be home this week."

"We just didn't think it was tonight," he added.

Gabby could have elbowed him.

Rachel only chuckled. "Sorry about that."

"Noah cooked dinner," Gabby said. "He made plenty. Please come join us."

Rachel hesitated, but Noah slung an arm around her shoulders. Gabby followed the siblings into the dining room.

"Let me just wash up," Rachel said, heading for the bathroom.

Gabby threaded her arm through Noah's and squeezed. "Should I leave? You could make some kind of excuse about why I was here."

"I'm not hiding anything, Gabby. Stay and get to know Rachel."

But Noah seemed to avoid her eyes as he spoke, and she didn't know what to make of it. Was he embarrassed to be having a fling with her? Though he was a guy, maybe what he'd do in Pittsburgh wasn't what he'd do in Spencer Hollow.

He'd told her they didn't need to hide from his friends and family, so she'd just have to take him at his word.

Chapter 8

Noah was almost disappointed that his dinner with Gabby had been interrupted. Already he was far too fascinated with her.

But this was his sister, Rachel, whom he'd barely seen this last year except for Christmas. She came back into the kitchen, and he was happy that her eyes lit up at the Ratatouille he'd been warming up in the pan.

"That looks and smells delicious," Rachel murmured, leaning against his shoulder as she bent over the stove and inhaled.

"Would you like a glass of wine?" Gabby asked.

"I think I'll grab a bottle of cider."

"Do you like the new Fairfield product?" Gabby took a sip from her glass.

"It's delicious." Rachel pulled a bottle from the fridge and opened it. "I remember when Carlos first started fermenting cider. Dad was against the whole concept, but he's come around."

"I wonder why he had a problem with it," Noah said with a faint air of bitterness. "I'm not sure Amy and Tyler would have cared about his opinion."

Rachel took a swig from the bottle and eyed him. "They were in charge. I can't blame them."

He carried her plate into the dining room, and both women followed. He sat back down at the head of the table, and the women sat down on either side of him, as if they were facing off. The thought almost made him laugh.

"The twins pretty much saved the orchard, right?" Gabby asked.

Noah thought Rachel stiffened. *Uh oh*. Rachel had been working at the orchard her entire life.

"Rachel worked hard to keep the orchard from floundering," he said, "after our dad let his drinking nearly ruin everything our ancestors had worked to build for two hundred years."

Both Rachel and Gabby stared at him, and he realized how bitter he sounded.

"Alcoholism is a disease," Rachel said coolly. "You know that, Noah. Dad worked really hard to overcome it. I'm proud of him."

He took a sip of wine and didn't answer. Rachel had been the one to pick up the slack when their dad couldn't, when Noah and his siblings had left. Noah had taken the easy way out, but he'd had to get away. His dad had eleven years of sobriety—and Noah still hadn't put it behind him.

"I know you're not proud of him," Rachel continued softly. "You never have been."

"That's not true," he insisted. "He overcame it, with Mom's help and patience, and there are people who never manage that. And I know he's sorry." He paused, realizing that was something he'd never thought about before. "But it doesn't negate everything he did to all of us, Rachel."

She stabbed her fork into a piece of eggplant and ate it, chewing a little forcefully.

"Look, I didn't mean to bring up memories that can't be changed," he continued, suddenly tired of all the baggage their dad's drinking made everyone carry around.

Gabby broke the tense silence, saying brightly, "Then let's talk about those two hundred years. Rachel, you must have come home to celebrate with the family."

Rachel seemed to really look at her for the first time. "That's one of the reasons. And there's only so much traveling one can

The Apple Blossom Café

do before homesickness sets in. You, of all people, must understand that."

Gabby nodded and took a sip of her wine before speaking. "When you first start traveling, it seems amazing that you get to see the parts of the world you'd only glimpsed in pictures or movies. It's exciting and fascinating and awe-inspiring."

Rachel was nodding, her smile becoming more relaxed. Noah found himself glad that Gabby seemed to know exactly how to distract them.

"After a while, you miss home," Rachel murmured, gazing into the candlelight, her eyes a bit unfocused.

"Yes, you do." Gabby added quietly.

Rachel suddenly focused on Gabby. "I've heard you plan to call Spencer Hollow home."

"I do," Gabby agreed, smiling. "I like L.A. and New York, but...I need some peace and quiet between jobs, and I don't get it there."

"And Noah is helping you with that?"

Rachel turned innocent eyes on Noah, and he felt the teasing just below the surface. Gabby looked at him as well and waited with both amusement and expectation for how he'd describe what he was doing with her.

He cleared his throat. "Gabby has become a friend."

Rachel's smile widened. "So it's Gabby not Gabrielle?" she asked, turning back to the other woman.

"Gabrielle is my given name. It's sort of become my stage name, too, if that makes sense. My friends call me Gabby, and I hope you will, too."

"Gabby, it is," Rachel said, reaching across the table to shake hands.

Gabby briefly clasped her hand, her purple eyes sparkling.

"What does *Noah* call you?" Rachel asked innocently.

"You heard me call her Gabby," he said.

"You agree with Noah that you're friends?" Rachel prodded.

"We are," Gabby said.

Gabby didn't look at him, but Noah heard the quiet warmth of the words. It felt...good.

"Well, that's good to know," Rachel said. "Seems like you're a bit more than friends."

"Eat your vegetables," Noah said, biting into a forkful of zucchini.

Rachel laughed. "Is it supposed to be a secret? Because let me tell you, it's not a secret once you spend a couple minutes with you both."

Gabby was watching him now, a faint, alluring smile on her lips. Not that she was trying to be sexy. It was just a natural part of her. From the moment she'd first walked onto his TV screen, she'd been sexy, a riveting presence one didn't forget.

Rachel snapped her fingers in front of his face. "Hello."

He blinked and looked at his sister.

She laughed. "You'd better figure out what your answer will be to questions about the two of you, because it's pretty obvious something's going on."

He shrugged. "We're having fun, casually dating, whatever you want to call it. Remember, I'm leaving soon."

Rachel rested her chin on her palm. "You'll just open the café and then leave it?"

Both women focused their attention on him. He didn't lower his gaze or give any attempt at hesitation.

"I will. I know you guys will watch over it and let me know how things are going. I'll stay in touch with the general manager and the chef."

Rachel slowly nodded. "Sounds good." She took another bite of her food. "Damn, this is delicious. We're going to have a very successful café. Thank you for doing this."

He frowned. "Of course. I'd do anything for the family."

The Apple Blossom Café

"Except put Dad's past behind you," Rachel said quietly.

He stiffened, feeling Gabby staring at him in worry. "Rachel, that's enough," he said.

Rachel raised both hands. "I'm sorry. I worry about you."

"Worry about *me*? It seems you're really worrying about Dad."

"Well, of course I'm worried about Dad. He's a recovering alcoholic and always will be. I worry only because I know he's overcome an incredible, difficult challenge. I don't think every moment of the day, 'Is he drinking?' like I did the first few years. I've worked at his side for over a decade. You can trust my judgment, Noah. Dad is doing fine. But you…"

"I'm doing fine, too," he said coolly.

Rachel's gaze narrowed in sudden curiosity. "I know that."

It was abundantly clear that he'd made her suspicious. She'd always been too good at reading him. Why the hell couldn't he let the past go? Why couldn't he just tell Rachel and Gabby the truth about the restaurant in Pittsburgh?

Because…he couldn't. He could picture their shock and concern, remembered too well the pity he used to receive from teachers and family friends when it was obvious his dad had been drinking. He hated that feeling, and he wasn't going to experience it from Gabby, the woman he couldn't keep his hands off of. He wanted her to look at him as if sex was on her mind, not pity.

"So tell me about the plans for the grand opening," Rachel suddenly said.

"Now that's a transition." Gabby's smile bloomed.

Rachel clasped Noah's hand. "Seems my baby brother is prickly tonight. And it's my homecoming. I don't want to upset him."

"You could never upset me…much," he said grudgingly, his smile faint.

"Good. Now about that grand opening?"

~oOo~

The grand opening became Noah's focus for the rest of the week, and Gabby tried to be there as much as possible. It was fascinating to watch him in command like a captain of his ship. He and the general manager trained the staff; other times he worked with the line cooks, prepping for each menu item, timing out how long everything took, and figuring out the food shipments and different ways to use the same ingredients. She was impressed by all the meetings with local food sources, the linen company, serving wear representatives, and an advertising firm. He'd even hired a local potter to make custom plates and cut a deal by featuring the artist's work in the orchard's country store.

A couple times Noah interviewed chefs, but nothing came of it. Gabby learned not to even question him about it, because he became even more mono-syllabic, with an occasional grunt thrown in for good measure. Was he too picky? Or was there truly not enough local talent? It was a mystery.

Something in her softened whenever she saw him consulting over desserts with his grandfather or listening to his grandmother's thoughts as she taste-tested from the menu. Gabby wasn't certain she'd ever dated a man who was so much a part of his family, and she liked it.

She received a few interested glances from Amy and Tyler, and she wondered what Rachel had told them. None of them asked questions, as if it would disturb Noah's equilibrium.

Between the café and the theater guild, she was exhausted each night, and so was Noah. Though she saw him every day, there was no time for conversations or relaxation, and by the end of the week, she missed that. She was looking forward to the end of the stress and long hours.

The Apple Blossom Café

But would it end? Though they planned to stop serving food by five, since the orchard closed at 6, the siblings had begun to talk about extending their hours for the summer season.

The night before the soft opening, the rest of the family began to arrive, and they stopped into the café as if it was a right of passage. She reacquainted herself with Noah's other brothers, Logan and Michael. The Fairfields turned out good-looking men, she thought. She wondered when it would be their turn to come back home and help the family orchard, as all the siblings had vowed to do last year. Of course, Logan had been instrumental in supplying the capital for the recent improvements, which all the siblings had insisted be a loan and not a gift.

The Fairfield parents didn't arrive until the afternoon of the soft opening, while Gabby was home changing into nicer clothes. After the conversation with Rachel, she'd realized that Noah's anger with his father ran deep.

She couldn't be surprised that she didn't know everything about him, she thought as she drove back into the orchard parking lot and parked her car. It took months and years to get to know a person. She'd only been in the same room with him for a few weeks total. But…there was something between her and Noah, a chemistry, of course, and an understanding, too, though that sounded clichéd. They each had a past with a difficult parent, which made her sympathize with him even more.

The orchard had already closed for the day, but a photographer didn't heed the sign as he parked behind her. She knew he was following her, snapping pictures, and she didn't raise a fuss—it would only make her look bad, and after all, it was publicity for Fairfield Orchard.

When she took the few steps up to the café terrace, he had to stop, and she soon forgot about him. She caught her breath as she saw the tiny lights wound through many of the plants that interspersed the tables. There was a warm glow through the windows, and when she opened the door, the most delicious scents wafted out toward her.

Servers wearing black buttoned-down shirts carried trays of appetizers among the dozen people mingling. Gabby tried one, an apple, honey, and goat cheese crostini, she was told, and could have melted through the floor at the flavors bursting on her tongue.

"Gabby."

She turned to find Noah coming toward her in his white chef coat. Tall, serious, handsome, he made her catch her breath as she remembered his strong bare shoulders, and the force of his arms holding her close, the heat of his mouth on her—

But his eyes were crinkling in the corners as he looked at her, and a smile tugged at his lips. To her surprise, he leaned over and kissed her cheek in front of family and friends.

"Thanks for the invitation," she murmured, inhaling the smell of soap and man she'd come to think of as his alone.

"I did consider leaving you off the list," he said.

She arched a brow, waiting.

He smiled. "Just kidding."

"So what's our plan?" she whispered, noticing all the stares that tried not to be stares.

"Amy and Tyler already asked me about you, and I said 'seeing each other.' Hope that was okay."

"Of course, whatever you want."

It was his turn to arch a brow, and he murmured, "You'll be whatever I want? Now that's an interesting challenge."

She gave him a playful elbow to the stomach, her smile unchanging for their very curious audience. "I don't see your parents."

"They're in the kitchen with Rachel, checking things out. I guess I better get back there."

The Apple Blossom Café

"Don't sound too excited about it."

"I'm happy to see them. They're tan and relaxed and truly happy about the resurgence of the orchard."

"Even the serving-alcohol part? I remember hearing that it was difficult for your dad."

"He's adjusted. And he's seldom here."

"Just like you're seldom here?"

He frowned. "Let me guess—you've played a psychologist before and you just can't help yourself."

She laughed softly. "No, I promise. And you're right, I'll stay out of it."

"I didn't say that."

She eyed him in surprise. "You didn't. Thank you. Now go."

She gave him a playful push toward the kitchen, but just then, his parents and Rachel emerged. His mom saw them, gave a delighted smile and waved.

Gabby glanced at Noah, unable to control her curiosity. His expression was smooth and pleasant, and she realized he wasn't too bad of an actor when he wanted to be. Perhaps it was just years of practice. Yet…it reminded her about her feeling that he was keeping something a secret. Eyeing his approaching parents, she wondered if she wasn't the only one he was keeping it from.

His mother took Gabby's hands, her smile an expression of true delight. "Gabrielle, how wonderful to see you again!"

"Thank you, Mrs. Fairfield."

"Oh, please, call me Patty." She looked around the restaurant. "Isn't this just incredible? Noah told me what he had in mind, but I never dreamed how beautiful it would be."

Noah cleared his throat. "It's not like I was the architect, Mom."

"You had the vision," his father said with quiet firmness. "You told them what you wanted and you made it happen."

Noah shrugged with an endearing awkwardness. Gabby patted his forearm. Then she realized that Mr. Fairfield was watching her, his head cocked with curiosity.

"And before you 'Mr. Fairfield' me, I'm just Bruce." He reached out to shake her hand.

"Bruce, it's good to see you again."

He continued to study her as if she were a new variety of apple, and she couldn't help wondering what he thought of her. She'd dated his older son, gotten him involved in a scandal that had almost ruined his reputation, and now here she was, "seeing" another of his sons. To make things worse, she was moving to Spencer Hollow, where the Fairfields could very well think she meant to cause even more trouble for their family. It became a little harder to keep her smile in place, even though she reminded herself that "seeing" Noah was only a temporary thing.

To her surprise, she felt sad about the tenuousness of their relationship. She wanted to bask in her happiness for Noah, to stand at his side and support him, but that wasn't her role in the production that was their relationship.

"Whatever it is, you're over-thinking it," Noah suddenly said to her, his tone full of amusement.

"What?" she said, startled.

His parents chuckled and exchanged a glance she couldn't read, even as Gabby felt her cheeks heat with a blush. She was always a person who strived to be in the moment, to never take for granted her contact with people, because it was easy to feel separated and alone, as the object of so much attention by strangers.

"I'm sorry," she said. "I didn't want this to be awkward, and I'm the one making it awkward."

"Nonsense," Bruce said. "It's my fault. It's not often I get to meet a girl—"

"A woman," his wife chimed in.

The Apple Blossom Café

"A woman," he agreed, "whom my son is dating. Please don't think I'm looking you over with anything other than curiosity."

"I wouldn't blame you," Gabby said quietly. "After what happened last fall, you'd have every right to be suspicious of me and my motives."

"Tyler told us everything that happened, and why," Patty insisted. "There's nothing for you to worry about."

"It's hard to forget," Gabby couldn't help saying.

"My brother is hard to forget?" Noah asked lightly.

"Noah!" She knew that he was teasing, but it wasn't a subject she took lightly. "Thanks for trying to make this unimportant, but it's—"

"In the past," he interrupted. "You're overthinking, as I said."

"Overthinking?" she asked, a little affronted.

Patty took her hands again. "Everything has been explained, and it's all worked out for Tyler and Brianna. We don't hold anything against you, and I'd be sad if you continued to hold something against yourself. If you're going to be living in town, you can't let regret be a constant shadow."

"That's something I struggle with every day," Bruce said, "so I understand."

Though he wore a kind smile, Bruce spoke solemnly, not looking at Noah, who frowned at him. Gabby wanted to elbow Noah again, but perhaps his father didn't notice.

"I don't think I deserve your understanding," Gabby said, "although I appreciate it just the same. And your advice, too. I'll take it."

"Good." Patty squeezed her hands and let them go. She turned to her son. "So, where are you going to hang your award?"

Noah looked startled. "Award?"

Both of his parents stared at him in amazement.

"The Drayton Award," Patty said in exasperation, glancing at her husband. "How did we ever raise such a humble son?"

"It's probably hanging in the restaurant in which he won it," Bruce said. "The owners would want to show it off for customers."

"Oh, of course," Patty responded. "I still wish it could be here. We're so proud of you, Noah!"

Gabby noticed Noah didn't bother to say anything at all. There really was something going on with him, and tonight only seemed to make it worse.

As his parents were called away by Carlos Rodriguez, the manager of the orchard and Bruce's longtime friend, Gabby looked up at Noah. "What the heck is going on?"

"Huh?" He seemed to take a moment before focusing on her. "We're having a soft opening," he said with deliberate slowness, as if she couldn't understand English.

She kept her voice low. "Noah, you're keeping something a secret, and I just wanted you to know that if it's obvious to me, surely it will be obvious to the rest of your family."

He studied her impassively—too impassively. "Gabby, let's just enjoy the evening."

She put her hand on his arm. "But are you? Are you really?"

Something flashed in his eyes, a sudden pain that made her stomach clenched. Then it was gone, and he turned on the charming smile. Apparently Tyler wasn't the only Fairfield brother with acting skill.

And was it her business, demanding someone's secrets, when she had secrets, too? How easily she'd forgotten, after eight years of pushing her guilt down deep, where it gnawed on her darkest thoughts.

She squeezed Noah's arm and let him go with a smile. "I'm sorry—you're right. This is a celebration of the Apple Blossom

The Apple Blossom Café

Café, a longtime dream of yours. You keep your secrets. We all have them, right?"

He nodded. "I have to get back to the kitchen. Time to oversee the next course."

"Can I watch?"

"Of course."

He leaned near her ear, and his breath warmed her skin.

"As long as you say something like that when we're alone."

She gave a soft laugh. "I don't think I want to watch—I want to participate, thank you very much."

It was his turn to laugh as he led the way to the kitchen. Before they could reach the doors, they heard raised voices coming from around the corner. Noah glanced at Gabby with a frown, and they looked into the corridor that connected the café with the tasting room. Rachel and Amy were facing each other, and from the tense lines of their bodies, Gabby didn't think it was a friendly conversation. Uma paced nearby, furry head hung low.

"I'm sorry we don't do it the way you used to," Amy said, her voice strained.

Rachel spoke with exasperation. "I'm not saying the old ways are the best—I'm not ninety years old! I just thought that when you made a change, you'd consult the rest of us."

"You left us in charge, Rachel." Amy threw her hands wide. "You sounded sick of me asking your opinion, so I just...stopped."

And then the two women noticed Gabby and Noah, and blushed.

"Everything okay?" Noah asked.

With two identical nods, Rachel and Amy walked by them and back into the café. Amy found her fiancé Jonathan, and Rachel joined her other brothers. Uma leaned against Amy's legs as if offering support.

"What was that all about?" Gabby whispered.

"I was worried something like this might happen," he whispered back. "Rachel ran the orchard with our father for so many years. I'm think she's feeling defensive over all the changes, although it's just a guess. She hasn't been home long enough."

"She can't expect everything to stay the same, not after she backed out. I assume you're preparing yourself for the same."

"What do you mean?"

"When you go back to Pittsburgh." She chuckled. "It's as if you've forgotten."

"I haven't forgotten. Let's get to the kitchen."

She followed him, studying those broad shoulders with a curiosity that was hard to push down. But she forced herself.

Chapter 9

An hour later, Noah came out of the kitchen and paused, taking in the view. His family and friends were scattered about the tables, talking and laughing, while the servers moved smoothly among them, refreshing drinks and bringing more bread. The café would have good food, and be a place to come and relax, another reason to visit Fairfield Orchard—and he had helped make it happen. The feeling of satisfaction was a balm to his soul, as if a ray of sunshine had heated him from within.

He had to admit that these last few weeks had helped him form new memories of Fairfield Orchard, and that wasn't a bad thing. He'd enjoyed working alongside Amy and Tyler. He glanced with fondness at them, where they sat at the same table with the people they loved, Jonathan and Brianna. Noah had envied them the achievement of making hard cider and bringing so many new customers to the orchard. They'd found a new purpose, and both of them had left behind their old lives, successful though they were.

Was that something he should consider?

He shook his head. That would be admitting he'd failed in Pittsburgh, and he couldn't do that.

A faint frown narrowed his gaze as he noticed Rachel sitting on the far side of the room with their parents. Seeing the tension between Amy and Rachel had not surprised him. The two strong women were going to have to learn to work side by side, and Noah suspected it might be a bumpy road.

His father was laughing at something Rachel said, as if he didn't have a care in the world. And he didn't, not any more. When he'd wanted to retire, he'd left a business that was shaky because of his negligence—although to his credit, he'd worked hard the last eleven years after he'd sobered up for good. Why couldn't Noah focus on that, like so many of his siblings did? Why did he keep remembering what it felt like to hear his father stumbling drunkenly through the house late at night, when Noah couldn't sleep?

"You're supposed to look happy at your grand opening."

Noah shook himself out of his melancholy and turned to Tyler, who was watching him with amusement.

"I can be serious and happy at the same time," Noah said.

"That expression is serious?"

Noah arched a brow.

"Okay, I'll take you at your word." Tyler's smile slowly faded as he continued to regard Noah.

"What?" Noah said with exasperation.

"Just thinking about you and Gabby."

Noah sighed. "I know. It feels…weird because you and she used to…" His words trailed off. This was what he'd feared, tension with his brother. Noah wouldn't have thought anything was worth that, but then he remembered Gabby smiling up at him, Gabby teasing him out of a serious mood.

"She and I used to what? Kiss? Frankly, it was pretty awkward."

Noah was jarred out of his own awkwardness. "What did you say?"

"Awkward? Yeah, a strange word for two such pretty people as Gabby and me." He elbowed Noah.

"Awkward how?"

"Just…awkward. After weeks making out in front of a camera, we thought we were hot for each other. Then after one date and a kiss in a dark corner, we just knew it was all wrong. Awkward, you know?"

Noah tried not to gape. "You only kissed? You never…"

The Apple Blossom Café

"Slept together?" Tyler shuddered. "No."

Relief settled over Noah, and he took a deep, easy breath.

Tyler lowered his voice. "You thought we'd slept together? Why didn't you ask Gabby?"

"You don't ask what you think you already know. And like I wanted to talk about it?"

"Huh." Tyler studied him. "It bothered you and yet you still went for her?"

"I tried not to want her. But…"

They both turned to stare at Gabby, who was sitting with Carmen and Theresa, Brianna's sister. Gabby was listening intently to Carmen, her face alight with interest and amusement. Her skin glowed with warmth, her lavender eyes shone, and when she laughed, Noah felt something deep in his gut.

He came to when Tyler elbowed him again.

"Yeah, I can see how little resistance you have to her," Tyler said, shaking his head. "So are you going to keep dating after you go back to Pittsburgh?"

Noah turned away from Gabby. "I don't know. Probably not."

"Don't assume. Maybe you've got a good thing going."

"It's only been a week or so. That doesn't mean anything."

"Maybe."

Then Brianna waved at them. Tyler waved back.

"I'm going to marry that girl," Tyler said to Noah.

"I know." Noah couldn't help smiling. "Have you asked her?"

"Not yet. I have to think of the perfect way."

"Besides just getting down on one knee?"

"Have you no imagination?" Tyler demanded with amused exasperation.

"Guess not. If she loves you, she won't care." His gaze went to Gabby without volition, and now she was looking at the two of them, head cocked in curiosity.

And then Noah saw an uncomfortable truth about himself. He'd been using Gabby's and Tyler's supposed relationship as a way to keep his distance, sort of. It hadn't worked physically, but mentally, it had been an obstacle…and now it was gone.

"You know Gabby saved my life once," said Tyler, who'd been watching Noah closely.

"Saved your life? Why haven't I heard about this?"

"You haven't been around much, and it wasn't like she pulled me from a burning building. She saved my life just the same. Our characters on the soap were just taking off, and we were suddenly popular. I was pretty reckless, partying too hard, drinking too much. This woman I was flirting with offered me a ride home from a party, and it was Gabby who noticed she was drunk. She refused to let me get in the car with her. I was drunk myself, and accused Gabby of being jealous, but she held her ground. The woman ended up getting in a car accident, the passenger side all smashed in. I would have died, I'm sure of it."

"Wow. You're lucky you had her."

Tyler winked at him. "I could say the same to you. She's pretty special."

When his brother sauntered off toward Brianna, Noah watched him go, frowning. Gabby was studying Noah, and with her finger, she traced the smile on her face, encouraging him, he knew. Why was everyone so worried he wasn't having a good time?

Maybe because he usually didn't have a good time at the orchard, especially when his father was around. He hadn't wanted people to worry about him, and now he felt almost guilty. He usually would have told himself it was his father who should feel guilty, but the thought just made him tired. He'd been carrying around his anger for so long. Why couldn't he just get over it?

The Apple Blossom Café

He realized that this was the first time he actually *wanted* to get over it. Maybe that was a good start.

~oOo~

As the evening wound down, and guests left, Gabby watched with satisfaction as Noah circulated among his family. Though they always made her feel welcome, she was enjoying hanging back, watching the Fairfield siblings tease each other in a loving way. She hadn't had this kind of childhood, and it always amazed her to watch it in action. You couldn't replicate the closeness of people who'd grown up together. She found herself thinking of her brother and wondering how he was doing.

"Now who's looking sad?" Noah asked.

Startled, she said, "I'm not sad, just watching your family together."

"And that makes you sad?"

She gave his arm a push. "Not sad, just...regretful. You don't know how good you have it, with siblings as close as you all are."

"My dad's alcoholism brought us together," he said shortly.

"Maybe that's part of it, but not all. I bet it's more working together in a family business, being able to play on a farm together, having both parents."

She held her breath, wondering if he'd get defensive again, but he didn't seem to. That was an improvement.

He looked down at her for a long moment. She was getting to know him better, and his pensive expression wasn't angry or distracted, but...focused. On her.

She shivered.

"Cold?" he murmured.

"Not at all." She kept her voice low and husky.

He was looking at her mouth.

"They all know we're dating, right?" she asked quietly.

"Yes."

"Then if I take you out beneath the stars for some fresh air, it won't be too suspicious, right?"

"It will."

"Do you care?"

"No." He took her arm and walked her toward the door.

Brianna called out good-bye. Since Gabby wasn't even wearing a coat, Brianna came up short, then simply grinned. Gabby grinned back at her as Noah pulled her along.

Outside, the warm spring day had cooled, but when Noah gathered her into his arms beneath the shadows of the vine-covered trellis, her goosebumps had nothing to do with the temperature. They kissed for minutes, feverish mouths meeting, tongues entwining, moans exchanged. She could have kissed him forever, never tiring of the mystery that was Noah.

A few minutes later, they rested their foreheads against each other, breathing heavily, shakily.

"So...what's the plan?" Gabby asked.

"Since I can't bring you back to the house with Rachel and my parents there, I'm going to take you back to your house and do unspeakable things with you."

She chuckled softly. "Well, that wasn't what I was talking about, but I'll take it."

"Good."

He kissed her cheek, her chin, behind her ear. She sighed at the heated warmth of his mouth.

"Are you going to ask what I meant?" she whispered.

He bit her earlobe. "Do I want to know?"

"Maybe not. But the café is open, and you don't have a chef to replace you. That means you can't go back to Pittsburgh anytime soon."

Did he stiffen? It was so subtle, she could hardly tell. He spoke with casual ease.

"I have some finalists. I'll narrow it down this week."

The Apple Blossom Café

"Oh, that's nice. Can I be there for the interviews? Will they cook for you? It'd be fascinating to watching."

He rained gentle kisses on her mouth, speaking between them. "I thought…you only wanted…to watch me."

"Oh, of course you're right."

"Stop talking," he murmured, then gave her a lingering, deeper kiss that put everything else out of her mind.

"Hey, you two!" Amy leaned out of the open door. "Come on back in. We have hours of celebrating yet to do."

Noah lifted his head, called, "In a minute," and went right back to kissing Gabby.

She fairly tingled at the passionate way he focused on her. It had been a long time since she'd felt like there were no other distractions for a man when he was with her.

Finally, she broke the kiss. "We should go in. Your parents won't be in town that long. They obviously miss you."

"All right, all right," he said with good-natured reluctance.

Linking arms, they walked back toward the door. It made her realize that she'd soon be missing him, too.

~oOo~

The next morning, as he ate breakfast, Noah was scrolling through his phone when he saw that Gabby had tagged him on Instagram. He stiffened when he saw his beautiful café, full of people, the lights twinkling overhead, as a backdrop for the selfie Gabby had insisted they take together. He hadn't even thought she'd make it public.

He knew she'd been trying to boost publicity for the café, and under normal circumstances, he couldn't fault her. Yet his life was anything but normal. What if someone online brought up that he'd been fired? The disappointment and pity would surround him, and then Amy and Tyler would lay into him about staying at the orchard. The awkwardness with his father last night had only reminded him of why he liked his life in the city.

Noah found Gabby at the café, charming the line cooks as they all chopped vegetables together. He was a night owl, after working dinners for years. Apparently Gabby was not. She was fresh and enthusiastic, and he could have winced at her cheerfulness. When Noah had been entwined with her in her bed last night, she'd promised to hang in the kitchen for his public grand opening, before heading to the theater to work with the kids. She didn't talk about that much, though he sensed there was more to her volunteering than she was letting on. Since she didn't pry into his secrets, he wouldn't pry into hers.

Telling her to stop putting up photos of him might make her even more curious, but he was going to have to risk it.

When she saw him in the doorway, her smile was so radiant it could have gleamed off the chrome appliances.

"You made it on time," she said.

The line cooks laughed at some private joke.

Gabby grinned. "I was telling them I didn't think you liked the early hours prepping for lunch."

"You look like you're not having a problem with it."

"We shoot at all hours," she said. "I'm good at adjusting to whatever time I have to."

Noah watched her knife work for a while, and though he was still upset about the Instagram post, he felt even more relaxed with her now that he knew she hadn't slept with Tyler. He hadn't realized it had lurked in the back of his mind until he'd been relieved of the burden.

Just before the café opened for business, he drew her into his office when the rest of the staff was in the middle of last-second preparations.

She cocked her head, her smile curious.

"I saw the Instagram post," he said with no preamble.

Her smile started to fade, and he knew she was reacting to his serious tone.

The Apple Blossom Café

"Should I have asked your permission before posting?"

"I wish you would have. Part of your job is being on constant display. Maybe you like it more than you think."

"Oh." She put her hand on his arm. "I thought I was promoting the café."

"I know that. I'm not angry."

"Really? Because I'm not so certain."

He took both her hands and looked hard into her eyes. "I'm *not* angry. Although I admit, I don't know if I'm ready for the whole world to know about us." That was the truth...mostly. "Family and friends—that's fine. Let's just keep everyone else out of our business for now."

She blinked at him for a moment, then smiled again. "Okay, I get it."

"Thanks for understanding. Now let's get out there and impress the customers." He squeezed her hands and let her go.

Gabby returned to the cold line, helping prepare salads. Noah tried not to watch her, wondering if he'd hurt her feelings. He hoped not, but he didn't regret explaining things to her.

During the noon hour, though it was the height of craziness, Noah was used to it; he thrived in it. He was in control of his kitchen. He'd been away from this feeling for a few weeks and hadn't realized how much he missed it.

Though he was focused, even he couldn't miss the commotion in the dining room, voices raised in excitement.

Gabby looked through the pass-through and winced, glancing at him with regret. "I'm sorry, Noah."

"Sorry about what?"

"A friend of mine I invited for lunch and a reporter who's spending the day with her. I cleared the reporter with Amy when I couldn't reach you," she added when she saw his expression. "I was only thinking of the grand opening. And who better to bring some excitement than Melanie Archer?" she added gamely. "I promise—no pictures of the two of us together."

Noah knew the name, heard the excitement in the rest of the staff. He looked into the dining room and saw the crowd gathering around the actress. Melanie was almost Hollywood royalty, with two Oscars to her name, and the regality of a woman who'd not only aged well but enjoyed the satisfaction of her accomplishments.

At his side, Gabby straightened her shoulders as if to brace herself. "People are taking pictures. Soon the news will be everywhere online, and think of all the curious people who'll stop by. They'll eat, they'll swoon as their taste buds explode." She squeezed his arm. "The grand opening will be even more of a success than it already is."

Because of Gabby, Noah thought. Without her, he wouldn't even have known how successful it was for a few days, if the word-of-mouth had spread, if a reporter or two from Charlottesville bothered to come and put a small blurb in a paper somewhere. He should be happy for her help—if only it didn't lead to complications. How would he ever know if the café's success was due to his talent rather than her stardom?

Gabby drew him out of his kitchen to meet her guest. Although his staff insisted he go, it was the first full day; what if things got behind? He didn't have a choice. Melanie Archer was a kind woman, who'd already sampled some dishes and raved. He accepted the praise quietly, but made sure he wasn't in any photos with Gabby.

He mingled with his family, his proud parents, his brothers and sisters. It was a big day for all of them, he reminded himself. Noah was helping turn the orchard around, something Logan, Tyler, and Amy had begun.

This was everything he'd worked for, and he did feel satisfied. Then he overheard the reporter asking his brothers Logan and

The Apple Blossom Café

Michael about which of the Fairfields Gabby was dating. Gabby shot Noah a wide-eyed, apologetic look.

He went back to his kitchen.

After lunch, when the crowds had died down a bit, he entered the office to check out the computer and decide what food they'd need to reorder. Gabby followed him inside.

"No sex on the desk," Noah said, not even taking his eyes from the computer screen.

She laughed and took a seat next to the desk. "Okay, okay, if you insist. I'm glad you're not mad at me."

"I appreciate what you tried to do."

"Do you? That reporter—"

"Was being a reporter, stirring up a story. I get it."

He looked back at his computer. She didn't speak for a long moment. He kept focusing on the screen, though he wasn't comprehending a single number.

"That was an interesting lunch rush," she said, a little too brightly.

"Busier than it'll end up being on a daily basis."

"And you were in charge. It was sexy."

He gave her a dubious glance. "Come on."

"No, really, it was. I like a man in command. Surely that was why you got into cooking."

He gave her half a smile. "I liked the creativity, the experimentation, the instant feedback." *And getting away from Dad when I'd been suspended from school.* But he wasn't going to say that out loud.

"And it made you popular with all the girls."

"Not back then. I had brothers who were sports stars—now *that's* popular. Some girls thought I was gay because I liked to cook."

"I don't believe it. They had no gaydar at all." She sighed. "And much as I'd love to keep chatting—"

"You have to leave for the theater—or should I say the church hall?"

"No teasing. Bri will do a good job transforming that church hall when it's time for the show to go on."

"I know she will."

Gabby leaned in and kissed his cheek. "Gotta go. Have fun at the rest of your grand opening." She hesitated and her smile faded. "Maybe you don't want to hear this, but I'm a little sad you've hit this milestone."

"Sad? Why?"

"Because it means you'll leave Spencer Hollow. I'll miss you."

This time she kissed him on the mouth, touched his arm, and left. Noah stared at the doorway as if she was still framed there.

Chapter 10

At the church hall—the theater, Gabby reminded herself with a silent laugh—it was the first day of actual rehearsals. Auditions had happened the previous week, and though some kids were disappointed not to get the leads, it was an ensemble show where no one had a huge part.

And she needed the distraction; otherwise she kept berating herself over her stupidity with Noah. She still flinched when she remembered his words about liking being on constant display. Did she? Maybe it was time to start rethinking the balance between her career and her private life.

She thought she'd been helping promote the restaurant, but now she could see the truth—her mere presence was a risk any man who dated her took. Of course he didn't want to be seen in public with her; maybe no man would ever want that. The reporters would write about Noah like he was just another Fairfield brother she was working her way through. She shuddered.

"Miss Gabrielle!" someone called.

She shook herself back into focus. Her enjoyment of the theater pushed her self-doubt back into the dark place where it belonged. The kids were used to her now; even their parents came up to talk to her about their children, as if she was just another teacher. Without the distraction of eager fans, she was able to work with one group of children on the character breakdowns while Aaron worked with the leads.

And she could still catch glimpses of Sarah, who was helping to build the set. Her little sister had one of the leads, and Sarah occasionally glanced at her with pride. Gabby looked at the little girl, too, but couldn't bring herself to think about the girl's name. What were the odds that she'd be the same age as Gabby's daughter, with the exact same name?

Gabby found herself breathing shakily and had to take deep breaths. She stepped away from the kids, raising her water bottle as if she just needed a drink. Instead, she was drinking in the sight of Sarah's sister, the way her curls bounced when she laughed, how she slung an arm around another girl's neck with innocent friendship. They made funny faces at each other, then quickly tried to be good when Aaron gave them a mock serious look.

Gabby forced herself to look away. Her gaze found Sarah again, and she was startled to notice that there were shadows beneath Sarah's eyes, and strain in the grim set of her mouth when she thought no one was looking. Even her shaggy hair with its blue stripe looked limp. When Sarah walked quickly toward the back hall, Gabby played a hunch and followed her, leaving her students with another volunteer.

She found Sarah in the women's bathroom, bracing herself on her arms over a sink, her head hung low, shoulders shaking.

"Sarah?" Gabby said with concern.

The girl stiffened. "I'm okay." Her expression was grim, her eyes haunted.

"I don't think you are," Gabby said, her concern deepening. "Can I help?"

Sarah met her gaze in the mirror and spoke with brave resolution. "I'll be all right."

"But—"

And then Sarah darted into the nearest stall and threw up. Frozen, Gabby hoped the teenager was merely sick. Some instinct told her otherwise. Gabby felt herself tumbling back through time, like it was yesterday, staring at the pregnancy stick

The Apple Blossom Café

while everything around her faded away, replaced by the terror of not knowing what to do.

When Sarah emerged, pale and trembling, she gave a start upon seeing Gabby. "You're still here."

"I am. Would you like to talk? I'm a good listener, and anything you say will remain between us."

Sarah washed her face and rinsed her mouth before turning to face Gabby. "I'm fine. You don't have to worry about me."

"You're not fine," Gabby said gently. "Are you pregnant?"

The girl covered her mouth, eyes wide and glistening above her hand.

"It will be all right." Gabby moved closer and put her arm around Sarah's trembling shoulders.

"It won't be all right, not ever again." Her whisper was anguished. "I'm only a few days late. But I've been sick to my stomach in the mornings…" Tears overflowed her eyes.

Gabby pulled some tissues out of the box on the counter and handed them to her. "Let me help. Have you taken a pregnancy test?"

After blowing her nose, Sarah shook her head. "Someone would see me buy it."

"Then that's what we're going to do. Right now. You might not be pregnant at all, and you need to know. Let's go."

"My sister—"

"I'll tell Bri to keep an eye on her until your parents arrive, because you're not feeling well. It's the truth, right?"

"Yes, but…everyone stares at you! They'll notice what we're doing—they'll think *you're* pregnant!"

Gabby smiled without much humor. "You haven't seen the back seat of my car. It's *full* of disguises."

Sarah blinked at her. "Why are you helping me?"

"Because you need help. And women have to stick together. Wait here, I'll be right back."

Brianna accepted Gabby's story with a distracted nod as she watched two kids reading through their lines on stage. "That's nice of you. Hope she doesn't throw up in your car."

Gabby found Sarah in the hall near the doors, hugging herself, looking skinny and very young.

"You used to ride a bike here," Sarah said.

"Not today. I had errands. And I'm starting to bore most of the paparazzi. How many photos can they get of me in yoga pants?"

Sarah gave a faint smile. Luck was with them, probably because they were leaving practice early, and no photographers were in sight. Gabby hurried to the car and got in, followed by Sarah, who buckled her seatbelt.

"Is Crozet far enough?" Gabby asked as they started to drive down the hill leading from the village. "Or should we head to Charlottesville?"

"I can't be gone that long. My mom would be upset. Although she'll really be upset when I tell her..." She trailed off and her eyes welled with tears again.

"Crozet it is. And stop thinking that way. You don't know anything. Do you feel like you might get sick again? I have a bag somewhere."

Sarah quickly shook her head.

Gabby went right back to the heart of the matter. "So you didn't use protection?"

She nodded. "I did. He didn't put it on right away. I had to make him."

What an ass. "That was a brave, smart thing you did."

"But useless," she whispered. "Letting myself get in this situation was *not* a smart thing. I didn't even love him. My mom always says you should be in a *committed, loving relationship*. I can just hear her saying those words," she added miserably.

"If you didn't love him, why did you agree?"

The Apple Blossom Café

With a helpless shrug, Sarah looked out the window. "Because everybody had done it except me, and he's really cute and I couldn't believe he was interested in me. But he wasn't interested in *me*. He's barely talked to me since."

"Some men are scum. Not all men, I promise."

They didn't say anything more for the fifteen-minute drive into Crozet. Gabby actually got Sarah to smile in the parking lot of the drug store, when she tried on several different hats she pulled from the back seat, including a big floppy beach hat. But they both agreed the best look was pulling her ponytail through a Virginia Cavaliers ball cap and wearing sunglasses that looked more like regular glasses with tinted lenses.

"I hope no one recognizes you," Sarah said nervously. "You're buying a *pregnancy test*!" She almost whispered the last two words. "I should do it myself."

"No, stay here. I don't care what people think." Well, that was an exaggeration.

Sarah's lower lip trembled. "You're being so nice to me."

"I've always been impressed by you," Gabby said simply. "The way you take care of your sister…I had to take care of my brother when I was your age. I didn't handle it with anywhere near your grace."

Sarah just stared at her before whispering, "Thanks."

Gabby patted her hand. "I'll be right back."

Gabby wandered the aisles until she found the pregnancy tests. She bought some crackers for good measure, and the clerk gave her a sympathetic smile as she rang her up. Gabby was back in the car, feeling triumphant at once again fooling people with her acting abilities—and a disguise.

And then she saw Sarah's white, strained face, and remembered the seriousness of the situation. "I had no problems at all," Gabby said. "Let's go to my house and do this right now."

"I've been Googling it—morning is best. If I'm at least four weeks pregnant, afternoons would sort of be okay. It's been four weeks since...since I was stupid enough to—"

"Stop punishing yourself. The past can't be changed, but our reaction to it can. You don't know for certain yet. Let's hope for the best."

It was obvious Sarah didn't have much hope, and Gabby was worried she was right.

When they turned down the drive and approached the house rising above the banks of the creek, Sarah said, "This is really nice."

"I know, which is why I'm going to buy it."

"You really want to stay in Spencer Hollow?"

It was obvious Sarah thought that a fate worse than death.

Gabby smiled as she turned off the car. "I've lived in a lot of big cities. They can be wonderful, but don't underestimate the appeal of peace and fresh air."

Sarah didn't look convinced, and when she picked up the drug store bag, she became even more glum. Once they were inside, they read the directions together, and then Sarah disappeared into the powder room off the great room.

It was a long ten minutes, and Gabby paced, imagining Sarah rereading the directions and taking her time. She knew just how the poor girl felt but didn't think it was wise to distract Sarah with her own story. If Sarah ended up pregnant, Gabby would share her experiences.

Relive her experiences, she reminded herself. She'd spent her entire adult life trying to forget the hardest decision she'd ever had to make, giving up her own daughter for adoption. But she'd tell Sarah about it, if that might help.

She had this sudden weird fantasy about offering to adopt the baby—that was crazy! She had already decided that her life was

The Apple Blossom Café

too uneven to subject a child to it. Why, now, did her mind play tricks on her by hinting otherwise?

Gabby couldn't believe her own outrageous thoughts.

Sarah reappeared, near tears.

Oh no, Gabby thought.

Sarah shook her head and smiled. "It says I'm not pregnant."

She flung herself at Gabby, who caught her and hugged her tight. Though the girl was thin, she felt strong and resilient.

Gabby pulled back and held Sarah's shoulders so she could look into her eyes. "I'm happy for you, but you have to promise me you'll do the second test tomorrow morning. It works best then, all right?"

Biting her lip, Sarah nodded, her expression sobering. "I can't thank you enough for your help."

"Any time. Get out your cell and add my number. I want to hear from you tomorrow."

Sarah gave her a shy smile. "Okay, I promise. Guess I've just got a stomach bug."

"Guess so. Maybe you can get some rest now that you know the truth. Let's get you back to the theater before your parents arrive. I think we can just make it in time."

When they pulled into the parking lot, Gabby stopped Sarah before she could jump out of the car. "Promise me you'll be much more prepared the next time you decide to be intimate with someone."

"Believe me, I will," Sarah said vehemently. "I got into UVA. I need a career before having a baby."

"That's what I like to hear. Remember, you can call me anytime, about boys or anything."

Sarah smiled. "Thanks."

Gabby stayed behind the wheel, watching as Sarah disappeared inside. She let out her breath slowly, then leaned forward until her forehead rested on the wheel. She'd been able to help someone, without using her fame or her money. She was determined to find more ways in her life for such quiet satisfaction.

She heard something outside the window, and turned to see a camera pressed to the glass, clicking away. She sighed, wondering what the headline would be if they used the one with her head down: *Gabrielle contemplates suicide; Gabrielle nearly in a car wreck.*

Whatever. She drove off, barely resisting the urge to flip the bird. Now *that* would be making a statement.

~oOo~

Noah was surprised and pleased to get an invitation from Gabby for dinner that night, anticipating sitting back while she did all the cooking.

But as he walked toward his SUV in front of the family home, he was startled when a woman and a man approached him.

He frowned. "The orchard is closed, and you're on private property, not the public grounds."

The woman gave a friendly smile. "Mr. Fairfield, this will only take a moment of your time."

And then the man lifted a professional camera that he'd been hiding.

Noah stiffened. "What is this about?"

Surprisingly, the man didn't start taking pictures. Instead the woman held out a stack of what looked like 5x7s.

"Mr. Fairfield, we thought you'd be interested in these. Perhaps you'll give us a statement?"

"I'm not interested." He clicked open the car door locks.

"But they're of Gabrielle Holt taken just a few hours ago in Crozet."

Crozet? Gabby had told him she was going to the theater. Regardless, it wasn't any business of the paparazzi. "Please leave or I'll be forced to call the police. You're trespassing."

He opened his car door.

The Apple Blossom Café

"Is the baby yours, Mr. Fairfield?"

Baby? He froze, his brain taking a moment to begin firing neurons again. Was Gabby pregnant when she arrived, and she hadn't told him? Because it certainly couldn't be his, not this soon. Or could it? He didn't know how quickly accurate tests were nowadays.

The woman shoved the photos at him, the photographer started clicking away, and suddenly he was looking at a picture of Gabby wearing a ball cap and sunglasses, going into a drug store. The next showed her coming out with a bag, and a third one was of her very up close, her head resting on the steering wheel as if she were too upset to function.

"This is all you have?" he asked coldly. "You're making assumptions about a woman's private life because she went to a drug store?"

"I talked to the clerk," the woman rushed to say, sounding eager, "and when she realized I was right about Gabrielle's identity, she admitted what she'd bought."

Noah forced himself to chuckle. "Nice try. Now please leave or I'm calling the police." He tossed the photos onto the ground, got into his SUV, and started the engine.

The woman retrieved the photos, said something to the man, and started trudging back toward their car, farther up the path. He was tempted to follow her way too close, hurrying them along, but he could see himself being sued if she accidentally tripped in front of him. He made sure their car disappeared down the road away from the orchard, waited ten tense minutes, then took a back route to Gabby's.

The whole time he drove, his mind raced faster than the car. He couldn't believe she wouldn't have told him if she was pregnant when she arrived—and he also couldn't believe she could really be pregnant. But what if she'd actually bought a pregnancy test?

The fact that the paparazzi came right to him meant it was already common knowledge they were seeing each other. So much for asking her to keep their relationship out of the public eye. Soon, everything about him would be fodder for the fans, every one of his flaws magnified, all of his private concerns revealed.

She was in the kitchen when he arrived; steam moistened the air. She was wearing a tank top, her flawless skin glistening with perspiration. He thought of her pregnant and knew she'd be just as beautiful.

There might be another man involved, and Noah would have to step back. That was what he should want, right?

She waved him away from the stove. "I'll take care of this. I decanted a bottle of rosé out in the great room. Help yourself."

He reached around her and turned off several burners on the stove while she was still sautéing.

"Hey!" She gave him an incredulous look.

Between gritted teeth, he said, "I was confronted by some paparazzi a few minutes ago."

Her face blanched. "Oh, Noah, I'm sorry."

He angrily waved her apology aside. "Is this a nice dinner to prepare me for the results of the pregnancy test you bought this afternoon?"

She gaped at him as if with incomprehension. "They were following me?"

"You really bought a pregnancy test?" he demanded. "How could you be so foolish? You're watched every moment of the day! Haven't you heard of online shopping?"

She winced as if he'd slapped her. "Don't you think I know that? There's a damn good reason, if you'd just give me a chance—"

"Are you pregnant or not?"

The Apple Blossom Café

To his surprise, he felt a bit...conflicted over what the result would be. And that was as shocking as hearing about it from reporters. He wanted to hang onto his anger, his sense of invasion.

"The test wasn't mine," she insisted. "I'm not pregnant, and I don't even suspect it. But that explains why my assistant keeps calling me. I was going to get back to her after dinner. Damn."

Her expression was pensive, and he imagined that damage control was already on her mind. He couldn't think about that now.

"You're not pregnant," he said stiffly.

"No."

He sank down on a stool near the island, dazed, his heart touched by a faint echo of sadness. He wanted kids, but he should be relieved that he wasn't going to have one with Gabrielle. What was wrong with him?

He still wasn't positive Gabby hadn't slept with him just to get what she needed for her career. A baby would have tied him to her forever. They might have made a go at being a couple for the baby's sake, but what movie star's relationships ever work out?

She shook him out of his thoughts when she stood up to his anger and spoke in a sober voice. "The pregnancy test was for one of the teenagers at the theater."

It took a moment to register. "One of your students?"

She nodded. "Thank God, it was negative. I won't fully relax until she lets me know tomorrow morning after she takes the second test."

"How the hell did you get involved in that?"

She told him what had happened, and he listened without asking more questions. He was impressed by her understanding and her sympathy; he wasn't surprised by it, of course, but the depth of it seemed...unusual. How had she guessed the teenager's problem?

He stared into her eyes for a silent moment when she was through. "There's something you're not telling me."

She turned back to the stove and lit the burners. "I don't know what you mean."

Something was wrong, and all of his frustration and anger drained away. She was hurting. "Gabby?" he asked softly. "Tell me what you're thinking, why this meant so much to you."

"I told you that Sarah reminds me a lot of me at that age, reluctantly watching her sister, but doing a far better job than I ever did. And the thought of her pregnant at 17...I just...I just..."

Noah took her by the shoulders and turned her around. There were tears shining in her eyes, and it hit him hard. He was a selfish ass. "Gabby? What is it?"

"I..." At last she met his gaze. "I got pregnant when I was a teenager."

He swiftly inhaled.

"Her dilemma brought back everything I went through. And I'm praying hard the test is still negative in the morning, because dealing with what I had to...it's not something any woman wants to face."

He put his arms around her, and he didn't blame her for remaining stiff after his hot-headed display. As if she needed to stand on her own, she only leaned her forehead against his shoulder and trembled.

He kissed her head and spoke quietly, as if she were a frightened fawn. "What did you do?"

"I gave the baby up for adoption. My daughter. I held her once."

The last words were so forlorn that Noah's throat tightened with sorrow.

The Apple Blossom Café

The words kept tumbling out. "I couldn't take care of her. I had no money, I was sleeping on the couches of people I barely knew. I couldn't do that to her!"

She looked up at him with pleading eyes as if he'd disagreed with her.

"I'm sorry you had to go through that," he said, his voice husky. "You made a good decision."

"I always thought so, even though lately I've had a hard time justifying it to myself."

"What do you mean?"

"It's stupid, I know. I think of what I have now, what I could offer her…"

"And would you have any of this to offer her if you'd been a struggling single mother?"

"I know," she said with a sigh. "But my mind plays tricks on me."

"*Were* you a single mother? Did the father want to be involved?"

She shook her head. "He gladly signed papers to give up the baby for adoption. We weren't together. God, I was so recklessly stupid…getting pregnant." With a sigh, she continued, "I know I gave her a life with two loving parents who could take care of her. I force myself to remember that when my regrets are at their worst. I thought enough time had passed, that I was better able to handle the memories, to be around children again."

"Is *that* why you got involved in the theater?" he asked in surprise. "Were you testing yourself?"

"That makes it seem like I'm only there for myself," she added with a little spirit.

"I don't mean that."

"Okay, that's part of it. I wanted to help Bri, to help the kids. I thought I was ready. And I was. It's been okay, even good for me. Much as I love the kids, I think it's finally proving to me once and for all that I shouldn't be a parent."

"What?" he asked sharply.

"No, I've made up my mind. This has helped me find some peace." She pulled away from him and turned the burner back on. "It's as if I was meant to be there to help Sarah. And that's a good thing. But as for being a parent? No, I don't think so." She hesitated. "What about you? Do you want children?"

"Yes, I do," he said quietly.

She gave a brisk nod. "Even more reason why we can't be a long-term thing. Now why don't you refill my glass? I could use some wine."

He watched her bustle about the kitchen as if she hadn't just confessed what might be her most tragic secret to him. As if she hadn't just said she would never be a mother. It seemed even sadder, since he'd always pictured himself having a bunch of kids.

He imagined her as a young frightened girl all alone, feeling like she had no one to turn to. That girl had made a decision that had affected the rest of her life. She'd made it alone, and since then, she'd built a career alone. Did she continue to think she had to do *everything* alone? Or was she punishing herself, as if she didn't *deserve* to have someone special in her life or to be a mother?

As she finished cooking dinner, she was unusually quiet, and she didn't eat all that much the first few silent minutes. She took a half-hearted forkful, and accepted his compliments on her cooking while she kept staring into her wine glass. He was so curious, but asking personal questions went against everything he'd trained himself to be. Yet…if she was going to think about it, maybe she needed to talk about it.

The Apple Blossom Café

"Did you have to drop out of school?" he asked, realizing too late that he should have eased back into their serious conversation.

She didn't seem at all surprised, only sighed. "I'd already dropped out long before I was pregnant. We're going to keep talking about this?"

"It's hard not to think about it. But if you don't want to, I'd understand."

"No, it's all right. I'm sitting here trying to decide how I feel about spilling the truth like I just did. I told you something I've never talked about since the day I gave my daughter away."

"Not with anyone?" he asked, surprised.

She shook her head.

He felt...awkward and uncomfortable to be the recipient of something so personal. Well, *sex* was personal. They were sharing that, weren't they?

This was different. He tried to lighten the mood. "I don't have as much to share from when I was young and stupid. I was suspended for a couple weeks."

She gave a brief laugh. "No! You? Tell me about it."

"First you tell me why you dropped out."

She took another sip of wine, her fork twirling in her pasta, though she didn't eat it. He wanted her to eat, to relax, to let the past go. He hoped talking about it might accomplish that.

"I told you my brother Kevin was an addict," she began slowly.

He nodded.

"And that I had to watch over him after school. My mom...I can't fault her for working two jobs to take care of us, but I could always tell she blamed us for how hard she had to work. She was short-tempered and angry, and discovering that Kevin had gotten in with a bad crowd made everything worse. She blamed me and made me quit the high school theater group I was involved with. If I wasn't working on the weekends, I was home with Kevin after school and all evening. I was pretty miserable—Kevin and I were both miserable, and we took it out on each other. I'm not proud of that, and the fact that we could have a good phone conversation the other day…that was important to me. But back then…he started doing drugs. Mom came down on me even harder, like it was all my fault. So I just…left. I was bored in school, and I thought the cost of college was beyond me. Quit school, stayed with whatever friend would let me crash on their couch for a while, picked up more hours waitressing. I don't know what I thought I'd accomplish that way. I was happier…at first. Then came the uncertainty of my situation, feeling like I was intruding on friends, but couldn't afford my own place…feeling like I had to say yes when a guy…"

They didn't speak for a long moment. He hadn't had the best childhood, but his parents had been there, had helped him pay for some of culinary school. He'd never felt he had no place to go, even when he was certain he didn't belong.

"And then I got pregnant," she said bitterly. "My own fault."

He reached out to squeeze her hand and sighed with relief when she squeezed him back.

"Needless to say," she continued, "I realized my life was crap, and I couldn't keep going on the way I was. After…the adoption, I moved to New York City to start over. I vowed to make my life better, to never let myself be so helpless again."

"You made that happen," he said emphatically.

"I did." She nodded and seemed to shake off her soberness. "Your turn. You were suspended. Wait—let me guess why."

He took a bite of pasta and watched as she made a pretty display of thinking. He didn't mind playing the game, glad to distract her in any way he could. He had once thought her blessed with beauty and brains and talent, that nothing bad could

The Apple Blossom Café

have happened to her before America thought she was cheating on the memory of a beloved actor. Noah could be a self-absorbed idiot, sometimes. He took a sip of wine.

"You slept with a teacher."

He choked and almost spit his wine onto his plate.

Gabby was watching him, wearing a half-smile that showed she clearly enjoyed surprising him.

"No," he said hoarsely, and gave a cough.

"I thought I had you there."

After wiping his mouth with a napkin, he said, "Try again."

"You stole an opposing team's mascot and barbecued it."

"You think I'm capable of animal cruelty?" he demanded.

She laughed.

"Trust me, it wasn't all that unusual. I was caught drinking."

Her eyebrows rose. "Drinking?"

"Yeah, I know what you're thinking. A guy with an alcoholic dad being stupid enough to drink."

"Apparently it happens a lot," she said quietly.

"I know. The principal made it worse when he went on about how disappointed he was in me, that he didn't want me to end up like my dad."

She winced.

"So I flipped his desk."

"Wow. You seem a lot more in control of your emotions now."

"I've worked hard at it."

She lifted a glass to him. "To maturing."

He clinked his glass to hers. "Wish there was an easier way."

"Guess we both had to be knocked over the head to have it sink in."

They looked at each other for a long moment as they sipped their wine.

"Another thing we have in common," she murmured, her unusual eyes smoldering at him.

And though he was turned on, he was also uneasy. He didn't need to find a lot of similarities between them. He wanted her; she wanted him. Every emotional tie between them was one more that would have to be severed when he left.

But he hadn't gotten around to making plans to leave. He should, he knew it. Every day's delay from now on would just make people suspicious.

"About the paparazzi," he began.

He saw the way her shoulders tensed, and her eyes went soft with sadness, and he felt like a jerk.

"I'm very sad this has spilled over onto you, Noah," Gabby said at last. "I know you want to keep us private, as do I. But reporters make connections, and then hope we'll react in a way to give them a better story."

"I didn't say much to them, so don't worry."

She put her hand on his. "I didn't think you would."

"It was pretty terrible how they asked a clerk about your purchase—and she just told them," he added indignantly.

"So that's how they knew," Gabby mused. "When I'm not pregnant, they'll just forget they ever made the accusations, until the next time. God forbid they apologize. And to involve you…"

"Yeah, I wasn't happy about it. I'm not used to people knowing my business."

"And you don't want that, I know."

She sounded sad, resigned even.

"No, I don't. But I don't blame you."

He reached for her hand and pulled her out of her seat and around to his side of the table. Damn, he wanted her. When she straddled his lap, he forgot all his reservations, the uncertainty of his life. There was only Gabby, and the desire for her that

The Apple Blossom Café

simmered inside him every day, never going away completely, just waiting to be fanned back to life like flame from an ember.

Their kiss was hot and urgent; he cupped her breasts, even as she ground her hips into his. After unbuckling his pants, she reached inside and gripped him with her warm, firm hand.

Noah groaned. "Gabby, what you do to me."

"Condom?" she said against his mouth.

"In my pocket."

She gently bit his lower lip. "Always prepared."

They made love on the kitchen chair, and again in front of a fire in the great room. Afterward, he drowsed, stretched out on his stomach, head pillowed in his arms. He'd heard his phone buzz a few times and ignored it. He didn't know if the paparazzi had made public their suspicions about his and Gabby's supposed child, but he wasn't ready to deal with it. He watched her silhouette as she sat staring into the fire, seeing a touch of melancholy in her gaze. He imagined she would not easily suppress the memories she's brought up tonight.

She'd revealed her soul, and all he'd told her was an old high school story. Why couldn't he confess that even though the café was a success, he felt like a failure? He thought he'd been indispensable, almost a partner, at the top of his game when he won the Drayton Award. It had all been an illusion.

Was his success at the café an illusion, too? Was it only because of Gabby's presence?

Chapter 11

Gabby awoke at eight the next morning, alone. She'd tried to convince Noah to spend the night, but he'd said it would be an early day, that the family was taking advantage of being together to plant trees. When she'd asked to come along, he'd chuckled, as if she was kidding, then relented when she'd insisted she could work as hard as he could. Men.

Or maybe he hadn't spent the night because he'd seen his phone messages. Because of her, everyone was wondering if he'd got her pregnant, or if she'd had an affair while carrying another man's child. For herself, she didn't mind as much. These things flared up and would die down when it was obvious that she wasn't pregnant. The previous year they'd said far worse things about her after Brock had died and she'd been caught a few months later kissing another man. One tabloid claimed she'd gotten rid of Brock's baby. No one had known how devastated that had made her feel, as all her guilt rose up to suffocate her.

Noah, so private with his personal life, might take this intrusion hard. Yet he'd still asked her to enjoy the day with his family. To her surprise, he was going to trust one of his line cooks to oversee the café kitchen for a couple hours. She wondered if that was the first step to him letting go, to going back to Pittsburgh. It made her sad. Every day they were together showed her even more how much she'd miss him. And now she'd told him her biggest secret. Perhaps her subconscious was trying to tell her she'd miss him a lot, that this was more than just a temporary fling, that maybe she'd have to take some trips to Pittsburgh. Would Noah welcome her and the unflattering spotlight that shown on anyone around her?

The Apple Blossom Café

She wasn't going to think about it and ruin a day with his family.

Gabby kept her phone in the bathroom while showering, but Sarah never called. Thank God. She would assume the girl wasn't pregnant but would still look into her eyes the next time they were together to make sure. Sarah would have a chance to learn a valuable lesson without suffering the terrible consequences Gabby had. She hoped the girl wasn't upset about the tabloid pregnancy rumors, which she'd feared would happen. Gabby would make it clear that this hadn't bothered her.

Though Gabby had confessed her past to Noah, she hadn't told him everything, especially what it was like to carry a child within her, unable to enjoy every phase of its growth. Every kick had been a reminder of the decision she hadn't known how to make, of her mistakes, of her shame. The last couple weeks of the pregnancy she'd been unable to work and had to resort to a friend's kindness just to survive. It had reinforced even more how little she would have been able to care for a baby.

As she dressed, she once again wrapped up her aching memories and put them away on a closet shelf in her mind. It was a little harder today, after sharing it with Noah.

And a little easier, too. He hadn't been appalled or disappointed. He'd been sad for her; he'd understood. He was a good man, and she would miss him when he left her.

When he left the Hollow, she reminded herself. She didn't want to think he'd be fleeing her.

~oOo~

Noah could barely keep his eyes off Gabby, as she stood in the back of the trailer wearing jeans and a dirty tank top, her blond hair pulled back beneath a ball cap. He thought again of the cool, controlled woman he'd first met, her clothes elegantly casual, her manner restrained. Now she seemed like a different person to him, warm and funny and kind. He'd been let into her world, saw how she ached for a teenage girl she barely knew, how she suffered for the tragic mistakes of her past, how she had to put up with the world believing lies about her. Yet she held herself together, without the bitterness that often overtook him. He could learn a thing or two from her.

Gabby's job was to take a baby tree from the cluster of trees that looked like three-foot toothpicks with scraggly roots at one end, and hand it to Tyler, who stood over the long opening cut in the middle of the trailer. He dropped a tree in the long furrow dug beneath the front of the trailer, then blades swept the dirt back into the trench as they passed. Noah walked behind, stomping the dirt around the tree where the blades couldn't safely reach. Somewhere nearby, their parents drove one of the old pickups, wooden bins full of trees stacked in the bed.

It was April in the orchard, and bees buzzed noisily as they went about their work of pollinating. Uma ignored them, romping through the rows of trees as if it were her own private maze. The air was scented with blossoms, the pure blue sky framed the Blue Ridge Mountains, and the good memories of Noah's childhood overtook the bad ones, even if just for the afternoon.

And looking at Gabby made everything worthwhile. She was wearing little to no makeup, although a lot of sunscreen, she insisted. After calming his concerned family about the tabloid pregnancy rumors, he'd asked them not to bother Gabby with it. Consequently she was smiling and chatting with Amy, who drove the tractor, following the GPS course they'd programmed to follow the land. After a few days of planting, they'd string wire between posts to support the weight of the dwarf trees. People often mistook the young trellised trees for grape vines, but that was the modern way to grow apple trees.

Rachel walked beside Noah, looking over the newly planted trees that now stretched far behind them. Dozens more rows

The Apple Blossom Café

awaited planting this spring. Though the tractor was loud enough that they couldn't easily talk to anyone on the trailer, Noah was able to hear Rachel, who was giving him a curious look.

"So, you and Gabby," she said.

"Haven't we already had this conversation?"

"Yeah, but you brought her to spring planting."

"She asked to come."

"Even more revealing. Are you serious about her?"

"No."

Rachel arched a brow. "You did get her pregnant."

"Stop," he said with a grimace.

"You all right about this?" She eyed him as her teasing smile faded.

"Yeah, people will forget about it soon enough. The guys at Feel the Burn had some laughter at my expense." He *had* to be all right about it. What else could he do? This was what Gabby put up with all the time. He felt like a jerk being concerned about one stupid rumor and how it might affect him.

She chuckled. "Sorry."

"As for getting serious about her, that would be pointless. I'm leaving."

"So you say."

He stiffened, but said nothing, just stomped around a newly planted tree.

"And what does that matter?" Rachel asked. "Pittsburgh's not that far away."

"It's not like she lives here regularly."

"She'll be gone a few weeks here and there, occasionally a few months. The kids will be fine with you." Rachel smirked.

"She doesn't want kids." Noah couldn't believe he'd blurted that out.

Rachel's amused expression vanished. "I'm sorry to hear that. You want kids?"

139

He nodded.

"Your thoughts about her have gone that far."

He blinked. He hadn't realized it.

"I'm glad to hear you want kids."

His gaze shot to her. "You sound surprised."

"I am. After the way we grew up, and your reaction to it—"

"You make it sound like no one else had issues with Dad's problems."

"I didn't mean that, and you know it. We all had issues, in our own ways. I've never been certain about how it molded you. Tyler always tried to smooth things over, to look for the attention he never got. Amy tried to fix dad, and when she couldn't, ended up dating a man with alcohol issues. But you—"

"What about you?" he asked.

"What do you mean?"

"You're so quick to judge the twins."

"I'm not judging them!" She stomped hard around a baby tree.

"Let's call it diagnosing, then."

"My reaction was to stay here and help make things right. I was here every day for Dad's recovery."

"Except for the last year."

"That had nothing to do with Dad," she said with exasperation. "I'd barely had the occasional weekend away before this last trip. The twins had come home to help. Why should you and Logan and Michael be the only ones to benefit from that?"

He wasn't sure that was everything, but he wouldn't press the point, because she'd surely press back, right into his business.

"Switch!" Tyler suddenly yelled.

Amy stopped the tractor and Tyler took her place in the driver's seat; Rachel replaced Gabby on the trailer, and she came down to stomp dirt with him.

The Apple Blossom Café

"Amy," Noah called, "did you want me to drop the trees?"

"No, you walk hand-in-hand with your girlfriend," she said with a smirk.

Gabby smiled up at him but kept a careful distance. When he took her hand as they started to walk, she looked around worriedly as if wondering who'd see the display of affection. He'd made her feel that way, and it gnawed at him.

They had to drop hands for the next tree stomp.

"What happens next in the planting process?" she asked when Noah took her hand again.

"We have to put posts in the ground at intervals, and string wire to support the growing trees. Lots of fertilizer, too."

"Why do you plant dwarf trees?"

"More trees mean more yield; it cuts down on the spraying, and the individual apples get more exposure to the sun. They taste a lot better. And let's not forget how much easier it is to pick them when the trees are short."

"Spraying?"

"It starts next month and goes into the summer."

"Though you've been away for years, the knowledge is still there, huh?"

He knocked on his forehead. "Ingrained. Being a farm kid meant I could drive the pickup way before I turned sixteen. There were some perks."

"I'm glad to hear that," she said softly.

Though he shot her a look, she just continued on with her questions.

"Amy said you're putting in some new varieties?"

"Yep, specifically for the cider, like Winesap, Elstar, and Sonata. Carlos and Tyler have big plans for some new cider flavors. But it'll take a good three years before these trees are producing a decent crop."

She continued to eye him until he became uncomfortable.

"What?" he asked. "Is there dirt on my face?"

"No, I just like seeing you work with your family. And I like seeing you in charge of your kitchen. Maybe I just like watching you, period."

He gave a faint smile. "You're not so bad to look at, yourself."

She put a hand to her chest. "What a compliment!"

"Come on, people compliment your looks every day. It must get old."

"Or insincere."

"They're lying about how beautiful you are?"

"They don't know me. But when you compliment me, it means something." Though up ahead, the tractor rumbled, his family chattered, Gabby hesitated, her expression growing pensive. "I didn't ruin things by telling you about my past, did I?"

Noah frowned. "Ruin things? How could you ruin things by being honest about what happened?"

"I don't know. It's pretty…real. Some guys like the glamour and illusion, you know?"

He briefly squeezed her hand again before another baby tree got between them. "I like reality. I always have."

She gave him a grateful smile, and it rivaled the sun.

And then he heard himself. Reality? What was real about lying to her about his job situation? How could he keep lying when she'd been so honest? It had haunted him since she'd told him about the hardest decision of her life. He slowed his pace until the tractor began to pull away from them.

He stomped dirt around a baby tree and said, "It's pretty ridiculous for me to say I prefer reality when I've been lying to you."

The Apple Blossom Café

Gabby told herself to look interested, not too intrigued. She'd known Noah had a secret but hadn't imagined he'd trust her with it. He was a man who guarded himself well.

He sighed. "You know this extended vacation I've told everyone I'm on? It's no vacation—I was fired."

She only allowed herself a couple blinks of astonishment, instead of her mouth dropping open in shock. Her acting training was really coming in handy. "Fired? But you'd just won a prestigious award! What were they thinking?"

He shot her an amused look. "Thanks for not assuming I'd done something worthy of being fired."

"You love your work, Noah. Watching you run a kitchen has been really eye-opening for me. You're professional—none of that crazy screaming you see from some TV chefs. And the ways you combine ingredients, wow."

"Okay, okay, thanks for trying to make me feel better. The reason for my firing *was* something I did. I asked for some extended vacation time when I had barely even taken a weekend or two all of last year."

"*That's* the reason they fired you?"

He shrugged. "The owner wouldn't give me a reason. But he didn't want me to take two weeks all at once, tried to talk me out of it several times, each more forcefully than the last. I explained what was going on at the orchard; I had thought we were friends and could discuss things like that. Hell, maybe it was that I dared to open a restaurant. It's not as if we were in competition. I don't know. It doesn't matter anymore."

"Of course it matters. It matters so much that you haven't told anyone."

He said nothing, just stomped dirt around a baby tree. She watched the way his flannel shirt, open over a t-shirt, flapped in the breeze. He was wearing old jeans and work gloves, and he'd never looked sexier to her.

But he was hurting. He loved his work.

"Noah? Why haven't you told anyone?"

"Because they'll think I can stay here and run the café. I'm not doing that."

"You can just say no."

"They'll get their hopes up. They want us all to work here, one happy family."

"You can't blame them for that."

"I don't. And I'm flattered. I love them all, and I'm enjoying being here. But…I was making a name for myself in Pittsburgh."

She sensed it was more than that. How could she persuade him to tell her and perhaps release some of his pain? And every time Gabby had brought him into the public eye, he must have worried the firing would become news, and hurt his family. No wonder he'd been so tense.

"I liked the accomplishments and the success I'd achieved," he added.

She did not point out that he could achieve things at Fairfield Orchard, too. He knew that. There was more going on. When he didn't say anything else, she was left with the feeling that either he couldn't articulate it—or he didn't feel like he could trust her with the truth, though she'd trusted him with the pain of the loss of her daughter.

Discussing that with him had been *her* choice. They'd only been seeing each other for days, not months or years. She'd already felt close enough to him to confess her most painful secret. Apparently she was feeling a lot closer to him than he was to her. But that was her issue, not his.

"So what's the plan?" she asked. "When do you leave?"

"Rushing me out the door?" he asked lightly.

"You know I'm not. But surely your family will start getting suspicious."

"I know. I thought I'd stay until the end of the week."

The Apple Blossom Café

Just a few more days, she thought, surprised to feel an ache of wistfulness. "I'll miss you."

He gave her a crooked smile. "I'll miss you, too. We can visit each other—if you want us to."

"That sounds nice."

"You don't sound all that sure."

"I've been in long-distance relationships. They're difficult." *And lonely*. It had always played on her fear that her life would be nothing *but* long-distance relationships, since she'd have to be gone several months a year. And there was still Noah's insistence that their relationship stay out of the public eye. She heard herself say, "But with you, I'd like to give it a try."

He leaned around the baby tree and kissed her. "I'm glad."

When he touched her, it felt so good. He straightened, and then the melancholy started. She firmly pushed it away.

"No long-distance relationships, huh?" she said. "You've been suspiciously quiet about the women in your past."

"There's not much to tell—and that's not an exaggeration. I worked all the time. That's what's been so weird about being home here. I'm just not as busy—well, I wasn't, but now that the café is open..."

"You're getting off topic."

"You noticed, huh?"

She chuckled. "You know all about my relationships, thanks to the internet. Now it's your turn."

He gave an exaggerated sigh, then good-naturedly continued. "Seriously, there isn't much to tell. I was never with a woman for more than a month or two."

"Really?"

"Yeah, it doesn't make me sound like the ideal boyfriend. I never had time to put into relationships, so they tended to flare and then fade out quickly. The women usually worked days, and

Emma Cane

I worked every evening, but especially weekends. Without the chance to talk..."

"You had quick sex."

Did he actually blush?

"Well, I'm a guy. I didn't hate that."

She rolled her eyes. "Men."

"Hey, the women liked that part, too. I made sure of that."

"I know," she said in a sultry voice.

They looked at each other meaningfully.

"Speaking of quickies," she said, "I might need a shower after this."

He looked down her body with interest. Damn, she liked the way it felt to see admiration in his eyes. Why was it different with him? She knew people found her attractive. But with Noah, who guarded his emotions, it felt so much more important that he wanted her. She liked being with him and his family, doing something as important as shepherding the land into the future. All it had taken was her hard work, side by side with the Fairfields, no cameras around.

Noah was still looking at her body. "You do look very dirty," he said suggestively. "And sweaty."

She chuckled. "So much so that I might need help."

"If you insist..."

They grinned at each other before she remembered something. "Would you do me a favor before you leave?"

"Anything."

"Could I rent out the café tomorrow evening and have a small party? I'd love for you to cook for a couple friends of mine. We're doing a movie together soon, and we'd like to get together, since they happen to be in D.C. for a charity event. And trust me—they know how to remain quiet about what happens in our personal lives."

"Of course."

The Apple Blossom Café

He sounded a little unemotional, but she couldn't second guess everything he was thinking or she'd drive herself crazy. She had to trust him to tell her whenever he was uncomfortable. She briefly took his arm and squeezed as the tractor got even farther away from them. "Good. I want to show you off."

He patted her hand. "Anything special?"

"No, you can surprise me. I like everything you cook."

"Damn, a man can be led into dangerous thoughts with that kind of flattery."

"And a man would be right."

Just as they leaned in to kiss, a horn beeped. His parents pulled up beside them in the pickup truck and matched their slow pace.

His mom leaned out the window and called cheerfully, "You're falling behind!"

"Leave the man to his distractions," Bruce said. "We'll see you at the end of the row."

Gabby smiled as they sped up. When she glanced at Noah, she thought he hid the briefest touch of sadness behind a cheerful smile.

~oOo~

They all retreated to the new café for lunch, gathering a bunch of tables together on the terrace. Noah resisted the urge to check on the kitchen. Though he just tried to enjoy his family, his gaze kept straying to Gabby, who was shoulder to shoulder with Rachel, chatting about the joys of travel. They were talking about Machu Picchu in Peru and Ephesus in Turkey, but he found himself dwelling on his own thoughts.

He'd told Gabby about being fired—hadn't even asked her to keep it quiet. He knew he trusted her to do so.

Well, she had trusted him with the secret of the baby she'd given up for adoption. Maybe that had meant more to him than he'd realized.

They were all discussing what food they would order, when Tyler seemed suddenly distracted by his cell phone. "Hey, Noah, there've been a couple great local articles about the grand opening. Did you see them?"

"Mom kept sending me links last night," Noah said.

"You bet I did," said Patty. "I asked Tyler to put them on our Facebook and Instagram pages."

"I even tweeted," Tyler teased.

Patty grimaced. "There's so much to keep track of nowadays."

Tyler said, "And here's another article by that reporter who was here the other day with Melanie Archer. I'll text you the link."

Noah felt uneasy as he clicked on the link and it opened in his browser. As he started reading, there wasn't much about the event itself—they hadn't even mentioned the orchard name, he thought with regret. It was all about Gabby dating him after dating his brother. There was nothing about his past in Pittsburgh, thank God.

He glanced at Gabby, who was laughing over something Rachel had said. He didn't want to tell Gabby about it. Tyler met his gaze and gave a brief shake of his head as if he knew just what Noah was thinking.

Noah knew Gabby would blame herself, that she'd hoped to bring him nothing but good publicity.

He didn't like feeling so self-absorbed, something the last couple years of his life seemed to have made him. Though succeeding at his work had brought him local fame and an award, what had that really mattered in the end? When he'd felt bound to help his family, he'd been betrayed by a man he'd thought was his friend more than his boss. His life had become a crossroads, where he wasn't certain what to do next.

Chapter 12

The day of Gabby's private party, Noah didn't feel any pressure as he and his line cooks kept busy through the orchard's public schedule. The café had been doing brisk business the first few days since opening, and he'd seen plenty of repeat customers, which boded well for the future.

He'd even settled on a new chef, although he hadn't offered the woman the job yet. He still wanted to speak to Amy, Tyler, and Rachel about her.

"Gabrielle is here!" Juan was looking through the pass-through into the dining room.

Noah shot him an amused look. "She's worked beside you on the line for days now."

Juan shrugged, obviously embarrassed. "She seems different out there now. I mean, look what she's wearing—and look who she's with!"

Lindsey bumped shoulders with Juan to see. She covered her mouth with both hands. "That's Sky Becket! I just saw her in that superhero movie."

Juan's mouth dropped open. "And isn't that LaDavis Jones?"

Noah found himself mildly annoyed when Lindsey gasped, then fanned herself.

"He's incredible," she gushed. "I was sure he'd win the Oscar this year. And now he's in our café!"

"Let's get back to work," Noah said, keeping his voice mild but no-nonsense.

LaDavis Jones? Noah hadn't thought to ask who was coming. He pretended nonchalance as he glanced through the pass-through. He caught his breath. Gabby was wearing a diaphanous dress in gold and maroon and cream, rivaling even the most beautiful autumn at the orchard. The dress wrapped around her, making her seem like a butterfly come to life. Beneath, she was wearing cream tights and knee-high boots.

She was smiling up at LaDavis, who was tall, dark, and broad-shouldered, with the honed body of the football player he once was. Now he was known for his quirky indie films and the occasional blockbuster that made him a name on the lips of every female movie fan.

Damn, he was even better looking in person. And he looked at Gabby as if her words were gold.

Not that that mattered. As Noah had told Gabby the other day, he never had long relationships, and theirs wasn't going to prove any different. His relationships with women were over fast. With his all-encompassing career, what choice did he have? His days and evenings were filled with work, and most nights in Pittsburgh, he felt so wired he had a hard time falling asleep.

Not at the orchard, he had to admit. The stress wasn't as great, and there was something about the crisp, fresh spring air, and the smell of apple blossoms that filled his days and made him sleepy at night.

Or maybe it was all the great, athletic sex, he thought, shrugging out of his white coat. He eyed the trays of appetizers.

"Looking good," he called to his staff. "I'll see you out there."

Several servers followed him into the dining room, spreading out among their guests, who were taste-testing the new hard cider varieties Fairfield Orchard specialized in.

Gabby caught sight of him, and her face lit with a golden glow of a smile. He felt...bathed in her attention and admiration. She seemed to flow toward him, all grace, as she reached for his hand to pull him forward into the warmth that surrounded her.

"Noah!" she called, sliding her hand into his arm. "Come meet my guests."

The Apple Blossom Café

She introduced him to the four people gathered around her: LaDavis, as well as Sky, an up-and-coming young actress whose biggest role to date would be as Gabby's sister in the movie they were doing together. The other two guests were Bill and Jack, men in their late thirties who were obviously a couple, by the tender gazes they gave each other. Bill was a producer Gabby had worked with many times.

"This is quite the place your family has here," LaDavis said, gesturing toward the tall glass windows.

Though it was almost fully dark now, Noah knew he was referring to the public grounds of the orchard, with the hundred-fifty-year-old barn converted into the tasting room, as well as the café, which had been added on in a rustic, complimentary style.

"Thanks," Noah said. "It's been a labor of love for a couple hundred years."

"So we've heard," Sky said. "It's the 200th anniversary of the orchard, Gabby tells us."

"Actually, it's the farm's anniversary. Apple trees were only a small part of it back then. My ancestor bought it from Thomas Jefferson two hundred years ago."

Although most of the guests looked interested, LaDavis kept giving Gabby lingering glances. Not that Noah was surprised. She had that effect on men. She would *always* have that effect on men.

"You buying a house here—now that's unusual," LaDavis said to Gabby.

She shrugged her slender shoulders. "You've seen how beautiful it is, how peaceful."

Sky smiled at Noah. "And we've seen who else is here."

Noah raised both hands. "I'm not the draw here. I'm heading back to Pittsburgh by the end of the week."

He saw Gabby's expression turn wistful, even as LaDavis became intrigued, but it was Sky who brightened and said, "Hey, I'm from Pittsburgh!"

Noah's stomach tensed. "Really? What neighborhood?"

"Squirrel Hill."

"Not too far from me in Shadyside."

"What restaurant do you work at?"

For a split second, he didn't know how to answer. Then Gabby did it for him.

"La Folie. And he just won the Drayton Award for the Best Upcoming Chef in Pittsburgh."

Noah winced. There wasn't a single clue in her expression that she knew not all of that was true. Though she was trying to help him, he knew, Noah felt like the biggest fraud in the room full of talented people.

"Congratulations," Sky said. "I don't know the restaurant, but then I don't get home all that much lately."

Bill and Jack gave her sympathetic expressions.

Juan chose that moment to send out the first course, to Noah's relief. They all took their seats beneath the white lights strung through the beams. The table was elegantly decorated with tiny candles amidst twigs of newly picked apple blossoms, Amy's idea. She'd been so eager to make the ambiance special, to treat Gabby's friends well, to make Noah feel proud.

Noah always felt proud of his family and didn't need to show off. And then he heard his thoughts. He felt *proud* of the orchard, the place he hadn't been able to wait to escape. He'd kept tying up the place with his father's addiction, but that had been the wrong thing to do. He *was* proud, and being home had showed him that. The resurgence of Fairfield Orchard, the coming together of the siblings to make that happen, had lifted their family's spirits. Their struggling business had seemed to be a symbol of their struggle to move past all the ways that alcoholism had separated them.

It hadn't been all that difficult to be with his father; the anticipation had been the worst. Once they'd arrived, everyone had been busy. They'd all worked together on the spring planting, and Noah had thought that that was the reason everyone got along. They'd been getting along for a while, but worry about the orchard had overshadowed everything. The joy of planting, the renewal of the earth in spring, the knowledge that more and more customers would arrive and have a great time—and a great meal—had made them seem like a normal family. He'd never felt that way before.

Noah put aside his confusing thoughts and kept up his end of the conversation. Gabby's friends were nice people, even if LaDavis watched her like a dog tracking a bunny. Soon she'd be kissing LaDavis every day, since they'd be playing a couple in the movie. He thought of them having fake sex, and his gut churned. That was a part of an actor's life; they were all professionals.

And he had no claim on her, no reason to feel jealous. Yet it was jealousy he was feeling—for a temporary, *fun* relationship, he reminded himself.

But how many men knew the "real" Gabby, the woman who grieved a decision she'd made almost a decade ago? She'd trusted *him* with her vulnerabilities, her fears. He'd even let down some of his own defenses. When it ended between them, he would remember that sharing, something he'd never had with another woman.

Already, he missed it.

When she glanced at him, a little worry in her eyes, he squeezed her hand. "Sorry, thinking about the kitchen," he said. He didn't want to worry her, and he'd tell her his thoughts later, if she wanted to know.

Apparently, he was letting himself be an open book, as long as it was Gabby doing the reading.

~oOo~

Gabby's guests had spent the night in her home, and in the morning as she saw them off on their way back to Washington D.C., she admitted to herself that she'd been a little disappointed that Noah hadn't come back to the house with them.

He'd stayed at the café to clean up with his kitchen staff, but she thought that had been an excuse. Though he'd been gracious and conversational, he'd seemed a little distant, and she would have liked to find out what he'd been thinking.

But when she arrived to shadow him at the café, it obviously wasn't the right time. There was already a line to be seated, and the tables out on the terrace were full. Since it was a sunny April day in Virginia, that meant it was warm enough to enjoy the outdoors.

"You're late," Noah said gruffly as she slipped on a spotless apron.

"I don't suppose you want to hear about being chased by paparazzi from my doorway to here."

Two line cooks and the dishwasher gaped at her.

She gave them a bright smile. Noah glanced at her and went back to whatever was sizzling in his skillet.

Apparently her charm didn't work on Noah now that they were sleeping together.

Or was it something else?

She went to her station on the cold line and helped prepare the salads. There were apples everywhere, apples in the salads, in the appetizers, in the main courses.

"Gabby, I saw your photos of the café on Instagram," Juan called.

Gabby could have sworn Noah paused as he worked, but she must have imagined it. He didn't even glance up from the sauté station. She hadn't posted anything new since he'd asked her not to.

But she wouldn't ignore Juan. "Pretty, huh? The café looks gorgeous in the evening. Too bad you're not regularly open late."

"That's okay by me," Lindsey said. "I'm fine with a day shift." She glanced at Noah. "Did Chef see how popular that selfie of the two of you is?"

Noah didn't turn his head.

Gabby sighed.

"There are hundreds of thousands of responses," Juan gushed.

Instead of paying attention to his sautéing vegetables, Noah remembered the photo, the two of them with their heads close together, the warmth of Gabby's body pressed along the length of his. He'd asked her not to go public with their relationship, but never thought about asking her to delete the photo. It had been gathering responses and eyeballs for days, especially when the pregnancy rumors hit the internet.

He knew any relationship with her was public, even when she tried to hide. He'd had ample proof of that after what had happened to Tyler, just *pretending* a relationship with her.

Gabby had been trying to help him. And now her eyes were filling with growing worry. He gave her a smile he wasn't feeling, and it didn't ease her concern.

He couldn't help thinking that people might start flocking to the café because of her popularity. He wanted to be known for his cooking, not who he was sleeping with. He'd always been driven to succeed, to find his place in the world, having felt adrift much of his childhood. Being at her side would mean he'd never know if he could achieve something on his own.

~oOo~

That evening, as Gabby pulled into her driveway after an afternoon shopping in Charlottesville, she saw an unfamiliar car parked in front of her garage, the silhouette of a person in the driver's seat. This had happened before, a photographer trespassing on her private property. She'd called the police more than once.

As she pulled up beside the car and turned to frown at the intruder, she recognized that face, even in the waning light.

It was her brother, Kevin.

In the old days, her stomach would have clenched with dismay. But he gave a wave that was both hesitant and cheerful at the same time as he got out of his car. He wore his sandy hair short in that pseudo military style that was a little long on top. He'd lost the chubbiness his old lifestyle had given him, and in nice jeans and a Henley long sleeve, he looked good—really good. His sheepish smile was so infectious that she had no problem smiling back as she got out of her car.

Another car pulled up behind hers, and she recognized Noah. She felt a flutter of nervousness at the thought of these two men meeting. She smiled at Noah and took his hand, then turned to face her brother.

Kevin, eyeing Noah, put up both hands. "I know I didn't call. I'm sorry to interrupt. I didn't even think I'd be in your neck of the woods. But we had a client move out to the area from D.C., and we like to follow up and see how they're doing. Since I was done early, I just—"

She stopped his excuses with a big hug. "No need for explanations. I know it might have been hard to call me. I don't want it to be that way with us. I'm glad you came."

He looked so relieved that she felt guilty, then reminded herself that their relationship had been dysfunctional for a lot of reasons, and blaming herself or him didn't help things to go forward.

"Kevin, this is Noah Fairfield. Noah, my brother Kevin."

The two men shook hands.

"Should I let you two catch up?" Noah asked. "I could call you tomorrow."

"No, please join us." She glanced at Kevin. "If that's okay."

"I'm the intruder," Kevin said genially. "Whatever you want."

"You're spending the night, right?" she asked Kevin. "It's almost full dark already."

His eyes shown with delight at her invitation, and it made her feel good.

"Gabby, I don't mean to put you out. I just thought we'd have dinner together or something."

"And we'll do that. I'd take you out to dinner, but I've been followed a lot today, and I'd just rather enjoy a quiet conversation and a home-cooked meal." She rounded on Noah. "And I'm cooking, okay?"

"I wouldn't think of intruding in your kitchen," Noah said.

"Like I haven't intruded in your kitchen?" she teased.

"You did do that." Noah smiled.

"It all sounds great to me." Kevin grabbed a backpack out of his back seat and trailed behind her into the house. "I don't know how you do it, being followed all the time. Maybe it's paranoia left over from my drug days, but I'd hate it."

"It comes with my profession, so I try not to get upset." Except when it spilled over onto the man in her life.

In the kitchen, she tossed her purse and keys on the counter and turned to see her brother eyeing the house with interest. It felt like she'd be bragging if she offered to show him around.

"I can see why you want to buy the place," Kevin said. "It's great."

"It's right on a creek, too, where I can sit outside in peace. No honking horns and noise, unlike my apartment in New York."

"Isn't your place in L.A. quiet?"

She reddened, glancing at Noah who gave her an encouraging smile. She reminded herself that her good fortune had also helped Kevin get clean. "That's true, but there's something about this mountain air."

"And the people here?" His smile was amused as he looked from her to Noah.

"They're all very nice," she said primly, even as she put her head into the fridge to see what she could make for dinner.

"I'm glad to hear that," Kevin said. "I saw a picture of you with one of those nice people today, looking pretty close." He glanced at Noah. "You kind of look like him."

She was about to say they *were* close, but that wasn't true—not when one person wanted to get away, and soon. "Noah and I are having fun together."

Kevin arched an eyebrow, Noah gave her a smoldering look behind her brother's back, and she quickly turned to prepare dinner. As the two men helped, they all discussed the movie she'd just finished filming, and Kevin's work in D.C. It almost felt natural, as if she and her brother chatted all the time, instead of months—and once even a year—passing with silence between them.

When they sat down to dinner, she eyed Kevin closely. "How's it really going?"

He met her gaze, wearing a crooked smile, as if he knew exactly what she meant.

Then she realized she'd spoken in front of Noah, as if Kevin wanted to be on display, the way she let herself be. "I'm sorry, Kevin, I shouldn't bring up your personal life."

"No, I have nothing to hide. My problems are in the papers and all over the internet, after all."

"Because of me," Gabby said quietly.

The Apple Blossom Café

Kevin briefly clasped her hand. "Because of *me*. But it's going okay. There are days when I can almost forget the need. And then there are other days…"

She thought she glimpsed a weary bleakness in his eyes, and her own stung with helplessness. This was her baby brother in pain, the boy she'd played with in her childhood, who she'd resented in her stupid teenage years, who'd been used by their mother to keep Gabby in line.

"Frankly," Kevin continued, "working with people struggling with the same thing has really helped. It reminds me every day that I don't want to go back to that dark place again."

It was her turn to touch his hand. "I'm glad. I was worried that being around people using drugs would make it more difficult."

"Surprisingly not. It helps me confront what made me so desperate to escape my own life."

"Perhaps it was Mom." She'd meant it jokingly, then regretted making light of his problems. "I'm sorry, I shouldn't have—"

"No, I'm glad you did. I was going to bring her up."

"You were?" Her stomach plummeted. She'd wanted to reconnect with her brother, but her mom…

"Did you know she retired?" he asked hesitantly.

She rubbed her finger and thumb into her eyes, as if she could wipe away…so many things. "No. I haven't talked to her in about six months. Look, do we need to talk about her now?"

She glanced at Noah, who was chewing a bite of chicken, gaze lowered, as if he could make himself inconspicuous.

Kevin sat back in his chair, his head hanging for a long moment, until he met her gaze. "No, we don't need to talk about her. It's up to you. I was only going to bring her up because it's part of my therapy to face the past, to make amends."

"Make amends?" she asked sharply. "If anyone should make amends, it's her."

"I think that's what she's trying to do. She wants to see you, Gabby," Kevin said.

Something hot and uncomfortable seemed to rise in her chest, choking her with anger and resentment and the despondency of knowing her mother had had a part in everything that had happened to Kevin—and to her.

Gabby prided herself on being calm and laid back most of the time, but her mother always brought out the worst in her or helped her along to make the worst decisions. Maybe her dysfunctional upbringing had affected her more than she thought—maybe it *still* affected her.

And then she felt Noah's warm hand close over hers where she still gripped a fork like it was a weapon. She took a deep breath and tried to exhale all the anger.

Her voice sounded brittle as she spoke. "She wants to see me? I can't believe she had the nerve to call you. She's a lot of the reason you became an addict."

"I made my own decisions, and I've tried to stop blaming other people for what I did to myself."

"Then you're a better person than I am."

Kevin leaned toward her, eyes wide. "I didn't mean to sound like I was preaching at you."

"I didn't take it that way, I promise you." She gave Noah's hand a squeeze and let go.

"You probably think she wants something," Kevin said, "like maybe money—"

Gabby snorted.

"But she doesn't," he continued. "She just wants to settle things with you. Will you give it some thought?"

Her initial reaction was to say no. She hesitated, knowing that Kevin was only trying to help. She didn't want to ruin the evening with a disagreement about their mother.

The Apple Blossom Café

"I'll think about it," she said, "as long as you'll agree to change the subject."

He so visibly relaxed, she knew she was doing the right thing.

"It's a deal," he said, grinning.

She asked him about where he was living, and the conversation veered to his work, and his excitement in helping people as he'd been helped. His face was animated, eager, no longer haunted or sulky or defensive. She was glad to have helped in some small way, even though it was only with money that she'd offered. More than once she'd thought about giving up on him, but she hadn't. Though she'd clung to her faith in him, that was nothing compared to the hard work Kevin himself had put in to change his life, to resist addiction.

After a long day on the road, Kevin retired early, and Noah was a quiet presence at her side, helping to clean up the kitchen. Gabby kept telling herself to chat, to make light of things. She couldn't force out the acting required. And Noah said nothing, just let her think and stew. She kept glancing at him, but he looked calm and unconcerned.

Damn, she liked that about him.

"Your brother got his act together," Noah said at last, a towel draped over his shoulder. "You must be proud."

She leaned back against the counter beside him and spoke quietly. "I am. But…" She let that word trail out.

"But?"

She shrugged. "He's gotten clean before."

"And it didn't last."

"No. This has been the longest time clean. And he has a job he's kept for more than a month. Noah, I'm afraid to hope, afraid to believe in him—" Her voice broke.

He squeezed her hand. "I understand."

"Do you?" Then she faced him on a gasp. "Of course you do. Your father must have done the same thing."

"Only once or twice, that I knew of. My parents might have kept quiet, or he relapsed quickly. I don't know what happened between them, if my mom threatened him with anything."

"Did you expect her to leave him?"

He sighed. "I don't remember being angry with her. She took such good care of us, being both parents sometimes. Taking us away from him might have made everything worse. How can I second-guess her decision? It really wasn't until he almost had that tractor accident with the kids that he was scared sober."

"And even then, you must have been afraid to believe."

"I wasn't around a lot then. Culinary school."

A silence enveloped them as he dried the last pot and put it away.

Noah leaned back against the counter and said, "Your mom seemed a pretty sore subject."

She arched an eyebrow at him.

He put up both hands. "I'm not saying you should see her."

"You should understand better than anyone."

"And I do. But you know, since I've been forcing myself to be around my dad, I've been seeing it from a different angle, really looking at the family and how I fit in. And for the first time, I realize I want to get over my bad feelings, my grudge, whatever you want to call it. It's been a weight holding me down my entire life, keeping me away from the orchard and my family. I just don't want to live like that anymore. I looked at my mom riding in the pickup truck with Dad, and how happy she was. If anyone should hold a grudge for all the lost, wasted years, it should be her. But she loves him, she forgives him. And maybe I'm the one holding her back from the ultimate happiness."

Gabby couldn't keep from gaping at him. "The ultimate happiness?"

He winced. "I hear myself. Corny as all hell."

The Apple Blossom Café

"I think it's sweet you're thinking about your mom and her happiness, corny as you may sound."

"Not just her happiness; mine. I want to be happy, Gabby. It feels like it's been a long time since I was, and it's been better since I've been home. I know part of my unhappiness is recent, losing my job, I mean. I felt on top of the world for a few years, and that was a kick in the teeth. I don't think I was ever truly happy, because of how I dwelled on the things that went wrong when I was a kid."

Gabby stood beside him, staring out the window, but not really seeing anything.

"Damn, this sounds like I'm preaching," he said. "Sorry."

"No, say whatever you want. I like seeing you happy."

"Well, you're a big part of that." He put a hand over hers. "And I want you to be happy, too."

"I'm happy. And now I sound defensive," she added ruefully.

He gave her hand another squeeze.

"You think I'm dwelling on my childhood too much?" she asked.

He faced her, taking her upper arms in his hands. "I'm the last person to tell you what to do or feel. You've been patient with my moods."

"And now you are trying to be patient with mine?"

He closed his eyes. "I'm handling this all wrong."

She gave a small laugh and leaned into him, sighing as he put his arms around her. "No, you're being thoughtful, trying to help. But my mom isn't like your parents. Your dad's alcoholism is a disease; my mom's just...not a nice person. I know her, Noah. Any time we talk, my fame comes up, and I don't just mean a discussion of my life as an actress. She *likes* how the world knows who I am, that she can brag about me. And it's not because she's proud."

"Are you sure of that?" Under her ear, his chest rumbled as he spoke.

"Well, okay, maybe, but it's a selfish kind of pride. It's more about her, that she's my mom, that it makes her special or something." Her mom liked being in the spotlight—had Gabby subconsciously wanted the same thing? "When I'm with her, I feel almost alone, like the person I am doesn't matter." Her voice kept dropping lower and lower, and then it cracked as she said, "I always felt like she abandoned me, emotionally I mean. I'm so much worse, because I really did abandon my own daughter, emotionally, physically, body and soul." A sob rose up inside her as if from nowhere, uncontrollable and noisy. She buried her face in his chest and kept crying, and he held her tight, kissing the top of her head.

"Oh, Gabby," he whispered.

At last she lifted her head and leaned back to look up at him, wiping her face, trying to smile. "I'm sorry. I know I did the right thing—or at least I've always told myself I did. But every so often, the guilt just overwhelms me. Do you think I resist talking to my mom because it reminds me of that guilt?"

He tucked a strand of hair behind her ear with a gentleness that made her ache.

"Only you can figure that out," he said quietly. "Not long ago I would have told you to write off your mom, that she doesn't deserve forgiveness. Now…I don't know. Does punishing your mom end up punishing you, too? Hell, maybe for your own peace of mind, you *should* keep your distance. Some people are just toxic. I guess I just want you to be sure about your decision, so you can find some peace."

"That makes sense." She sighed. "I guess I'll call her. Your dad changed his life; maybe she has, too." *Although I doubt it.* She put on a smile. "You got into this for some casual dating. I bet

The Apple Blossom Café

you never imagined that meant I'd be soaking your shirt with tears. Such drama." She tsked.

"It seems I like drama. I've brought enough of it myself."

She almost said, *We're well-matched,* but knew how that might sound. "Can you spend the night?"

"I need to go home. My family's all still in town."

"Did I take you away? I'm sorry!"

"I drove here without even telling you I was coming, remember?"

Was she so full of doubt that she was apologizing for things that weren't even her fault? She searched his eyes. "Everything okay?"

"It is, thanks. Sometimes the loudness and togetherness gets overwhelming, but in a good way, I promise. When I get home, they'll be playing cards or board games like they're still kids."

"That sounds wonderful," she said softly.

He nodded, his smile crooked. "I was going to invite you, but Kevin seemed pretty beat."

She reached out to take his hand. "Yeah. Another time."

"It's a date."

He took her other hand and they stared at each other for a long silent moment. They'd discussed a lot of weighty things, but she felt lighter about it all. She'd never in her life shared so much with a man, and after only just starting what was supposed to have been a casual relationship. Though it had to mean something, she was afraid to contemplate it too deeply.

Afraid to get hurt, she knew. She'd spent a lot of her life running away from the sad feelings that could overwhelm her. She wasn't going to ruin the present any more than she already had.

She flung her arms around his neck and kissed him hard, surprising him, she knew. "Thanks," she said, and kissed him again. "Now go home and enjoy the family."

"You, too."

He gave her butt a squeeze and she wriggled against him.

With a groan he held her away from him. "Now it'll be an uncomfortable ride home."

She grinned. "Then you won't forget me."

His smile seemed to fade for just a moment, so quickly she might have imagined it.

He put a hand over his heart and vowed with exaggerated sincerity, "Never."

After Noah left, Gabby found herself restless. She took a glass of wine out onto the terrace, wrapped herself in a blanket and sat in an Adirondack chair. She could hear the sound of the creek chortling its way over rocks as it escaped the mountains. Insects buzzed, and overhead the sky was ablaze with stars. She leaned her head back with a sigh.

"Hey, Gabby?"

She sat up with a startled gasp, until she remembered she wasn't alone in the house. "Hey, Kevin."

He was dressed in his jeans and a sweatshirt, but his hair was rumpled as if he'd been lying down.

"Couldn't sleep?" she asked, gesturing to the chair. "Hope we weren't too loud."

He sat down. "Not at all. Just...buzzed from the day, I guess."

"Those pesky emotions of reconnecting with family."

He chuckled. "Maybe." He stretched his legs. "It's nice out here."

"I think so, too." She bolstered herself with a sip of wine before saying, "I'm really amazed and proud about how you're trying to fix the mistakes of your past."

He ducked his head. "Don't be amazed and proud—remember how many times I've tried to make this happen, and I couldn't."

The Apple Blossom Café

"You're doing it now, and that's what matters."

"I hope so."

"About Mom…" She let out a long sigh, and took another fortifying taste of her wine. "I've been thinking about her ever since you brought her up."

"Is that good or bad?"

They exchanged wry smiles.

"I've been thinking about how uncomfortable she makes me feel," Gabby continued, "and how much it might still be affecting me."

"What do you mean?"

"He asks in his best counselor voice," Gabby said with a smile.

"Now you're trying to distract us both."

"Maybe." She let her head fall back again. "She acts like she's proud of me. I've always taken it as a very selfish sort of pride, like she's showing the world what she created. She likes that sort of notoriety."

"Maybe."

"Am I any different than she is?"

He stiffened. "What are you talking about?"

"My entire career has been about getting myself noticed, and keeping myself in the spotlight, no matter who it hurts."

"You're making it sound like it's your own private addiction."

"Isn't it?"

"Gabby, your job is very public. No one's going to your movies if they don't know who you are. I can see that it can be a two-edged sword for you. Aren't you being a little hard on yourself?"

"You don't think our mom affected you, in sort of the same way? It was hard to get her attention, and we both worked at it in our own ways, trying to get in her spotlight."

"But you achieved unparalleled success, Gabby. I almost killed myself when the drugs got out of control. There's a big difference."

She reached across and squeezed his hand. "I don't mean to make comparisons between the paths our lives took. I know everything is mostly good in my life, that I've been lucky. But I've hurt people, Kevin, more than one person. And I'm worried I'll hurt Noah just as I hurt every man I've been with. My celebrity is a part of me; I even use it, just like Mom does. The spotlight can be harsh on those around me—you of all people know that. Your struggles might have remained more private if you weren't connected to me."

"And without your generosity and patience, I might be dead. You can't only look at the bad things, Gabby. You're not like Mom. Sure, fame probably has a down side—"

"Probably?" she interrupted with a trace of bitterness.

"You're not using it deliberately to hurt people. You're doing your best, just as we all are."

She gave another long sigh. "I'm trying."

"And you're certainly not trying to stay in the spotlight by moving to Spencer Hollow."

Her mouth quirked in a smile. "That's true. For me, maybe it's a way to…start over, to find a new way of living. I feel normal here, more connected to other people."

Kevin smiled at her. "My new job makes me feel the same way. It's not all about me, but about the people around me."

They looked at each other for a long moment. She reached again for his hand, and he squeezed hers in return.

"Thanks, Counselor Kevin. You've made me feel better."

"That's my job. Remember you can call me any time you feel an urgent need to…promote yourself unwisely."

Their shared laughter felt good.

Chapter 13

Monday after school, all the children arrived at the church hall, and Gabby was there waiting anxiously. She wanted to look into Sarah's face and see the truth written there. The girl hadn't called over the weekend, and Gabby took that as a good sign, but still...

Sarah's little sister came through first, chatting with her friends. *Zoe,* Gabby thought, calling a hello but unable to make herself say the name out loud. Several dozen more followed, many greeting "Miss Gabrielle," warming Gabby deep inside. She'd practically been afraid of children before this, and it had turned into one of the best experiences of her life. The children slowly dwindled to a few stragglers, and Gabby felt nervous. Though Brianna was giving her a strange look, Gabby ignored her.

Then at last Sarah appeared, lugging a French horn case, along with her backpack. Gabby rushed forward to take the case, and when Sarah met her gaze, she knew the truth—everything was going to be fine.

Sarah's smile was shy but radiant, and she whispered, "I feel a lot better. My mom ended up being sick, too. We hung out and watched movies together all weekend. I even got my period."

Gabby put an arm around her shoulders and gave a squeeze. "I'm happy for you. But you learned some good lessons, right?"

"Yes, ma'am," Sarah's face briefly sobered. "I won't ever make those mistakes again. And I learned how nice people can be when you need help." Then she looked stricken. "Miss Gabrielle, I'm so sorry. My mom told me about those awful rumors about you at the...drug store. I—I couldn't say anything." Her shoulders sagged.

"I would never want you to! Those rumors mean nothing to me, honey, I promise. They happen all the time and are quickly forgotten, especially since it'll be very obvious they're not true."

Sarah searched her face worriedly, and Gabby gave an encouraging smile. Before she could say anything else, Zoe ran up to get something out of Sarah's backpack. Sarah rolled her eyes and turned to deal with her sister, leaving Gabby wearing what she knew was a silly, relieved smile. At last, she joined the other volunteers.

An hour later, Theresa arrived to talk to Brianna, her little boy David toddling at her side as she clutched his hand. Gabby took one look at Theresa's serious face and knew something was up. The two sisters started to talk, and Gabby thought she heard the word "Dad."

David didn't care. He was tugging hard on his mom's hand, and soon he splayed his legs, trying to drop with all his weight to the floor.

Gabby rushed forward. "Theresa, want some help? I can take him while you talk."

Theresa hesitated. "Are you sure? He can be a handful. I could barely keep him away from the paintbrushes when they were painting the set."

"We'll find something to do." Gabby looked at David, who was still dangling from his mom's hand, red-faced, as if working himself up to a good cry. Though she wasn't sure how to appease a little boy, she squatted down to face him. "Hey, David, remember me? I'm Gabby. Want to go for a walk?" She held out her hand.

He looked at her for a long moment, and inside flashed her old insecurities. Could he somehow tell she'd avoided kids for

The Apple Blossom Café

years, that she didn't know what to do—hadn't *wanted* to know what to do, because it brought up so many awful emotions?

But then he reached for her hand, the tension gone from his expression. He trusted her, she thought happily.

Or he just wanted to explore, and he didn't care who took him. Well, that was fine with her, too.

The two of them walked slowly toward the young actors, who were preparing to work on a song sung by the entire ensemble. For a while, David was happy to be the center of attention. Whenever he waved, he expected people to wave back to him, and when they didn't, he pulled Gabby after them until they finally waved. The fact that he had such an obvious little personality was amazing to her. Then he wanted her water bottle, and they settled down on the stage stairs, while she let him take a messy drink.

~oOo~

Noah walked into the noisy church hall. Kids were singing on the stage in front of a partial set, Aaron Ho stood in front of them, listening intently, while the other adult volunteers milled in little groups. Noah saw Brianna and her sister talking alone with some intensity.

And then he saw Gabby, sitting near the bottom of the stage stairs next to little David, who was reaching for her water bottle. Since the front of his shirt was already damp, Noah guessed the battle had been lost long ago. Gabby was laughing as the little boy used his smile to try to get his way, and she gave in easily.

She seemed relaxed and carefree. Here she was, practically babysitting. Then she happened to look up and see him, and she blushed, making her even prettier, if that was possible.

Noah walked up to them. "Hi, David."

The little boy had to tilt his head back far, his chin gleaming with water. Then he reached out a hand and waved. Noah waved back, trying to hide how much he wanted to stare at Gabby.

Only two weeks ago, she'd been so awkward with David at the Fairfield tasting room, and now she was relaxed as any mom.

Of course, she *was* a mom, he reminded himself. Did she think of herself that way? Or maybe she'd at last accepted that about herself.

Gabby scooted to one side so he could sit a few stairs above her, while she gave David her water bottle again, this time with the top on.

"Open?" he asked her.

"You try."

He frowned in concentration as he worked to remove it.

"You two look good together," Noah said, then realized how that might sound. "I mean—"

"I know what you mean," she said, smiling, as she rested her arm across his knees. "He's pretty adorable. After I heard Theresa say something about their dad, I offered to give them some time alone to talk."

"And they're still talking," Noah said, frowning as he glanced at the two women.

"I know. Hope everything's okay."

"Mac's been pretty stable this last year. Tyler tells me the medicine can help for a while."

"Mr. MacDougall was the one who got Tyler involved in the theater, right?"

"Right. Tyler took the diagnosis hard. He's been glad to be here for the family."

"Especially Bri."

Noah gave a half smile. "Of course."

Gabby let a pause go by before she said quietly, "I called my mom this morning."

Noah raised his eyebrows. "How did it go?"

She shrugged. "Okay, I guess. Neither of us brought up the past. I asked her how retirement was going. Since I've been

The Apple Blossom Café

sending her money regularly the last few years, she said I was part of the reason she was able to retire while still pretty young. She was glad I called, so she could thank me."

"That was nice of you to help, considering you don't exactly get along."

"Well, she *is* my mom, and I have the money."

"How old is she?"

"Fifty."

"She was pretty young when she had you."

"I know." Gabby held out her car keys to David, who was losing his fascination with the water bottle. He let out a chortle of delight, and she smiled.

"That doesn't excuse how she treated you," Noah said.

"No, it doesn't."

"What are her plans?"

"Well, she didn't hint about moving in with me, if that's what you're thinking."

"That's a relief."

"She asked outright."

Noah winced.

"And I said no," Gabby said with unapologetic firmness. "She knows how quickly we start arguing when we're together. I'd prefer to work things out from a distance. Or maybe we can just learn to tolerate each other. We're adults. We can learn new behaviors, right? And then I called Kevin. He was relieved. And he was the one I most wanted to please anyway."

Noah laced his fingers with hers. "I'm glad."

"And what have you been up to today?"

"I settled on a chef and talked to Tyler and the girls about her. We're still considering what to offer."

"That's good." She hesitated, then looked up and met his eyes. "You definitely want to go back to Pittsburgh? You seem to be enjoying yourself here." She grimaced. "I'm sorry. You don't need any pressure from me. And it's none of my business."

"You aren't pressuring me, and you know I'd discuss even the dictionary with you."

She bit her lip in an adorable way and he couldn't help leaning down to kiss her.

"Hey!" David called, obviously needing their attention. He threw the keys and they landed at Gabby's feet.

Theresa rushed over. "I'm so sorry! I can take him now." She handed Gabby the car keys and picked David up. He promptly flung himself backward in distress, but she obviously knew all his tricks.

"If you still need help…" Gabby began, rising to her feet.

Noah followed.

"No, it's okay," Theresa said. "I have to get back home."

"How's your dad?" Noah asked.

Theresa sighed. "He's having a bad day. The doctor wanted to try a new medication, even warned us that it might not work as well, but we gave it a shot anyway. Dad didn't know who David was when he got up this morning. We're going to try something different."

"I'm sorry," Gabby said, giving the other woman a quick one-armed hug.

David launched himself toward Gabby, sending Theresa off balance before she could right herself. He came away clutching Gabby's hair, and she followed him to disentangle herself. They all ended up laughing.

"This little boy makes everything better," Theresa said, her smile lingering. "Dad is wonderful with him. I swear David is the best medicine, cliché as that sounds. I'll let you two continue talking. Thanks again, Gabby."

The Apple Blossom Café

She walked away holding David, who waved at them. Gabby waved back, and Noah wondered if she realized how soft and tender her expression was.

~oOo~

After dinner with Noah at the Spencer Hollow Diner, Gabby arrived home alone. Noah had headed back to the orchard for business discussions with his family about the chef he was recommending.

She listened to messages on her cell phone, and one of them was from her assistant, Cassie.

"Gabby, please call me. This is important."

Gabby sank onto a stool at the breakfast bar and speed-dialed her number. The fact that Cassie picked up on one ring increased her unease. "Hey, it's me, what's going on?"

"Hi, Gabby. Did you read your email?"

"Not yet. You said it was important to call you."

"One of the evening entertainment shows did a piece on you. I sent you a link to an excerpt. You can call me back after you watch it." The line clicked off.

Frowning, Gabby stared briefly at her phone. She hoped it wasn't about the pregnancy rumor. She was about to open her email app, then decided she might want to see whatever it was on a bigger screen, so she grabbed her laptop off the other end of the island.

In a few minutes, she stared in growing horror as the overly cheerful reporter practically did an expose on Noah, the "new man" in Gabby's life. He was an award-winning chef who'd mysteriously been fired—did it have something to do with Gabrielle, who'd left broken men in her wake before?

Gabby practically slammed the laptop closed, unable to find any words other than a frustrated groan. Broken men? What the hell was that about?

But their lies about her didn't matter at all compared to the truth they'd revealed about Noah. She forced herself to watch the rest of the salacious story, and realized it was even worse. They'd made Noah out to be a man who was using Gabrielle to resurrect his career with publicity gleaned from his association with her. There was even a hint that he might have gotten her pregnant on purpose.

Oh God.

He'd wanted to return to Pittsburgh on his own terms, and that might be sunk like a WWII battleship. If it wasn't for her, he could have told his family when he thought the time was right. Once again, a man's reputation was taking a hit all because he was in close proximity to her. She never gave enough thought to the consequences of her behavior on the people around her. Her stomach turned over with nausea and guilt. She wanted to rush right over there—maybe he hadn't even seen it. She didn't want to call and alert him, not without preparing him.

How could any man ever trust her? And how could she ever be worthy of a man's love when she only left the wreckage of people's lives in her wake?

She called Cassie back. "How the hell did this happen, do you know?"

"I think they followed a lead from the reporter who came with Melanie to the café's grand opening. She wasn't exactly complimentary about you."

Gabby smacked her forehead. "Damn. And here I thought I was giving the orchard some good publicity. I don't care about what they're saying about me—well, I care, but it's nothing new. I didn't know about Noah's job then."

"Noah's job?"

"He hasn't told his family he's been fired."

"Ohhh," Cassie breathed. "I'm sorry."

The Apple Blossom Café

Gabby propped her forehead on one hand and murmured, "Me, too." She sighed. "Anything else, Cassie?"

"Nothing that can't wait, if you need to take care of...something else."

"You mean some*one* else."

"I'm sorry, Gabby. You don't have the best luck with men. Oh—I shouldn't have said that."

Gabby didn't think her sorrow could get deeper; she was wrong. "It's okay. It's a fact, after all."

"Would you like me to fly out there and...help or something?"

"You're doing exactly what I need, Cassie. Stay there and run interference."

"You're still planning to be here in ten days, right? Simon keeps reminding me."

"And texting me," Gabby said. Her agent was relentless. "Of course I'm coming. But right now I have to talk to Noah and..." She imagined the look on his face. "I—never mind, I guess that's it."

"Bye, Gabby."

Cassie's voice sounded as forlorn as Gabby felt. She sat there for a few minutes, knowing she should call Noah, arrange to talk to him away from his family. Maybe his family hadn't seen it yet, and she could break it to him somehow.

There was no easy way to tell a man that the entire world knew he'd failed, and now thought he was the kind of man who'd use a woman for his own gains. She'd hurt him just like she'd hurt Tyler. She felt like some kind of medieval leper, who should be ringing a bell to warn men to keep away from her.

Taking a deep breath, she called him, but he didn't answer.

Chapter 14

Noah looked around at his family—the twins, Rachel, and his parents—as they all gathered around the fire in the family room. Uma was stretched out near the hearth, as if the heat didn't bother her at all. His family had taken the news that he'd settled on a chef with cheerfulness, but he'd disappointed them. He'd known from the beginning this would happen, so he wasn't surprised. It was the price he'd paid for being able to design the café and plan the first menu the way he'd always dreamed. The new chef would put her stamp on things, too, and he accepted that.

It had all been worth it, to see the building rise up from his dreams, to know that he'd helped Fairfield Orchard to thrive and continue on for another century.

After frowning down at his cell phone, Tyler got up and turned on the TV.

"What's going on?" Amy asked.

"A friend from our soap days told me that one of the entertainment news shows promo'ed Gabby before the commercial break. He said the background looked like our orchard."

Noah saw his parents exchange a pleased look. Tension tightened his shoulders, and he told himself not to assume the worst. No one said anything as a commercial played. Noah took a long swig from his beer.

And then the show was back, and behind the cheerful host was a gorgeous picture of Gabby from the grand opening of the café. Instead of discussing that, the host turned it over to a reporter, who began talking about the "new man in Gabrielle's

The Apple Blossom Café

life." There was that photo of the two of them that Gabby had shared online recently. Noah began to hope that this was just a filler piece about what Gabby was up to, since they mentioned the movie she'd be filming soon, where she'd be playing a chef. But no, there was a picture of him with his Drayton Award in Pittsburgh. Noah winced and took another nervous swallow of beer.

"Though Chef Noah Fairfield was making a name for himself in Pittsburgh, sources tell us that he was fired for mysterious reasons."

Noah briefly closed his eyes as his sisters gasped in unison. He opened his eyes in time to see his mother cover her mouth, her worried gaze on him.

"Noah?" his father said in confusion.

Noah didn't think it could get worse, but he was wrong.

"Is Noah using Gabrielle to resurrect his career? Is the publicity too enticing for him? Did he get her pregnant deliberately? Perhaps he has his eyes set on his own TV show. We'll bring you more as we know it."

Noah stared at the screen, surprised and furious at the slam on his character. They didn't know him; they just assumed he'd only want to use Gabby. This was everything he'd feared would happen if he got too close to her.

The host made some inane comment about the intrigue that always seemed to surround the glamorous Gabrielle. That's when Noah realized how Gabby was going to take this, how she'd blame herself. How was he going to break the news to her? He knew she only wanted to help him, but every time she tried, it had ended in disaster.

He realized he didn't want to focus on himself, that he didn't want to retreat into his shell of solemnity and regrets. It had never done him any good, and it certainly wouldn't help his family—or Gabby.

"Oh, Noah," Amy said sorrowfully, "why didn't you tell us what was really going on?"

He put down his beer with a sigh. "You know why—because you'd look at me like that. Then you'd spend all my time home thinking you could persuade me to stay."

Amy stiffened. "I would never—"

"Amy," Tyler interrupted. "I'm not excusing Noah misleading us, but he knows us well. That's exactly what we would have done, all of us." He turned to Noah. "I'm sorry this happened to you. It sucks."

Noah glanced at his phone. "Are you all getting texts like I am? At least I won't have to explain things to all of our neighbors and friends."

"You could explain it to us," his mother said quietly.

Noah leaned toward her. "I'm sorry, Mom. I really thought I could make it all work out, that you wouldn't have to feel bad about what was going on in my life. I would have found another job and then let you know about it."

"But you just won that award," Bruce said, bewildered. "Why the hell would they fire you?"

Noah glanced at Tyler, who winced.

"Because of the café," Tyler answered.

"Oh no!" Patty cried.

"I wanted a couple weeks off," Noah said, "and the owner didn't want me to have it."

"You never took vacations!" Patty said. "I used to worry you were going to burn out."

"Maybe I did burn out, because I called his bluff. And he fired me."

"Before you even came home?" Amy said.

Noah nodded.

The Apple Blossom Café

"So you've kept this to yourself the whole time," Amy continued. "Secrets are hard, Noah. I should know. It makes me sad you thought you couldn't share a bad spot in your life."

Noah pinched the bridge of his nose. "I'm sorry."

"Yet...you're still going back to Pittsburgh at the end of the week?" Patty asked.

"Mom!" Tyler, Amy, and Rachel all said in unison.

Noah couldn't help but laugh, and the tension in the room eased.

There was an insistent knock on the back door. Uma jumped to her feet and trotted over. When Bruce started to rise, Noah put out a hand. "Let me. I'm pretty sure I know who it is."

He opened the door to see Gabby, doing her best to hide her worry. Damn, she knew.

"We all saw the program," he said. "Secret's out."

Her expression crumbled into sorrow. She put her arms around his waist and hugged him tight. "I'm sorry."

"Don't be. It was going to come out eventually. My own fault for trying to hide it." Then he held her shoulders so he could look down at her face. "And don't you dare blame yourself."

"I forced my bumbling promo efforts on you. I shouldn't—"

She stopped, and he could see she'd caught sight of his family just behind. Her face reddened.

He took her hand. "Let's talk outside."

It was dark, so they sat on the wide porch swing. Noah put his arm around her as a buffer against the cool breeze.

"You're being too nice to me," she murmured.

"And why wouldn't I be? I'm the one who got fired and hid it from my family."

"You could have told them on your own terms, except for me. I brought that reporter to the grand opening, and her story made that stupid news show curious, so they started digging. I did whatever I wanted, though you had it under control."

"And when I asked you to pull back, you did. I appreciate that you listened to me."

"A lot of good it did. Oh, Noah, I'm sorry."

How had he thought his own foolish fears were worth hurting Gabby? He was an idiot, and the only way to apologize was with a kiss.

She froze then pulled back. "Noah Fairfield, don't think you can distract me so easily."

"And I just want you to know that I don't blame you one bit. Yet I'll blame you if you don't kiss me right now. It's what porch swings are for."

"But—"

"I'm coming in for another kiss," he said, leaning over her.

She gave a groan, but this time she allowed it. Finally she relaxed into his arms, and the kiss grew deeper, hotter.

"Though I want to go home with you," he murmured against her mouth, "I can't abandon my family tonight."

"Of course." She leaned her forehead against his. "Will I see you at the café tomorrow?"

"Where else would I be?" he asked lightly. "At least until everything is settled with the new chef. You don't need to come if you think it will be difficult for you."

That was the wrong thing to say.

Her eyes widened. "You think I shouldn't come? Will it make things even harder on you?"

"I didn't mean it that way. I'm handling this all wrong, but that seems to be my pattern lately. I was just thinking how hard you're taking this, and you're trying to blame yourself, when I don't want you to."

"I'll be at the café," she said with conviction.

"And I appreciate it."

"You appreciate me peering over your shoulder and asking questions."

The Apple Blossom Café

"I appreciate a lot of things about you, even that."

She gave a tentative smile. "All right then. I'll let you get back to your family." The smile faded. "I should apologize to them first."

"Gabby, you need to stop blaming yourself."

"I could say the same thing to you."

"Let's both stop. Go home and get some sleep. I'm going to work you hard tomorrow."

"Promises, promises." Her voice was sultry, but he could tell she was forcing it.

He walked her to the car, kissed her good-night, and watched her drive away. He went through the front door, only to find his father sitting in the living room alone, waiting for him.

"Hey, Dad," he said.

"Can we talk, Noah?"

"Of course." As he took a seat on a chair across from the couch Bruce sat on, Noah braced himself for a lecture, for disappointment, for—what? He really didn't know how his father was going to react, because he didn't really know his father at all.

They looked at each other for a long moment of silence. Beyond the dining room and kitchen, they could hear the soft voices of their family.

"We don't talk much alone," Bruce said.

What was there to say to that? It was true.

"Even when we call from the RV," Bruce continued, "it's a group call including your mom. I know you've been disappointed in me, and you've had every right."

Noah blinked in surprise, and his voice sounded rough as he said, "And now you're disappointed in me."

Bruce stiffened and leaned forward. "No! Why would you think that?"

"I got fired and I lied about it."

Emma Cane

"Getting fired—that happens to most of us at one time or another. And if you were hoping to spare our feelings until you had another job, I can't blame you for that either."

Noah tilted his head as he studied his dad, feeling even more curious. "Then why the big talk?"

"This isn't a big talk," Bruce said with a sigh. "I just wanted you to know you can talk to me about whatever you want, any time. I wasn't always there for you, and that's the biggest mistake of my life. I'll never get over my regrets, though I've had to learn to live with them. I let all of you down, but I don't want you ever equating yourself with me. You didn't let anyone down by losing your job. Life happens, and so do bad breaks. It's what you do afterward that matters."

Noah opened his mouth, unable to find the right words.

"Listen to me preach," Bruce said, shaking his head.

"It's not preaching, but it *was* a good speech. And I appreciate it, Dad."

Though neither of them said anything for a long moment, it was a companionable silence. Noah had never imagined experiencing a moment like this with his father. Something had changed between them, and he knew it was because he wanted to give his father the chance Noah had always denied him before.

Rachel stepped into the room, saw them, and did an immediate retreat. Noah and his dad both chuckled.

"You didn't want to come back to the orchard when you were young," Noah said.

Bruce gave a slow nod. "It's true. I know you've wanted to make your own way. I'm very proud of you for that, and I don't mean it as if you made it out of here when I couldn't. Yeah, I resisted the orchard, but some of that had to do with my experiences in Vietnam. No—most of it did."

The Apple Blossom Café

"I'm sure Michael understands more of that than I ever could."

"He does. I know military tradition often runs in families, but it was terrible to watch my own son join up. Though you may not have his experiences, you're not stupid. You know how such ugliness can affect a man. After a while, I didn't regret staying at the orchard. I loved your mother, and you kids came along. But by then it was too late, and drinking had me by the balls."

Noah barely held in a snort, and to his surprise, it was mostly amusement at his dad's choice of words.

Bruce said, "I just want you to understand that I know a lot about feeling like a failure. I wasn't good for this orchard, not like my own children have been."

"Dad—"

"I'm not finished. I just want to point out that much of my failure was brought on by my own actions. All you did was try to help your family, and you got punished for it, right when you should have been enjoying all the success you'd worked so hard for."

Noah's throat felt tight, and it was difficult to swallow.

"For whatever its worth, I'm very proud of you, Noah," Bruce said gruffly.

"Thanks, Dad." Noah's own voice was hoarse, and he cleared his throat. He stood up. "Guess we should get back to the family room before people start eavesdropping."

As they reached the entrance to the dining room, he put a hand on his dad's shoulder, and saw the man's eyes widen briefly with gratitude.

It had started as a crappy evening, Noah thought, but it hadn't turned out too bad.

~oOo~

Noah was feeling pretty good about stuff at home the next day. He hadn't realized how much keeping a secret had been weighing on him. The talk with his dad, though it hadn't solved all the family problems, had been a good one.

As he arrived at the Apple Blossom to help prep, he wondered if his staff had heard the news, or if they'd bring it up.

Juan had no difficulties. "Chef, heard about the restaurant in Pittsburgh. They're idiots. You stayin' here, man?"

All eyes turned to look at him.

"No plans to," Noah said nonchalantly.

Lindsey nodded. "Not much excitement in Spencer Hollow compared to Pittsburgh."

More nods, and Noah began to relax. Then Gabby walked in.

In a low voice, Juan said, "Chef, Lindsey might be underestimating the excitement around here."

Noah smiled. Gabby seemed almost hesitant as she glanced from Noah to the other employees, her forehead wrinkled with worry.

Noah tossed an apron at her. "It's about time. Let's get to work."

Once the café doors opened, the crowds surged in, and the hostess had to seat almost every table at once. Through the pass-through, Noah could see people craning their necks to see into the kitchen. Fans wanted to get a glimpse of Gabby, so the staff was busy for several hours. Noah should have been grateful.

Everything he'd hoped to prove to himself by coming home and making a success of the café was coming true, but did his own skills even matter? If he stayed with Gabby, it might always be like that, and he would have to find a way to live with it.

If he stayed with Gabby? Where the hell had that come from?

By the time they closed at 6, Noah was as exhausted as his staff. Gabby had left several hours before for the youth theater. He'd told her he wasn't sure what his plans were for that evening, but that was crap. He'd spooked himself by imagining being with her long term, and now he couldn't stop thinking

The Apple Blossom Café

about all the complications, as well as the rewards. And there was the kid issue—she didn't want them and he did.

He was alone, working at the computer, when he heard Gabby say his name from out in the hall as if his thoughts had summoned her.

"I'm in the office," he called.

He swiveled his chair when she appeared in the doorway and leaned against the frame as if hesitant to come in.

"I'm sorry to intrude," she said. "You probably have plans with your family, after everything that happened yesterday."

"Not sure yet. Come on in."

Smiling, she pulled up a chair near him. "It was very busy today."

"It was. I should thank you." He meant the words to be honest, but thought he heard a faint thread of irony.

She closed her eyes briefly, as if in pain. "Oh, Noah."

He reached for her hand. "I didn't mean that the way it sounded. I'm being an ass, and frankly, I don't like what I'm realizing about myself."

"What do you mean?"

"Because I can't accept the success of the café merely as a way to bring customers to Fairfield Orchard and make our family business thrive. It's somehow wrapped up in my own ego."

"Success usually is, to some degree. We all want people to acknowledge our hard work."

"But that's just it. Customers returning again and again should be about the food, the experience we created."

"Your food is delicious! Of course that's why they'll come back."

"Thank you, and part of me hopes that is true. This business about getting fired has messed with my head, and I don't like the insecurities that are coming out. Once I started cooking in restaurants and working hard, each success came a little too easily. I thought I was confident in my abilities, and I handled everything thrown my way. Though becoming an executive chef for the first time was thrilling and challenging, I always thought I could handle it. Then things changed when I was fired. I should have been focused on the Apple Blossom; instead, I started questioning everything about myself. I want the café to succeed, but my own sense of self-worth is now wrapped up in it. How will I ever know if the café is successful on its own, because of my effort, or if it's because people are just curious?"

She sat back. "You mean because of me."

He'd been able to read her expressive eyes from the beginning. He could tell he'd hurt her, and he never meant to. He'd been so focused on himself. "Gabby, I'm sorry."

"Don't be," she said firmly. "I'll just leave a little sooner than I meant to so you can have the last few days here on your own, without me drawing a crowd."

He blinked, confused. "What?"

"This has just been for fun these last couple weeks, right? I have a meeting in L.A. coming up. I'll be gone for a week or two, and by the time I get back, you'll be back in Pittsburgh. I think it's best we take a break."

She stood up and he did, too, feeling at a loss. "Take a break?" he echoed, unable to come up with other words.

"Sure. We knew this wasn't permanent, and it's obvious being with me isn't the easiest thing. Let's just…take a little time."

"But—"

"Look, we both know this hasn't been easy, after everything I put Tyler through. Maybe you've even been regretting getting involved with me."

"I have not," he said firmly.

"That's nice of you to say, Noah," she said.

Her soft, sweet smile seemed to lance a spot in his heart.

The Apple Blossom Café

"I'm not being nice at all," he insisted.

"I'll just go. I'm sure I can move up the flight."

"What about the Skyline theater—"

"They'll still be in rehearsals when I get back. As for you and me, let's talk then."

"You're saying I shouldn't call you?"

"I don't think you should." Now it was obviously her turn to be firm. "You're being sweet not to blame me for the turmoil in your life, but you might think differently with some time to consider things." She leaned up and kissed his cheek. "See you around."

And then she was gone.

Noah stood there, confused. Had she just dumped him? He'd been justifying himself, and she'd just walked away. He tried to remind himself that a Hollywood relationship never worked out, that famous movie stars' lives weren't cut out for this.

Surely she was making the right move. He wasn't staying, and it was better to end things cleanly. And how could he forget the biggest conflict of all—he wanted kids and she didn't. But he'd hurt her, and that weighed on him with an ache he hadn't anticipated.

Chapter 15

Gabby was crying by the time she got to her car. The ending of a casual relationship wasn't supposed to feel like this, like her heart was cracking open, like she'd never be the same without seeing him, talking to him, making love with him.

She put both hands on the steering wheel and told herself to get a grip. She had to update her travel arrangements and pack. She needed to apologize to Brianna for taking off early and put off some paperwork Amy wanted her to sign about the house.

But this was all trivia she was trying to distract herself with. She put her forehead on the steering wheel and the tears came again.

~oOo~

Ten days later, Gabby drove up into the Blue Ridge Mountains in the car she'd purchased right off the lot in Charlottesville. She'd brought a bank draft from L.A., and the dealers had only been too happy to make it all happen in an afternoon.

The car made her feel permanent, a Virginia resident. She wasn't going to change her mind.

Even her broken heart over Noah didn't alter her plans to buy the house. She loved the college town of Charlottesville, with its preserved Main Street of shops and restaurants; she loved the twisty mountain roads, where spring made everything vividly green. At the four corners of Spencer Hollow, she found herself smiling at the little diner with its dark green upholstered

The Apple Blossom Café

booths framed by chrome, at Forget Me Not Antiques, Books to Buy or Borrow, and the MacDougall General Store.

It wasn't just the buildings; it was the people within them, the relationships she'd begun to form. That's what she loved most about the Hollow. She'd been guarded after giving up her daughter, then became so famous everyone wanted something from her. She'd let no one get close to her until meeting up with Noah had made her realize what she'd given up.

Then she saw Feel the Burn, where she and Noah had flirted while they worked out, and Jefferson's Retreat, where she'd kissed him in the car before inviting him home. Her gut tightened, her eyes briefly stung, but she was sick of crying. She'd played the professional these last ten days, though it had taken every inch of acting ability to pull it off.

She felt...bereft without Noah.

But he was just a man who didn't need the complications she brought, she kept telling herself. Spencer Hollow was a small town; she wouldn't see him much, and soon he'd go back to Pittsburgh, if he hadn't gone already. It was where he thought he belonged.

It didn't matter if she thought otherwise, that he could have a more fulfilling life in his own restaurant with his family. She was the one who wanted a small-town life, not him. She wanted him to be happy, after all.

And he wasn't happy with her.

She arrived at the church hall just as the kids banged through the doors after school. She was surrounded by happy faces and voices, the balm she needed.

Some part of her seemed to step back and marvel at the change she felt in only a few weeks. She'd been nervous around the kids, thinking too much of her past, but they'd helped her to move on, to accept them for the individuals they were, not some kind of ghosts representing the choices Gabby had made.

She stood beside Aaron as the kids ran through several scenes. She was able to give her opinion yet cushion it in the ways Aaron had taught her when working with children.

Back stage, she met up with Sarah, who nodded and smiled at her, but was focused on her sister on stage.

"Isn't she good?" Sarah whispered.

Gabby glanced at the little girl. "Zoe has an innate ability you can't teach."

It was another few minutes before Gabby realized that she'd said Zoe's name aloud for the first time. It had been the private name inside her own heart, the only thing she'd ever been able to give her daughter. Now she'd said it out loud, letting the double meaning and sadness go. She'd always have her daughter in her heart; the name used by another couldn't change that.

As Zoe ran off stage, straight to Gabby, her face was full of the exuberance of knowing that she'd captured a character other than herself, feeling the power of moving an audience.

"Miss Gabrielle, I did it!"

Gabby cupped her face and kissed the top of her head. "You did! I'm glad I'm back in time to see the show."

Zoe gushed about the upcoming performance, which of her school friends was coming, how her grandma was flying in from Erie PA. Gabby met Sarah's gaze over her sister's head, and they both smiled.

Gabby prayed that as she helped these kids, someone was helping her own daughter with her questions as she approached her teenage years.

~oOo~

Noah had had every intention of heading back to Pittsburgh. He followed up on job openings, submitted his resume, even got a few nibbles. But the chef he'd thought to hire locally had already taken another job, so he was forced to back up a couple steps and look again at the other applicants for the Apple

The Apple Blossom Café

Blossom. He was surprised to find himself not too unhappy about that fact, and as each day went by, he paid attention to how he felt, trying to evaluate what he really wanted out of life.

Trying to think of anything but how much he missed Gabby.

Though he had his siblings, he kept thinking of how easily he'd been able to talk to her about his confusion, his hesitation. He wanted to see her face light up when she saw him, wanted to see her eyes get smoky and knowing when she wanted to sleep with him. He was starting to lose track of what he was doing, thinking about her.

Even as the Fairfields relaxed in the tasting room after hours, Tyler kept having to call his name twice to hand him a drink or pass a platter of Apple Cider Chicken Meatballs that Noah had been trying out on the family. Though Rachel kept giving him squinty-eyed looks, he just returned them calmly. His feelings of distraction were no one's business.

And then he heard himself. Not his family's business? Wasn't that what had gotten him into trouble, holding things back? But how could he discuss Gabby, when there might not even be a relationship to discuss?

He had to admit that his family had been surprisingly cool about him losing his job. They'd been angry on his behalf, teased him that he'd kept it a secret, and then they'd just let it go. He hadn't heard a word about it in a week; they'd even stopped asking where he'd applied. He couldn't decide if they were giving him space, or if it was their attempt to sway him. Either way, he'd appreciated it. He and Tyler had taken to running together in the mornings; it had been peaceful and easy being with his big brother.

This evening, as the sun set through the glass wall of the converted barn, Noah felt a melancholy loneliness as he watched Brianna and Tyler cuddle together on a couch, and Amy challenging Jonathan to a chess match, their dog Uma lying at their feet. Rachel, Carmen, and Theresa had their heads together, still catching up after their year apart. Little David held on to his mother's hand, reaching toward Uma, but his mother wouldn't let him go. Noah knew he could have joined any of them instead of wallowing in his loneliness.

Then the door opened, and in walked Gabby. Noah didn't even realize he'd come to his feet, staring at her. It was as if the sun came out from behind dark clouds. She gave him a smile, but it was only polite, and he damn well knew the difference. Her gaze barely met his as she waved to the crowd of family and close friends.

"Gabby, when did you get back?" Tyler called.

To Noah's surprise, she didn't go to Tyler, she went straight for little David, who'd giggled when he'd seen her. She swept him up into her arms and kissed his cheek soundly. The boy laughed and she laughed along with him.

"I arrived this afternoon," Gabby said. "Amy has some papers for me to sign."

So she hadn't come looking for Noah, and his shoulders seemed to deflate.

She looked good, relaxed with the little boy and her new circle of friends. Noah felt an urgent need to talk to her, but after promising not to call him, she hadn't. Maybe she didn't want to talk to him at all. He'd almost texted her dozens of times, but something had stopped him. He would have seemed pathetic, needy—in love.

He wasn't in love—was he?

He felt as if the floor tilted a little beneath him, and he sat down heavily on the bar stool. Tyler and Rachel were both watching him closely.

Amy rummaged in her bag. "Damn, I left the paperwork in the office. I can go get it."

The Apple Blossom Café

"No rush," Gabby answered. "I'm going to take this little munchkin out on the deck to admire the view. Do you mind, Theresa?"

"God, no," Theresa said emphatically. "No one will ever accuse me of being a clingy mother."

"Now wait a minute. I've had some panicky phone calls…" Brianna began in a teasing voice.

"Never mind," Theresa said, shushing her sister.

And Gabby went through the glass doors out onto the deck. Noah watched her go, not having said a word. Tyler only arched a brow at him and turned away, shaking his head. He realized this was a moment of truth—he could go out on the deck and face Gabby or he could stay inside.

~oOo~

Gabby felt like a fool, latching onto David the moment she'd walked in the tasting room. But it had been the only thing keeping her from throwing herself at Noah. He'd stood up when she'd entered, a Southern gentleman. She hadn't been able to read his expression. She knew how well he read hers, how hard it was to disguise her feelings for him. She'd felt as if she couldn't breathe, as if everyone was staring at the two of them, waiting for the curtain to rise.

Did they even know she and Noah had broken up? She hadn't told anyone, and he was famously close-lipped. She thought she'd be able to handle being in the same room with him, but apparently not.

She focused on little David, who was gripping her finger in one hand, and the spindles of the railing with the other. He let go and started pointing, as if showing her the unfolding view of springtime in Virginia.

"Yes, I see how beautiful it is," Gabby said. "Can you say apple tree?"

Before David could respond, she heard the door open and close behind her. She knew who it was.

Taking a deep breath, she looked over her shoulder. Noah was coming toward her, his expression sober, intent. The closer he got, the more her insides alternated between tensing and melting. He looked so good in a cream-colored Henley shirt and jeans. He stopped next to her with his hands in his pockets. For a moment, they just looked at each other, and the cool breeze ruffled his hair.

"Hi, Gabby."

His voice was smooth, deep, yet hesitant. She didn't want to be affected, shouldn't *let* herself be affected, but she was. Was this how she'd feel every time they saw each other, off balance, yearning, even despondent?

"Hi, Noah." She swung David up into her arms, worried she'd lose track of him because she couldn't stop staring at Noah. And then she started babbling. "You're still here. I thought you were heading back to Pittsburgh."

"I thought so, too. We lost out on the chef I chose. The job search started all over again. But that's an excuse. I think…I think I'm going to stay in Spencer Hollow."

She widened her eyes. "Stay at the café?"

He nodded and shrugged, his hands still in his pockets. "I kept looking at job postings, and though there were many I could have applied for, I kept finding reasons not to. I think I was too proud to just admit I'd changed my mind."

"Your family must be very happy," she said quietly. "Don't worry about me. I won't come around. You won't have any cause to think—"

"Gabby, stop." He took a step toward her, his eyes beseeching. "I was an ass. Please forgive me."

The Apple Blossom Café

"I—I don't know what I'd be forgiving you for," she began hesitantly. "I only caused you trouble. I wouldn't blame you for wanting nothing more to do with me."

"Wanting nothing to do with you?" He threw his hands wide. "I've been miserable without you."

She bit her lip and just stared at him. David put his thumb in his mouth and looked from one to the other of them as if fascinated.

Gabby's eyes were stinging again, and she was sick of crying.

"Give me David," Noah said, taking the boy out of her hands.

She almost protested, then realized she'd be using the boy as a shield. She was left alone and hugging herself, as Noah went to the door and passed off the child to someone inside. When he came back, it was hard to read his expression, the way the setting sun cast shadows on his face. Gabby felt like taking a step back. She didn't know what she wanted from him—she wanted too much.

What did he mean by being miserable without her? She was afraid to hope.

"Another reason I'm staying," he began. "I talked to you about my life and my family in a way I'd never done with anyone before. You made a lot of sense, especially about my dad and how he'd never abandoned us, how he was trying to change. I kept thinking it was easier to stay away from him, but all I was doing was isolating myself, letting my feelings fester. Just talking to him after he found out about my job…it felt good. Our easier relationship let me admit to myself that it's okay to be home, to see what it's like to live as an adult here, rather than the angry teenager I used to be."

"I'm glad, Noah." Helping him find peace at home was a good thing—then why did she feel like crying? "Are you going to stay in the family home?"

"For a while, I guess. I'll probably get my own place at some point. Not sure I want the orchard twenty-four hours a day."

"That makes sense."

When he said nothing, she started to think she'd imagined what he'd confessed about missing her. Then he took her hands.

"Gabby, you had every reason to break things off with me. After you left, I was in limbo, roaming the orchard after dark, or staying in the kitchen, angry-cooking and then dropping excess food off at a women's shelter. I might have had good motives for trying to prove myself in Pittsburgh, but success wasn't all I needed. I had a lot to learn about myself and my reaction to failure. I'm not proud of it. I don't know why proving myself seemed to matter so much. Maybe to prove I'd survived my dysfunctional childhood?"

"Your parents succeeded in raising good kids," Gabby pointed out. "I envy your family, Noah. What does professional success matter next to that?"

"And that's what coming back here helped me learn," Noah agreed. "I was letting other people's definition of success mess with my head. Each of us brought something to Fairfield Orchard, and to try to take individual recognition isn't the right way to approach it. It's a team effort, and Gabby, you're part of the team," he added earnestly.

She swallowed past the suddenly large lump in her throat. "I am? Even after everything that I've caused to happen to Tyler—to you?"

He shook his head. "I don't care about any of that. What I care about is that I'm falling in love with you, and I have to know if you think you can forgive me, if you can look past my stupidity, if—"

She slung her arms around his neck. "Oh, stop talking and kiss me!"

The Apple Blossom Café

They shared a long moment of fierce, hot kissing, lost in passion, in relief, in hope for the future. The kiss turned gentle, tender, and Gabby broke it off with a chuckle to wipe away tears.

"No crying," he said huskily.

"These are good tears, Noah."

"Then I haven't driven you out of Spencer Hollow? I was afraid to ask Amy if you'd cancelled the house purchase."

"Never, I love it here. And now I'll love it even more, because you're here." Her smile gradually faded as she searched his face. "You know now how difficult it is to be with me. You'll make the news, though I won't mean for it to happen. I'll try to shield you, but—"

"I don't want to be shielded, Gabby. If I'm with you, I want to be at your side, full of pride. Because that's how I feel." He bent his head to kiss her hands where they joined with his.

"I think I love you, too," she whispered. "And I'm so afraid of that. I've never been successful with a guy—"

"Because you've never been with me," he said, straightening with a confident, cocky grin.

She truly did melt this time, right into his arms. "Oh, Noah, you're sweet, but there are so many issues that will come. I don't know if I want kids—"

"Stop." He kissed the top of her head. "We're never going to let anything fester. We're going to tell each other the truth, even if it's hard. We'll talk about things like kids. We have time."

She nodded.

"We've worked through a few things these last weeks," Noah said. "No doubt, we had family issues. I think we've taken some good first steps, me with my dad, you with your mom and brother."

"I talked to her again. It went okay. I'm going to let her come for a visit—a short one—to see the new house." She hesitated then peered up at him. "And to introduce you."

He smiled. "I'd like that a lot."

"Maybe…would you think about coming to the movie premiere with me next month? Or is my career something that should remain separate from us? I'd understand."

"Gabby, I only want to be with you. You put up with my idiocy—why wouldn't I want to see you out in the world, showing what you've worked so hard to accomplish? I'm proud of you. I'd be humbled to stand at your side."

"Damn, you're making me cry again."

He kissed the tip of her nose. "No crying. We're only going to be happy from now on."

She knew his vow for what it was, a promise, but with the understanding that life could be hard sometimes, a challenge that needed to be worked through. She knew a lot about working through challenges and heartbreak and regrets. With Noah's help, she'd come a long way toward letting go of some of her guilt, understanding she'd done the best she could for her daughter all those years ago. It was time for her to have her own life, and with Noah, she knew it could be a good one. She deserved love, maybe she even deserved to have another child of her own, but she wasn't ready to consider that yet. There'd be time.

"I did some thinking while I was gone," she said quietly. "About my daughter—Zoe. That was what I called her. I think I'm going to put my name in the national adoption database, so that if she wants to find me someday, she can. What do you think?"

He cupped her cheek and stared down into her eyes with tenderness. "I think that's a wonderful idea."

They shared another sweet kiss that made her yearn for more. She anticipated many hours, weeks, months—a lifetime—of sitting by the little creek, with Noah at her side. She needed a porch swing. Maybe Noah would move in...but she was getting ahead of herself. She hadn't even signed the papers yet!

Epilogue

Within the month, Noah moved in with Gabby. He was waiting whenever she returned home from another trip, and the first thing they always did was head to the gazebo, sit in their Adirondack chairs side by side, and watch the creek flow by as they talked. At their feet lay Barney, the little beagle mix they'd adopted to keep Noah company when she was away. Barney lifted his head and sniffed, and that usually only meant one thing—he had the scent of a bunny.

Though Gabby and Noah talked every night they were apart, it was special when they were back together, discussing the most recent craziness on her movie set, or the newest recipe he'd created to package and sell in the Fairfield Orchard country store.

Her career only thrived and grew now that she was happy and at peace. It was all because of the love she shared with Noah, the sanctuary they'd both found by coming home to Spencer Hollow.

And it didn't hurt when a national food critic panned his old restaurant, saying they should never have let go of their brilliant chef.

~The End~

Thank you for taking the time to read **The Apple Blossom Café**, the third book in the Fairfield Orchard series. If you enjoyed it, please consider telling your friends or posting a short review wherever you bought the book. Word of mouth is an author's best friend and much appreciated.

Next, please enjoy the first chapter of **At Fairfield Orchard**, Book 1 of the Fairfield Orchard series, where Amy Fairfield's plans to turn around the family orchard are jeopardized by Jonathon Gebhart's archaeology dig—and her overwhelming attraction to the professor…

Then check out **A Town Called Valentine**, the first book in my Valentine Valley series. A young woman with a painful past and a rancher who's no stranger to heartbreak find love in a tiny western town known for happily-ever-afters.

Thanks again!
Emma Cane

Books by Emma Cane

The Fairfield Orchard series
At Fairfield Orchard
A Spiced Apple Winter
The Apple Blossom Café

The Valentine Valley series
A Town Called Valentine
True Love at Silver Creek Ranch
The Cowboy of Valentine Valley
A Promise at Bluebell Hill
Sleigh Bells in Valentine Valley
Ever After at Sweetheart Ranch

Novellas in the Valentine Valley series
"The Christmas Cabin"
(from the *All I Want For Christmas Is a Cowboy* anthology)
A Wedding in Valentine
When the Rancher Came to Town
Secrets in Valentine Valley

Turn the page for Special Bonus Excerpts from the Fairfield Orchard and Valentine Valley series:

Excerpt of AT FAIRFIELD ORCHARD

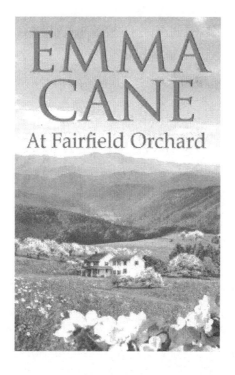

Published by HarperCollins Publishers

ISBN: 978-0-06-241135-8

Emma Cane

Chapter 1

Jonathan Gebhart got out of his car and breathed in the crisp air of Fairfield Orchard, ripe with the sweet scent of apple blossoms. In the distance, the Blue Ridge Mountains undulated into the disappearing mists of midmorning, their haze the mysterious blue they were named for. But everywhere else he looked, surrounding this oasis of buildings and a barn, the foothills were covered in the pink and white of blossoming trees, following long lines like the teeth on a comb. Had Thomas Jefferson known what would become of the land when he'd sold it almost two hundred years ago? Jonathan intended to prove it wasn't what other historians said it was.

He'd driven the half hour west from Charlottesville, Virginia, to Fairfield Orchard, rehearsing his most persuasive speech over and over. He wasn't known as the most outgoing of guys, but he was passionate about history and hoped that would be enough. But strangely, he didn't see a soul. A huge old barn that looked well over a hundred years old stood open and deserted. It had a lower level made of stone with its own entrance in the back, and the soaring upper level framed in weathered gray boards was stacked with crates and bins for the autumn harvest. A food shack and small store were obviously closed. There were picnic tables and benches, all positioned to take in the beautiful view of central Virginia during the harvest season. But in the spring, the public grounds were deserted.

Past a copse of towering oak and hickory trees was a dirt lane, which he followed around a curve until he saw a big house with white siding, blue shutters, and a wraparound porch around the

The Apple Blossom Café

original building. A two-story addition had been added to the right side. A battered blue pickup truck was parked nearby. He climbed the front steps, but no one answered the door. Jonathan hadn't called in advance, assuming that a request like his was better handled in person, but that had obviously been a mistake. There must be a business office or warehouse somewhere else on the grounds.

And then in the first row of apple trees next to the house, he saw a ladder disappearing up inside, and a pair of work boots perched on a rung, their owner partially hidden by branches and blossoms and bright green leaves. He'd done his research, knew that the owner was Bruce Fairfield, a Vietnam vet in his sixties.

"Mr. Fairfield?" Jonathan called as he approached the tree. "Bruce Fairfield?"

Sudden barking startled him, and a dog came up out of the straggly grass growing through a dark loam of what looked like fertilizer around the base of the tree. The medium-sized dog resembled a cross between a German shepherd and a coyote, its pointy ears alert.

"What's up, Uma?"

The voice from within the tree was far more feminine than "Bruce" should have. The dog sat down and regarded Jonathan, her spotted tongue visible as she panted, her head cocked to the side.

A woman pushed aside a branch and peered down, wreathed in pink and white blossoms, her sandy brown hair pulled into a ponytail beneath a ragged ball cap with the Virginia Cavaliers logo. She had a delicate face with a pointed chin, and a nose splattered with freckles. She was already tan from working outdoors, with eyes clear and deep blue and narrowed with curiosity. She wore a battered winter vest over a plaid shirt with a t-shirt beneath, and a faded pair of jeans with a tear at the knee. She held clippers in one hand.

"What can I do for you?" she asked, then added apologetically, "We're still closed for the off-season."

"I know. I've come from Charlottesville to speak with the owner."

Brightly, she said, "I'm one of them."

That rearranged his conclusion that she was just an employee.

"Hope you don't mind if I keep working while we talk," she added.

He blinked as her face disappeared behind the branch she released. Soon, he could hear occasional snipping, and saw a branch drop to the ground. She seemed like she was examining, more than pruning. He was used to talking to students who tried to hide their texting during a lecture, but he couldn't force this woman to pay attention to him. At least the dog watched him with expectation.

"My name is Dr. Jonathan Gebhart, and I'm an associate professor of history at the University of Virginia, with a specialty in colonial history, particularly Thomas Jefferson."

She gave a snort of laughter. "Of course."

He stiffened. "Of course?"

"Thomas Jefferson founded the university, right?"

Did anyone from the area not know that?

"I hear he might as well still be alive," she continued, "the way some people refer to him. I guess you're one of the worshippers."

"If you consider historians worshippers," he said dryly.

She peeked out from behind a branch and gave him an amused smile. "I didn't mean to offend, but you caught me on a bad day. I'm trying to remember my pruning skills. It's been a while, and it's not exactly the season for it."

"May I ask to whom I'm speaking?"

Her smile widened. "My, don't you have a pretty way of talking. I'm Amy Fairfield."

The Apple Blossom Café

"Daughter of the owner?"

"Technically one of the new owners, remember?"

She disappeared behind a branch again and continued pruning. Bees buzzed about her, alighting delicately on blossoms, but she ignored them.

"It's all a mess right now, of course," she continued. "My parents have just retired and left to have the time of their lives in the RV they always dreamed of." She peeked at him again. "Don't get me wrong, I'm happy for them, but they caught the whole family off guard, and now everyone has to decide who's coming back when, taking leaves of absence or quitting their jobs altogether, so we can keep the orchard going. And though I always worked weekends in the fall, it's been a long time since I was involved in the spring." She wrinkled her nose. "Way more than you wanted to hear, sorry."

And then she became silent as she examined her work critically. Her family problems were none of his business, though his curiosity began to formulate questions that he tamped back down.

"I'm here to ask a favor of you." He paused, but she didn't reappear. Taking a deep breath, he said, "I'm writing a book on the land Thomas Jefferson owned, and how selling it changed the course of Albemarle County and Virginia itself. As you know, your ancestors purchased this land from him."

"I know."

"You have an incredible inheritance here. One of our founding fathers walked this very land."

"I know that, too. But he walked a lot of land around here. I spent the last thirteen years in Charlottesville, sometimes running campus trails. I'm sure I walked lots of places TJ walked."

TJ? Though he corrected his students when they were so disrespectful, he found himself amused by Amy's irreverence. He

Emma Cane

well knew that Jefferson wasn't a saint, simply a flawed, though brilliant man.

But there were more important things on the line, like the book he needed to finish for his tenure portfolio. Without tenure, he could lose the career he'd worked so hard for, be let go from UVA. But even more important was his big hypothesis, the one that could turn his book into a bestseller and give him the prestigious career he'd always dreamed of.

"So what do I have to do with TJ?" Amy asked.

"I'd like your family's permission to interview them and look through the historical records you've kept through the years."

"Historical records?" she echoed. "Don't you find that stuff at courthouses or online?"

"You cannot find family Bibles or original land deeds so easily, not to mention family stories passed down through generations." He glanced at the house again, knowing it was far too recently built, and hoping Google hadn't misled him. "I believe there's an older house than this?"

"Yep, but we've closed it up to keep people from getting hurt."

A headache started to form. "Is it in disrepair?" He hoped Amy Fairfield and her family appreciated their own history.

"Not really, but no one is living there now, and we don't want vandals disturbing it."

The pressure between his eyes eased. "You get many vandals out here?"

"I didn't think so, but I'm not the one who made the decision. My father was. And then he left, leaving it to my siblings and me to continue family tradition—whether some of us wanted to or not," she added dryly.

He wasn't sure where she fit in on that spectrum, but it wasn't his concern. "Can I reach your father by phone or email?"

"Sure, but maybe you'd rather talk to my grandfather."

The Apple Blossom Café

He smiled with relief. The elderly had a better grasp of the importance of the past. "Do you think he'd speak with me?"

Amy spread the branches and gave him a long look from head to toe. He felt an odd connection, her gaze almost a physical touch. He was baffled to experience an awareness of her as a woman, when he could barely tell she was one beneath her farmer's garb. Those vivid blue eyes studied him as if judging him. He'd been judged and found wanting before, and he wouldn't go through that again.

"I can't speak for Grandpa, Jon, but—"

"Jonathan." He withheld a grimace, knowing that he shouldn't be correcting her when he needed her help.

"Sorry. I don't know if now's the best time to be stirring things up. The orchard ... well, we have a lot of work to do this summer, and it'll be time for the harvest before you know it. I just started working here again a couple days ago. How about next winter?"

"I can't wait until next winter," he said patiently. "This is the last section of the book, and I have to submit it by this fall to even have it ready in time for my tenure review next year. You do know what tenure is."

Those dark blue eyes narrowed, and she cocked her head. "Gee, maybe you better spell the word for me."

He briefly closed his eyes, knowing he was making things worse. "Forgive me."

He took a step toward her, trying to find the right words. He startled the dog, who jumped up and hit the ladder, which began to fall sideways. Amy let out a yelp and grabbed a branch even as the ladder crashed through several branches and hit the ground. Her feet struggled to find a thick enough branch to support her, and Jonathan reached for her. She was still too high to grab around the waist, but when he ducked under a thin branch and stepped beneath her, her toes brushed his shoulders.

"Step right on me," he urged.

For a moment, he thought she would refuse, but at last she let herself drop a bit, and her big muddy work boots settled on his shoulders. She wasn't even that heavy, and he realized she was probably smaller than he'd imagined, being half-hidden by the tree and wearing layers of warm clothing.

"If I was still a cheerleader," she said, "I'd have a spotter to help me jump."

At least she didn't sound upset with him. He needed her goodwill. "I'll squat, and you should be able to jump easily."

"You forget, I'm still in between all these branches."

"I'll go straight down, and you be careful." He sank slowly onto his haunches.

Using the tree for balance, she swung away from him and landed lightly on the ground. Still bent over, he came out from beneath the tree and practically ran right into her. Straightening, he stared down at her and she stared up, not six inches away from each other.

"You're taller than I thought," she said.

"And you're shorter."

"I am," she said ruefully.

Though smiling, she backed away as if he was contagious. To his surprise, he regretted that.

"I made a mess of your jacket," she pointed out.

He looked down at his shoulders. "It's just dirt. It'll come clean."

She flashed that teasing smile again, and he realized she might be flirting with him. The thought was surprising, a little disorienting.

"You'd say anything to get my cooperation," she said.

He looked into those intelligent blue eyes, and imagined many a man would. He would, too—for his research. Right now, it had to come before anything else. "Your cooperation is crucial. I

The Apple Blossom Café

have a theory that Jefferson might have escaped to here during the American Revolution, instead of to his land to the south."

She tilted her head. "But he didn't have a house here."

He widened his eyes in surprise. "No, he didn't. You know more about TJ than you let on."

He'd thought to put her at ease with a lighthearted tone, but those intriguing eyes suddenly seemed to shutter. He decided right then that going into detail about his research might put her off.

"No, I don't know all that much," she said, looking away.

"I'll be conducting research at the library at Monticello, and also here, if you'll permit it. I need to find proof that I'm right. Can I count on your cooperation?"

"I'll think about it."

She was already retrieving the clippers and righting the ladder. He tried to help, but she gave him a distracted smile.

"I can do it. This is my job now, you know."

"What did you do before?"

"Real estate."

He could see her as a friendly, outgoing saleswoman. "Did you always mean to come back to the orchard?" he asked, curious.

"Interesting question. I don't really know. As for your request, why don't you come back tomorrow, and I'll give you my answer."

And she maneuvered the ladder back into the tree and climbed up, disappearing within the spring blossoms until he could only see those muddy boots. He turned and strode back to his car.

~oOo~

Amy heard the crunch of gravel beneath Jonathan Gebhart's feet, and she ducked her head until she could watch him walk away. He'd been an interesting man, all sober and serious, and seemed a little taken aback when she'd teased him. She could still see his short, wavy black hair that looked difficult to tame. It was hard to forget his eyes, green as spring in the orchard—and that moment when he'd really looked at her as a woman. That had been surprising and unsettling. He didn't have laughing eyes—she imagined he didn't laugh much at all, which was a shame, when he looked so gorgeous.

Would he be one of those boring professors who droned on and on about something that no longer mattered to anyone? No, he'd sounded too passionate about his request. Maybe he brought that focus to kids who only needed his course as an elective, who stared out the window on a gorgeous day and wished to be anywhere else. That had been her, once upon a time…

But not where history was concerned. That was an interest she had once had in common with the professor. But she'd let it all go, pushed it from her mind just as she'd pushed her family and friends away. She was surprised how much the amateur genealogist inside her had tried to come creaking back to life when he'd told her his hypothesis about Jefferson and her family land. But she wouldn't let it.

When the professor reached his car, Amy saw that his broad shoulders were squared, and he moved like a man who always knew exactly what he was doing, had everything planned out. She always found confidence sexy. He'd been professionally attired in a buttoned-down shirt and chinos beneath the jacket she'd ruined, while she was grubby, with torn jeans and old shirts. He'd been dignified and educated, and she'd dropped out of college to spend her time with a man who hadn't proven worthy of the sacrifice. It hadn't been a sacrifice at the time, of course; she'd been giddy with what she thought was love. Amy knocked her forehead into the nearest branch, as if that could

The Apple Blossom Café

knock some sense into her. It had taken far too long for that sense to take hold, and it had proven costly.

She heard his car start, and then he was gone, dirt rising up behind as he traveled at a respectful speed down toward Spencer Hollow, the little village between the orchard and Crozet, the nearest small town. She used to take the quiet dirt road as an invitation to speed, roaring down the hill, the rolling countryside stretched out below her, rows of apple trees rising and falling as far as the eye could see. Life had been full of excitement and possibilities then—full of the promise of foolish mistakes, too, but she hadn't known that. Otherwise, she would have stayed holed up in her childhood bedroom forever.

She was back there now, in that same bedroom, her cheerleading trophies and school certificates still on the wall. She'd chosen this path, of course. When she'd gotten the call that her parents had wanted to retire, she'd been only too glad to run home for a fresh start. She'd been so excited to help her family, to spend more time with her siblings, to prove that they were all so important to her. But underneath all those good reasons she had to admit that coming home also meant pretending she hadn't let her life get so horribly, humiliatingly out of control as she'd spent years with a man who'd developed the same issues with alcohol that her dad had once had.

No one knew, of course, not even her twin brother—which Amy worried was causing a certain distance between them these last few years. But no one was ever going to know how foolish she had been. Her ex-boyfriend, Rob, certainly wouldn't tell; he'd moved on to the next woman, one even more malleable than she'd been. Amy had quit college for that idiot, she thought, groaning aloud. But at the time, it had seemed like a great move. Her grades had suffered because all she'd wanted was to begin a life with Rob, to live with him and make a home.

Emma Cane

It was Rob who'd introduced her to real estate, his family business. She'd started learning the ropes while still in college, helping out agents part-time. She discovered she loved working with people, and had a knack for knowing how to find the most important reason why someone looked for a home, and then delivering on it. She didn't need college for that, so she'd dropped out. Gradually, as things with Rob got worse, it was harder and harder to be a part of his family business. Breaking up with him had meant eventually quitting her job, and it was almost a relief to be done with anything to do with him.

Now she was facing a new future, and she didn't want to look back, to see again the mistakes she'd made.

But the professor wanted to talk about the past—her family's past, and the memories weren't always pleasant. Did she really want such a reminder? And, of course, there was the fact that she was always so quick to help a guy out, she thought with dismay. But she wouldn't let her own hang-ups interfere with her promise to give his request some thought. He was right about her family's link to Thomas Jefferson. If he had discovered new information, how could she deprive him of finding out the truth?

To clear her head, Amy took a deep breath of the apple blossoms all around her. This was the scent of springtime, fragrant and lush, of her childhood, of her family obsession for generations. She'd been molded by the rhythm of the seasons, of planting baby trees with her father in the spring, of morning walks through the orchard in the fall, examining apples to predict when each variety would be at peak ripeness. There definitely was a history here, the good kind—and the bad. She just didn't know if she wanted to talk about it with a stranger, for there were dark episodes, like her father's drinking, that warped some of her memories.

Yet being back at home with her twin brother, Tyler, made her feel all about family right now. Late last year, her mom,

The Apple Blossom Café

Patty, had had a breast cancer scare, and though it had turned out to be a benign lump, everything had changed for her father. Though sober for the last ten years, he'd never forgotten how his wife had taken up the slack when he'd been hungover, when he'd forgotten family events, when he had to be guided home after parties. Now Patty deserved the retirement she'd always dreamed of, and Bruce had intended to give it to her—even though the orchard's finances were shaky. He couldn't just give the orchard to his children and leave; there was no money for that. He would have had to sell it, and the thought had horrified the whole family. As the professor had pointed out, there'd been a Fairfield on this land for one hundred and ninety-nine years—Amy did know a lot more of her family history than she'd let on. It was their heritage, their history, their children's future. Their sister Rachel, who'd been Dad's right hand for years, couldn't resurrect it all on her own.

So Amy's oldest brother Logan, who'd made a fortune as a hedge fund manager in New York City and was now a venture capitalist, had offered a financial gift to their parents so they could buy their RV and begin their adventures. He'd insisted it was his right to share what he'd earned, and they'd reluctantly, graciously accepted. But Amy and the rest of her siblings had balked when he'd tried to bail out the orchard, too. After all, he was in business with several partners—it should be an official investment, a loan. The siblings even insisted on offering a business plan for what they intended to do to make Fairfield Orchard a success again.

And Amy, who'd been away from the business for a good ten years—except for working weekends at the height of autumn harvest—was beginning to feel a bit overwhelmed. Coming up with a new idea to change things up at the orchard was now going to fall on her, Tyler, and Rachel. Thank God for Rachel, who knew everything there was to know about the family business. With her help, they'd come up with a great way to position Fairfield Orchard for the twenty-first century.

Amy took a step higher in the ladder so she could look across the tops of the other pink-draped apple trees and see the Blue Ridge Mountains, the backdrop of her youth. She took a deep breath of the sweet fragrance and momentarily closed her eyes with happiness. It was so good to be home.

"Hey, are you still up the same tree?"

And then there was Tyler. Amy looked down to find her twin leaning against the tree, arms folded across his chest. He was giving her that killer smile that had won over legions of soap opera fans before the show had been canceled. He'd played Dr. Lake, dreamboat hunk and dedicated neurosurgeon—who always seemed to be in the ER to treat every other kind of trauma, too. Both twins had the same light brown hair and blue eyes, but his short hair seemed tousled naturally, rakishly—although she knew he spent a half hour in front of the bathroom mirror every morning, complaining the whole time about the necessity. His agent had several screen tests lined up over the next few months and was confident they would lead to work. Most of the time, Amy couldn't even be bothered to blow-dry her hair, just tossed it up in a ponytail. Tyler took good care of his body, and had already been after Amy to start running with him. As if she could keep up.

They talked or texted several times a week where once it had been several times a day. When Tyler said he'd come home to help her run the orchard, she'd been so happy knowing they'd spend time together again. College and life had separated them, and it had been jarring at first. He was a part of her.

In many ways, he was the same old Tyler, charming and happy, but in other ways, she sensed … something else. Was he hiding part of himself? But of course, she hadn't told him what had happened with Rob either.

The Apple Blossom Café

"Have you been watching me?" she called.

"You can see a lot from the house."

"But not enough to come join me."

"I'm here, aren't I?"

"After sleeping in," she teased.

He shrugged. "We famous actors have busy evening schedules. Have to see and be seen, you know—however annoying it is."

"No one to see you here at the orchard." She climbed down the ladder. "Or did you go out last night after I'd gone to bed? Oh, wait—didn't I see a Tweet about watching a TV show? Me and your thousands of followers?"

He rolled his eyes, then nudged her elbow with his. "It's part of the job, and my agent keeps hounding me about it. Keeping track of me?"

"Always," she said fondly, smiling. "It's my job as your big sister."

He snorted. "By five minutes."

"It's still five minutes," she said sweetly. "Think we'll have any groupie interruptions today?"

He grimaced. "I hope not. Sorry."

Yesterday, a group of forty-something women had supposedly been on a wine tour of the region, and "accidentally" gone out of their way to see Tyler. He'd signed autographs, chatted personably, and Amy had gotten to watch her brother in action. He'd always been good with fans, just as she'd always been good with clients. Just another thing the twins had in common.

"I don't want them to interfere with the orchard," he said. "Come fall, when we're officially open, I can't guarantee what will happen. The public is welcome, after all."

Her smile fading, she touched his arm. "This is a temporary job for both of us. Six months. No one's asking you to leave Manhattan permanently."

He gave her a crooked smile. "I know. But I'm as glad to be here as you are. We're both running away from something, aren't we?"

Her eyes widened in surprise. "Tyler—"

But he already had the ladder in both hands and was walking to the next tree. "It's been a while since I checked for disease. Let's remember together."

She followed him, and soon they were trying to remember spraying schedules, how to keep ahead of apple scab, and when the beekeeper was supposed to arrive. Those were some of the topics of her childhood, and they should have felt safe as they prepared questions for their sister Rachel. But the topics were also part of the past, and it was difficult to feel safe there, when their father had so often let them down.

A couple hours later they went back to the house for lunch. Afterward, Tyler retreated to his room to return phone calls and messages, and so did she. It wasn't easy to abruptly walk away from a real estate career. She'd been a little concerned that it would be difficult not to be out in the community every day, dealing with buyers and sellers, being in a crowded office on occasion. So far, so good. It was peaceful to be with only a handful of longtime employees. And when the fall season began, she'd have more people around her every day than she knew what to do with.

For a moment, she stood still in her old bedroom. The sun shone through the windows, glinting off her MVP trophy from her senior year of competitive cheerleading. There was a good-citizen certificate from the Rotary Club, a cross she'd been given for her First Communion. There was even a stuffed animal some boyfriend had won her at the county fair. The blue-and-white

The Apple Blossom Café

checked comforter matched Rachel's old one, from when they used to share bunk beds in the same room. It felt familiar and comfortable. She was home, ready to begin her new—perhaps temporary—future.

She looked through the photos pinned to her corkboard: prom group shots, lots of photos with her siblings, especially Tyler, and then the family shot they'd taken at the fair, where they'd all dressed up in nineteenth-century clothes and posed with serious expressions.

She'd once had another photo just like that. Only it had been real and rare and a hundred years old. The professor would have liked that, she thought hollowly. Once, genealogy had been a passion of hers, and she had spent hours talking to her grandfather, going through old letters and photos with him. The discovery of this photo had been the culmination of her private research, a way to surprise her grandpa with a picture of his own grandfather and his family.

She reached behind the desk for the manila envelope where she kept the small pieces that were all that was left of the photo, of her attempt to do something to honor her family history for the two-hundredth anniversary next year. Her stupidity had ruined it all. She couldn't keep the evidence here where Tyler could find it; she couldn't throw it away, because it was proof of a life she never wanted to return to, of what her mistake had cost her. She'd find a hiding place, perhaps her old one in the barn. Now, the future had to be all that mattered.

But not to Professor Gebhart. He was all about the past—he wanted her family's past, and it only felt like another reminder of her mistake in trusting a man who didn't think he had a drinking problem.

Find **AT FAIRFIELD ORCHARD** at your favorite bookstore!

Excerpt of A TOWN CALLED VALENTINE

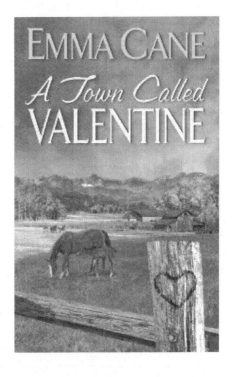

Published by HarperCollins Publishers

ISBN: 978-0-06-210227-0

The Apple Blossom Café

Chapter 1

The car gave one last shudder as Emily Murphy came to a stop in a parking space just beneath the blinking sign of Tony's Tavern. She turned off the ignition and leaned back against the headrest as the rain drummed on the roof, and the evening's darkness settled around her. *The car will be all right*, she told herself firmly. Taking a deep breath, she willed her shoulders to relax after a long stressful day driving up into the Colorado Rockies. Though the trip had been full of stunning mountain vistas still topped by snow in May, she never let her focus waver from her mission.

She glanced up at the flashing neon sign, and her stomach growled. The tavern was near the highway, and wasn't the most welcoming place. There were only a two pickups and a motorcycle beside her car on this wet night.

Her stomach gurgled again, and with a sigh, she tugged up the hood of her raincoat, grabbed her purse, and stepped out into the rain. Gingerly jumping over puddles, she made it beneath the overhang above the door and went inside. A blast of heat and the smell of beer hit her face. The tavern was sparsely furnished, with a half dozen tables and a long bar on the right side of the room. Between neon signs advertising beer, mounted animal heads peered down at the half dozen customers. A man and a woman sat at one table, watching a baseball game on the flat screen TV—at least there was one other woman in the place. Another couple men hunched at the bar, glancing from beneath their cowboy hats at her before turning away. No surprise there.

Emma Cane

When she hesitated, the bartender, a man in his thirties with shaggy dark hair and pleasant features, gave her a nod. "Sit anywhere you'd like."

Smiling gratefully, she slipped off her raincoat, hung it on one of the many hooks near the door, and sat down. She discovered her table was opposite the only man at a table by himself. He was directly in her line of vision, making it hard to notice anything else. He was tall, by the length of his denim-clad legs. Beneath the shadowing brim of his cowboy hat, she could see an angular face and the faint lines at the corner of his eyes of a man who spent much of his day squinting in the sun. She thought he might be older than her thirty years but not by much.

When he tipped his hat back and met her eyes, Emily gave a start, realizing she'd been caught staring. It had been so long since she'd looked at any man but her ex-husband. Her face got hot, and she quickly pulled the slightly sticky menu out from its place between a napkin dispenser and a condiment basket.

A shadow loomed over her, and for a moment, she thought she'd given the cowboy some kind of signal. Maybe her presence alone in a bar late at night was enough.

But it was only the bartender, who gave her a tired smile. "Can I get you something to drink?"

She almost said a Diet Coke, but the weariness of the day overtook her and she found herself ordering a beer. She studied the menu while he was gone, remembered her lack of funds, and asked for a burger when he returned. Some protein, some carbs, and with lettuce and tomato, it made a pretty well-rounded meal. She had to laugh at herself.

"I didn't know the menu was that funny," said a deep voice.

Not the bartender. Emily glanced up and met the solitary cowboy's gaze. Even from one table over, she could see the gleam of his green eyes. His big hand lifted a bottle of beer to his lips, yet he never stopped watching her.

The Apple Blossom Café

Was a cowboy trying to pick her up in a mountain bar? She blinked at him and tried to contain her smile. "No, I was smiling at something else," she said, trying to sound polite but cool.

To her surprise, the cowboy simply nodded, took another swig of his beer, and glanced back at the TV. She did the same, drinking absentmindedly and trying to pretend she liked baseball. Her ex-husband had been a fan of the San Francisco Giants, so she'd gone to an occasional game when one of the partners couldn't attend.

By the time her hamburger arrived, she'd finished her beer. The cowboy was watching her again, and she recklessly ordered another. Why not? Though she hadn't eaten much today, the burger would certainly offset the alcohol. Hungrily, she dug in. The two men at the bar started to play darts, and she watched them for a while. The cowboy did, too, but he watched her more.

She studied him back. "Don't cowboys have to get up early? You're out awful late." What was she doing? Talking to a stranger in a tavern?

But she was away from home, and everything she'd thought about herself had gone up in flames this past year. Her belly had warmed with food and the pleasant buzz of her second beer. Emily Murphy would never talk to a man in a bar—but Greg had made sure she didn't feel like Emily Murphy anymore. Changing back to her maiden name would be a formality.

And then the cowboy gave her a slow smile, and she saw the dimples that creased the leanness of his cheeks and the amusement hovering in those grass green eyes. "Yes, ma'am, it's well past my bedtime."

She bit her lip, ready to finish her burger and scurry back to her car, like the old, properly married Emily would have done. But she wasn't that person anymore. A person was made up of what she wanted, and everything Emily had thought she wanted had fallen apart. She was becoming a new woman, an independent woman, who didn't need a husband, or a mother, to make a success of her life.

But tonight, she was also just a single woman in a bar. And who was that hurting if she was? She could smile at a man, even flirt a bit. She wasn't exactly dressed for the part, in her black sweater and jeans, but the cowboy didn't seem to mind looking at her. She felt a flush of reaction that surprised her. How long had it been since she'd felt desirable instead of just empty inside? Too long.

"You'll hear this a lot if you stick around," the cowboy continued, "but you're a stranger around here."

"Yes, I am," she said, taking the last swig of her beer. Her second beer, she thought. "I've just driven from San Francisco."

"Been here before?" he asked.

She grinned as she glanced at the mounted hunting trophies on the walls. "Not right here. But Valentine Valley? Yes, but it's been a long, long time. Since my childhood in fact. So no one will know me."

"Don't worry," he said dryly. "Everyone will make it their business to fix that."

She eased back in her chair, tilting her head as she eyed him. "You don't like that?"

He shrugged. "It's all I've ever known." Leaning his forearms on the table, he said, "Someone waiting for you tonight?"

"No." A little shiver of pleasure stirred deep in her stomach. She wouldn't let herself enjoy this too much. She was a free woman, flirting in a bar to pass the time after an exhausting day. It didn't mean anything. The bartender brought over another beer and she didn't protest. "None of my family live here anymore."

The Apple Blossom Café

For a moment, the cowboy looked as if he would question that, but instead, he glanced at the bartender. "Tony, since the dartboard's taken, mind if we use the back room?"

Emily gaped at him.

The cowboy grinned as if he could read her mind. "Pool table. Do you play?"

She giggled. Oh, she'd really had too much to drink. But it was dark and raining, and she had no family here, and no one who cared what she did. She got to her feet and grabbed her beer. "Not since college. And I was never good. But if you need a reason to stay up past your bedtime…"

His laugh was a pleasurable, deep rumble. As she passed his table, he stood up, and for the first time she got a good look at the size of him, the width of his shoulders thanks to whatever work he did, the flannel shirt open over a dark t-shirt, those snug jeans following long legs down to well-used cowboy boots. Damn. He could really work a pair of jeans. And who would have thought she'd find cowboy boots hot? She'd always been drawn to a tailored suit and the subtle hint of a well-paid profession.

The back room was deserted on this stormy night. Low central lights hung over the table, brightly illuminating the playing surface, but leaving the corners of the room in the shadows. Emily set her beer down on a nearby table, and the cowboy did the same.

He chose a cue stick. As she was pulling her hair back in a quick ponytail, he turned and came to a stop, watching her. His hungry gaze traveled down her body, and though she realized her posture emphasized her breasts, she didn't stop until her hair was out of her face. It had been so long since a man looked at her with admiration and desire and need. Surely she'd be flustered—if it wasn't for the beer.

She took the cue stick from him and smiled, saying, "Thanks," knowing he'd chosen for himself.

He laughed and put several quarters in the table to release the balls. She watched him, drinking her beer and having a handful of mixed nuts from a basket on the table. Normally she never would have eaten from food that could have been sampled by anyone. Tonight it didn't matter. She was a new woman.

"Do you have a name, cowboy?"

He'd been leaning over the table to rack the balls, but he straightened and looked at her from beneath the brim of his hat. "Nate."

No last names. She felt a thrill of danger. "Emily."

"Pretty."

Though she normally would have blushed, this new, adventurous Emily smiled. "Thank you. But then I had no say in it."

"I wasn't talking about your name." His voice was a low draw, his eyes narrowed and glittering.

Had it gotten warmer in here? she wondered, unable to stop looking at him. Though there were several windows, they were streaked with rain, and it would be foolish to open them. Her sweater felt like it clung to her damply.

"So, Nate," she said brightly, "are you going to take me for all my money?"

"I'm a high roller," he said. "I might bet all of a dollar."

She snorted, then covered her mouth.

"Or I might bet a kiss."

She stared at him, still smiling, playing this game and not thinking. She was so tired of thinking. "Is that the prize if I win, or what I owe if I lose?"

He chuckled. "Depends, I guess. Am I worth it?"

She couldn't seem to take a deep enough breath. "I don't know. Guess we'll have to play and find out."

The Apple Blossom Café

They didn't speak during the game, only watched each other play. Emily had to be honest with herself—she was watching him move. She liked the way his jeans tightened over his butt, how she could glimpse the muscles in his arms when he stretched out over the table. He took his hat off, and the waves in his black hair glinted under the light. The tension between them sizzled, and she wouldn't have been surprised to hear a hiss. They walked about the table, about each other, as if in a choreographed dance of evasion and teasing. This was flirtation as a high art, and he was far better at it than she'd ever been.

But the beer was helping. When it was her turn to lean over the table to line up a shot, she knew he was watching her hips, knew what, as a man, he was thinking. And although she would *never* have sex with a stranger, the thought that he desired her gave her a heady, powerful feeling. This new Emily, in the next stage of her life, could be lusty.

But not with a stranger, she reminded herself.

And then she lost the game, as she knew she would. She still had so many balls on the table as he sunk his last one and slowly straightened to look at her.

"I'll take that kiss," he said, coming around the table.

Oh God. She was breathless already, looking up and up into those narrowed green eyes. He stopped right in front of her, her breasts almost touching his chest. She could feel the heat of him, the tension, the tug of danger, but it wasn't exactly him she was afraid of. She was drunk enough that she was afraid what she might do if she tasted him.

But she was also drunk enough to try it. As she stepped forward, their bodies brushed. His inhalation was sexy in itself, letting her know that she could affect him. She waited for him to lean down over her, arched her neck—and then he put his hands on her waist. She gasped as he lifted her off her feet and set her on the edge of the pool table. With wide eyes, feeling breathless, she watched him, unaware that she kept her legs pressed together until he leaned against them.

He smiled, she smiled, and then she parted her knees, holding her breath as he stepped between them. Their faces were almost level now.

He leaned in and very lightly touched his lips to hers. "Breathe," he whispered, softly laughing.

She did with a sudden inhalation. What was she supposed to do with her hands? She was beginning to feel nervous and foolish and that she was making a mistake. And then he put his hands on the outside of her thighs and slowly slid them up, past the roundness of her hips to the dip in her waist.

"So delicate," he murmured huskily, and kissed her again.

Part of her had expected a drunken kiss of triumph, but he took his time, his slightly parted lips taking hers with soft little strokes. Soon she couldn't keep herself from touching him, sliding her hands up his arms, feeling each ripple of muscle with an answering ripple of desire deep in her belly. Her thighs tightened around his hips, she slid her hands into his hair, and then as one, they deepened the kiss. He tasted of beer, and it was an aphrodisiac on this lost, lonely night. The rasp of his tongue along hers made her moan, and he pulled her tighter against him. She was lost in the heat of him, the feel of his warm, hard body in her arms. He tugged the band from her hair, and it spilled around her shoulders. She had no idea how long they kissed, only reveled in feeling absolutely wonderful. It had been so long.

He leaned over her and she fell back, body arched beneath him, moaning again as he began to trail kisses down her jaw, then her neck. His big hands cupped her shoulders as he held her in place, her own hands clasped his head to her as if she would never let him go.

The Apple Blossom Café

Deep inside a whisper grew louder, that this was wrong. Another languid voice said no, they both wanted this, just a little while longer…

His mouth lightly touched the center V of her sweater; his hands cupped her ribs, his thumbs riding the outer curve of her breasts. The anticipation was unbearable; she wanted to writhe even as his hand slid up and over her breast as if feeling its weight. His thumb flicked across her nipple and she jerked with pleasure. His hips were hard against hers, her legs spread to encompass him…

On a pool table, where anyone could walk into the back room and see them. The thrill of danger and excitement receded as guilt and worry rose up like hot bubbling water.

She was leading him on; he probably thought he could take her home and—

Torn between passion and mortification, she stiffened. "No," she whispered. Then louder, "No, please stop."

His hand froze, his head lifted until their eyes met.

She bit her lip, knowing she looked pathetic and remorseful and guilty. "I can't do this. Our bet was only for a kiss."

As he let his breath out, he straightened, pulling her up with him. He stayed between her thighs, watching her mouth. "Are you sure?" he whispered.

When she nodded, he stepped back as she jumped off the table. She stood there a moment, feeling shaky and foolish.

"I should go," she said, turning away and heading back to the bar.

At her table, she couldn't bear to wait for her bill, knowing that the bartender and the two dart players might have heard her moan. Her face was hot, her hands trembled, and she prayed the TV had been loud enough. She threw down far more money than was probably necessary, but she just couldn't face the bartender. Grabbing her raincoat off the hook, she ran out into the rain, jumped into her car, and sat there, feeling so stupid. She'd never done anything like that in her life. That man—Nate, she remembered—must think her the worst tease.

After a minute's fumbling in the depths of her purse, she found her keys and slid them into the ignition. The car tried to turn over several times, but nothing happened. Emily closed her eyes and silently prayed. *Please, not now.*

She turned the ignition again, and although the engine strained once or twice, it wouldn't start. She stared out the rain-streaked windshield at the glowing sign for Tony's Tavern. She couldn't go back in there. Her brain was fuzzy from too much alcohol as she tried to remember what she'd driven past when she left the highway. A motel perhaps? She'd been so worried about her car and the pouring rain and her growling stomach. How far could she walk at midnight in a strange town in a storm?

With a groan, she closed her eyes, feeling moisture from the rain trickle down her neck.

Find **A TOWN CALLED VALENTINE** at your favorite bookstore!

About the Author

Emma Cane grew up reading and soon discovered that she liked to write passionate stories of teenagers in space. Her love of "passionate stories" has never gone away, although today she concentrates on the heartwarming characters of Valentine Valley and Fairfield Orchard.

Now that her three children are grown, Emma loves spending time crocheting and singing (although not necessarily at the same time), and hiking and snowshoeing alongside her husband Jim and their rambunctious dog, Uma.

Emma also writes *USA Today* bestselling historical romances under the name Gayle Callen.

Visit Emma's website: EmmaCane.com

Made in the USA
San Bernardino, CA
11 May 2019